BERTRAND

He lost everything that proved he existed—except the story you're about to read.

By

MARK BERTRAND PhD

This book is a work of nonfiction. Every effort has been made to ensure the accuracy of the information presented. The author and publisher disclaim any liability for any loss or damage resulting from use of the information in this book.

For permissions, contact:
admin@notarealpublisher.com
First Edition
ISBN: 979-8-9931043-2-4 Ebook
ISBN: 979-8-9931043-3-1 Paperback
Published December 15, 2025 by Not A Real Publisher LLC
www.markbertrand.com

Forward

This is not a novel in the traditional sense.

Names have been changed. A few timelines adjusted. Some dialogue has been recreated from memory. But the systems, the betrayals, the losses, and the fire at the center of this story—those are real. I lived them.

Bertrand **is the second installment in a trilogy that traces the arc of one life moving through—and often against—systems designed to consume it. You don't need to read the first to understand this one. But if you've ever felt the quiet dread of playing by the rules only to realize the rules were designed to keep you in place... you're already where this story begins.**

Much of what you're about to read took place between the late 1980s and early 2000s, during a time when America was transforming from an industrial society into a financial one. I was inside that shift. On the factory floor. In the corporate backrooms. In meditation halls. And in conversations that never made it into company records but shaped everything.

Some will call this story political. Others will call it spiritual. A few may think it's cynical. I don't care which frame you bring. All I ask is that you don't mistake survival for surrender—and that you understand what it means to be brilliant in a world that doesn't want you to be.

This isn't about being a victim. And it isn't about being a hero. It's about what happens when you realize the system was never designed to reward merit, and that morality—untethered from power—is often just another word for starvation.

If you've ever felt like the rules were written in someone else's handwriting...
If you've ever been told to "breathe through it" when what you really needed was a match and a can of gasoline...
If you've ever been too good at a job that didn't want to pay you...

This story is for you.

And if none of that applies to you—then consider this a document from the other side of the glass.

—M.

Chapter 1: The Machine and the Man

Cross-legged in lotus pose on a worn meditation cushion, my spine taut with a tension that refuses to dissipate, my hands gripping my knees harder than they should. The room is dim, the faint smell of incense mingling with cedar in the air—a mix that might calm anyone else. Around me, the participants are cloaked in their silent battle for inner peace. They seem at ease, unaware that the sanctuary we're in is a fragile illusion. Even here, in the hallowed halls of the Hillcrest Buddhist Abbey, my thoughts churn, venomous and unyielding.

Outside the abbey, the late afternoon sky in February drapes itself in a soft, humid haze—a balmy lie that made the world feel kinder than it was. Every few minutes, a breeze would sneak in through the cracks in the old walls, carrying with it the faint sting of ocean salt. It was the kind of day California sold to dreamers—air warm enough to conjure hope, gusts gentle enough to stir the prayer flags without shredding them. But I knew better. Even the wind lied here. Even the weather conspired to pacify.

The first bell chimes softly and deliberately, cutting through the quiet like a razor through silk. I close my eyes, trying to find my breath. Inhale. Exhale. My chest tightens, and every breath is more labored than the last. My mind rebels instantly, dragging me down a familiar, suffocating spiral of anger and futility. The breath is supposed to anchor me, but today, it feels like drowning.

How did I end up here? Not in this abbey, but in this agonizing limbo between ambition and mediocrity. My life is a mockery of effort—a relentless grind that's yielded nothing but disappointment. I'm average. Average height, average strength, an athlete who never quite made it. High school track, college soccer—but too slow, too unremarkable. The world doesn't reward the average. It rewards brilliance, and I've spent my life clawing at its edges, desperate to be seen. Even a pending PhD in epigenetics and transcriptomics, a supposed pinnacle of achievement, feels like a cruel joke. Years of study, crippling debt, and what do I have to show for it? A meager stipend at the abbey, barely enough to scrape by, and a side gig running an internet advertising agency. My dreams, reduced to crumbs.

The bell chimes again, like a passive sonar ping in a war I never consented to fight, mocking me with its serenity. Focus, it says. Return to the breath. I try. God knows I try. Inhale. Exhale. But the bitterness boils over.

Don't get me wrong. I'm not whining about it. Quite the opposite. The justification for all the actions that will put me into the success lane. I had to come at life from way behind. Born poor and raised by parents who couldn't help themselves much less their children. My only advantage is the ability to learn and retain memory. It's my superpower. Photographic memory and an accurate sense of intuition. What some consider as logic. Intuition is far more complex than basic logic. Combine perception and observational skills to apply my intuition practically.

This isn't just about me. It's about using the system. A machine designed to crush the likes of me beneath its relentless gears. When did the rot set in? The 1980s, when Reagan sold the American Dream to the highest bidder? He wasn't a leader; he was a goddamn auctioneer, handing the keys of power to corporations while gutting unions and turning truth into a commodity. Reaganomics was a con, a smiling charlatan's promise that tax cuts for the rich would trickle down to the rest of us. They didn't. They never have.

I shift on the cushion; the movement betraying my growing unease. Reagan didn't just hollow out the middle class; he entrenched a caste system. If you weren't born into wealth, you were expendable. The myth of meritocracy is a cruel lie, a dangling carrot that keeps us running in circles while the rich grow fatter on the spoils. Call it out, and you're branded a socialist, a threat to freedom. Freedom? Freedom's just a code word for letting the rich hoard while the rest of us scramble for scraps.

I bite back a growl, forcing myself to focus. Inhale. Exhale. The anger doesn't dissipate; it sharpens. Hard work doesn't guarantee success—it guarantees exhaustion. I've watched friends, colleagues, and strangers break themselves against the promise of a better life, only to be betrayed by a system that rewards privilege over effort. And it's not just individuals. Entire communities are hollowed out, schools reduced to underfunded shadows, and healthcare dangled like a luxury for the few.

My brother, the older one, had severe mental issues, but they weren't just in his head. It was genetic. Years of denial about his homosexuality led him to seek shelter in the arms of his lord and savior. He went fanatical about Jesus. He went orthodox, old school. No television, no radio. He had his own church and gathered his own flock. Usually, a handful of men he was attracted to. Sexual abuse was his aim. Like the Catholics, he used a hocus pocus approach to religion that spun a web of deception around his hypocrisy. It had fried his brain, leaving him in a cycle of psychosis, paranoia, and violence. Homosexual to the bone, but his mother insisted God would damn him for it so he married three women in Utah and had four kids. Troubled to the core, he was.

The doctors called it substance-induced psychotic disorder—hallucinations, delusions, erratic outbursts, the whole package. He was in and out of jail, fighting with cops, fighting with ghosts. The medications that could have stabilized him were expensive, and Reagan had gutted mental healthcare, shutting down facilities that once kept men like him from falling through the cracks. Tens of thousands of veterans, many of them addicts trying to self-medicate their trauma, were left untreated, lost in a country that sent them to war but wouldn't save them after. The highest suicide rates in America belong to servicemen, and my brother was no different. One night, early morning—2 a.m. They thought he had a gun, but he was just reaching for a stick of gum. Seventeen bullet holes later, he was in the ground. Preventable, if mental healthcare had been treated as a right instead of a handout. Preventable, if Republicans hadn't funneled those funds into tax cuts for the rich—the men who already had everything.

A cough snaps me back to the room. My eyes trace the meditators, the serene faces of the participants grating against my nerves. They're here to find peace, to detach from their burdens. I'm supposed to guide them. Me, the one carrying a storm in his chest, the one whose thoughts are a battlefield of righteous fury and creeping despair.

My gaze lands on a young woman in the front row. Early twenties, neat bun, perfect posture. She's a mirror of who I used to be—idealistic, hopeful, naïve. I wonder how long it will take for her to see the truth. No degree, no effort, no goddamn bootstraps will save her from the tide pulling her under. She's swimming in an ocean designed to drown her.

Then there are my two lovers. The women I live with and who believe in me no matter how poor we are. They are seated side by side, holding perfect lotus poses and silent minds. Teresa, I sometimes call her sister Teresa. She's bipolar and frequently stops taking her meds. On her left is Ana Lorena. She's a Jennifer Aniston look-alike, with a huge double D chest. I paid five thousand dollars to a surgeon for those implants. Her days begin and end with shots of Yukon Jack whiskey. Vodka when she has to be around people.

Teresa's dad became my namesake. He is my hero. She told me many stories about him but today I remember a story of how he would sacrifice anything for his children. Nine kids he and mama Bertrand brought into this life. They never had enough money, and Teresa was the youngest, so she had a lot of people looking out for her. Papa Bertrand was the owner of a spin forming manufacturing business in Detroit. When the United States auto industry was collapsing, his business was nearing bankruptcy. It was about then that the second-youngest was hospitalized. A heroin addiction that destroyed her dreams had near taken her life. He couldn't afford the treatment and the medication that would help her beat the addiction. But he wasn't about to lose his daughter.

He sold the house and the business. Went to work at his own company as an hourly paid worker so he could use the money to heal his daughter. The events seemed like something out of a storybook. Compared to my upbringing and what my parents taught me about family, this man was the closest thing to a saint ... in the flesh. I was and am jealous of her and all her siblings.

It reminds me of the cruelty and hatefulness in this country and how I've been drowning my entire life. And somewhere along the way, I stopped playing by the rules. If the system is corrupt, why shouldn't I be? Why shouldn't I claw back what little I can? Corporations do it. Politicians do it. Even the justice system is complicit, stacking the deck against the poor while letting the rich rewrite the rules. So I stopped caring about what's "right" or "lawful." Survival isn't about morality; it's about adaptation.

They call it transparency now. It's as if financial privacy were some medieval indulgence, like dueling or lighting a cigar with a twenty. But starting in the mid-'90s—after the Clinton administration got cozy with Treasury-hired code experts and international "harmonization" treaties—the game shifted. FATF guidelines, Know-Your-Customer initiatives, and that sweet little love letter called the Suspicious Activity Report—everything got tighter, slower, stickier. Not for the banks. For us. The independents. The ghosts who moved clean money through gray fog.

They weaponized the Internet, not with speed—but with drag. Every transaction now moves like it's wearing ankle weights. Mid-'95 saw the launch of FinCEN's regulatory task force, ostensibly to combat terror finance, but really it was a slow suffocation of anyone operating outside the fluorescent-lit corridors of Goldman Sachs. You couldn't wire a hundred grand from a Swiss trust to a Nevada sub without lighting up more nodes than NORAD on Christmas Eve.

They turned the financial system into a glass coffin. And they didn't do it all at once—they did it algorithm by algorithm, like boiling a frog with compliance. That was the genius. They didn't ban freedom. They just audited it out of existence. Now I can't even transfer lunch money between two Panamanian shells without waking up a Latvian AI and some bored analyst in a Virginia data bunker. This isn't oversight—it's digital predation.

Now every transfer feels like dragging a bloody briefcase across a velvet floor. Silent. Traced. Weighted by suspicion.

You want to know the American Dream in 1997? You're trying to buy your own offshore time without getting waterboarded by paperwork. The government doesn't ask where you got your money—they assume you stole it. They don't hunt criminals. They log them. Index them. Store them until they're useful. We live in a state that lets millionaires offshore billions through Delaware blind trusts, but God forbid I try to move donor funds through Curaçao without a papal blessing and two notarized prayers to Janet Reno's ghost.

I'm not laundering money. I'm laundering distance. Distance from eyes, from flags, from the click of a keystroke that flags me as anomaly. And in this game? Anomaly is guilt.

The Republican Party isn't a political entity. It's a criminal organization, a cartel masquerading as governance. They don't govern; they loot. Their policies are a manifesto of greed, written for CEOs, hedge fund managers, and media moguls. They've turned the American Dream into a rigged lottery, and anyone who questions them is branded an enemy of the state.

The bell chimes again, a futile call to stillness. My mind is a raging inferno. If the rules are written to ensure my failure, then breaking them isn't just logical—it's necessary. Every shady deal, every ethically questionable decision I've made is my way of fighting back. The guilt that stirs in my chest isn't guilt; it's fuel. The thrill of outsmarting the system, of flipping the script on those who've stacked the deck, is intoxicating. It's the closest thing to justice I'll ever taste.

Another cough, another shift. The room is alive with subtle movements, the struggle for peace palpable. For them, this meditation is an escape. For me, it's a confrontation, a reckoning with the truths I'd rather bury.

The bell rings again, signaling the halfway point. I open my eyes briefly, catching the young woman's tear-streaked face. Her serenity infuriates me. She doesn't know. She doesn't feel it yet. The rage. The hunger to tear down the walls.

A sigh ripples through the room as the bell fades. I rise, smoothing the creases from my robe—the ceremonial armor of a man I barely recognize. In a few minutes, I'll step up to the dais, lift my hands in that slow, deliberate gesture of peace, and spin the same polished lines about breathing, acceptance, and surrender.

Inside, I'm spitting blood. What I really want to say?

"Breathe all you want. Meditate until you glow. It won't change a goddamn thing. Not unless you bend the system until it screams."

But I don't say it. I smile the calm smile. I lower my eyes. I play the part, because sometimes the only way to win is to wear the mask longer than anyone else can bear.

There are two enemies that stalk me every hour, closer than the scent of my own skin. The first is the small-world enemy: the useless sense of right and wrong, a vestigial organ of a world that no longer exists. It tries to tug me back, whispering warnings about decency, fairness, restraint. It would have me lay down my arms in a fight that was never fought fair to begin with.

The second is the behemoth—the mega-antagonist that hums beneath every sermon, every courthouse oath, every grave: the belief in a final judgment. The terror that no matter how cleverly I move, some ancient ledger is being tallied against me. That at the end, there will be a reckoning, and I will stand naked before a tribunal I can't outsmart.

I have to kill both enemies. Every day, every breath. Kill the need to be righteous. Kill the fear of eternal punishment. Only then can I survive this crooked world long enough to steal a sliver of it for myself.

I close my eyes again, my breath trembling. And yet ... There are nights it gnaws at me. Nights when even the whiskey-burned laughter of Ana Lorena can't drown out the sound of the tribunal in my head—an ancient court, cold and unblinking, scribbling down every betrayal, every sin, every shortcut I swore I had the right to take.

They don't wear robes. They don't carry gavels. They wear my stepfather's disapproving stare. My old professors' sad glances. The blank, frozen faces of people I couldn't save. Every small theft. Every betrayal of my younger self's impossible dreams.

The law says I'm a criminal. My conscience says I'm a survivor. Somewhere between those two lies the abyss I live inside.

I adjust the hem of my robe. The meditation bell hums again, a sound so soft it almost sounds like forgiveness. I don't believe in forgiveness anymore. Only in winning. Inhale. Exhale. Maybe one day, I'll find peace. But not today. Today, I'll guide them, let them believe in the illusion. And when the session ends, I'll step back into the fight, armed with my fury, ready to claw back what this world has stolen.

Most people don't even see it. They don't feel the devastation that's been wrought in their lives because they've been too dazzled by the spectacle. Reagan's Hollywood sheen, his polished charm, his camera-perfect smile—it seduced them. They loved him for it, for being the cowboy, the movie star, the symbol of American exceptionalism. That act got him elected governor of California and then swept him into the White House. People ate from his hand, bought into his myth. Even as his policies gutted their futures and sold their children's dreams to the highest bidder, they worshipped him. They still do. And that's the cruelest joke of all.

This isn't a story about politics. It's not a story about religion or Buddhism either. It's the story about a million dollars. It wasn't enough to make a million. Everyone does that. Every company goon and corporate slut makes millions of dollars for the wealthy. I had to learn to not only make a million for myself but to hang on to it. That is the hardest part.

~~~

I take my place at the front of the meditation hall, my eyes scanning the room again. Everyone is still here. So far, so good. Half of them will be gone before the end of the ten days. They always slip out during a sitting meditation. The air is thick with the scent of cedar and incense, mingling with the unspoken anticipation of the participants. It's the second day of the retreat, and I know this is when the veneer of peace cracks. The silence, the rules—no eye contact, no speaking for three days—are weighing on them. The actual work is just beginning.

I clap my hands softly. "Good morning, everyone. I hope you're settling into the rhythm of our retreat. As you know, today marks the start of our silent observation period. For the next three days, we'll avoid speaking and eye contact. This isn't about avoiding each other; it's about looking inward, focusing on your thoughts and feelings without external validation."

A few participants nod, their faces show a mixture of apprehension and resolve. I continue, "We'll still meet one-on-one daily to discuss your progress and any hurdles you're facing. Remember, these sessions are confidential. Use them as an opportunity and a quiet space, to be honest with yourself and me."
~~~

Several minutes later, I wait inside the one-on-one room. The first one-on-one session is with Greg, a middle-aged man with thinning hair and a nervous twitch in his left eye. I invite him to sit on a cushion across from me.

"How are you finding the retreat so far?" I ask, keeping my tone neutral but probing.

Greg shifts uncomfortably. "It's... harder than I expected. The silence is deafening. That no-eye-contact rule is unnerving."

I nod. "That's a common reaction. We're so used to constant noise and validation that silence can feel like a threat. However, the truth also emerges there."

Greg's shoulders sag. "I feel like my mind is a war zone. I keep thinking about work, the economy, my mortgage. It's relentless."

"Let's unpack that," I say. "You're not alone in feeling this way. Corporate-owned media and government policies have created a society where stress is the default. It's by design."

Greg frowns. "What do you mean?"

I lean forward slightly. "Take healthcare, for instance. The Reagan administration gutted federal funding for mental health in the 1980s, shifting responsibility to states that were ill-equipped to handle it. The Mental Health Systems Act of 1980, which aimed to build community-based care, was repealed almost immediately. What followed was a surge in homelessness and untreated mental illness."

Greg's eyes widen. "I remember that ... barely. But how does that connect to today?"

"When people can't access mental healthcare," I explain, "they're left to cope alone. They turn to retreats like this, self-help books, or worse, they self-medicate. That only addresses mental health. Reagan's deregulation of the media, with the repeal of the Fairness Doctrine in 1987, allowed multi-millionaires like Rupert Murdoch and Michael Bloomberg to consolidate control over information.

They've shaped public perception, feeding us narratives that keep us stressed and obedient."

Greg's twitch grows more pronounced. "It's ... a lot to take in."

"It is," I say. "Understanding the system, however, is the first step to liberation from it."

Sarah sits across from me, eyes red and swollen, her breath shallow like she's trying to keep something buried. I see it all over her—the weight of it, the quiet desperation that turns into a slow suffocation. She's too young to look this defeated.

"Sarah, what's on your mind?"

She hesitates. "I can't stop thinking about my student loans. I'm drowning in debt, and I... I don't see a way out."

I nod, keeping my expression even. "You're not alone."

"I know that feeling. The sinking certainty that the system was never designed to let you escape. It starts long before the debt collectors come knocking. It starts in the lessons you were—or weren't—taught as a child.

"My mother believed higher education was a worldly distraction. A trap. She used to say that life itself was a test of suffering, a trial to endure until we got to heaven. The idea of preparing for the future? Of building something? That wasn't in her theology. She saw work as an obligation, money as a necessary evil, but real ambition? That was vanity. Pride. A danger to the soul."

Sarah looks up, her brow knitting in confusion.

"She had five children," I continue, "and not a single one of us was prepared for the real world. Not college, not work, not relationships, not money. Because what was the point of learning how to build a life if life was nothing but a temporary trap to begin with?" I exhale sharply. "When it came time to leave, we didn't just lack opportunities—we didn't even know how to look for them."

Sarah swallows hard. "That sounds familiar."

"Of course it does," I say. "Because the system that saddled you with that debt works the same way. It doesn't just take your money—it robs you of the knowledge you need to escape it. My mother's religion told me life wasn't worth investing in. The government told you college was the only way forward, but it let the banks rig the game against you. And here we are."

She blinks rapidly, her shoulders rising and falling in shallow breaths. "I didn't know it went that far back."

"It does," I say. "Reagan deregulated the banking industry so institutions could take greater risks. The Garn-St. Germain Act of 1982 was the beginning of it—banks were suddenly free to gamble, to trap people in loans they could never escape. First, it led to the savings and loan crisis. A decade later, it set the stage for the student loan bubble you're caught in now. They dangle the idea of a better life in front of you, and then they chain you to it."

Sarah wipes at her eyes. "So we're all just ... pawns?"

"No," I say, shaking my head. "But we are part of a system that values profits over people. Recognizing that is painful, but it's also liberating. My mother believed real life was a distraction, so she never taught us how to navigate it. Banks believe your debt is more valuable than your freedom, so they make sure you can't escape it. The more you understand that, the less power they have over you."

Sarah lets out a slow, shuddering breath. "But what do I do now?"

I lean forward. "You cut the strings."

The most heated session of the day is with Dan, a retired factory worker in his sixties. He enters the room with a scowl, arms crossed tightly over his chest.

"What's the point of all this?" Dan demands before I can speak. "Meditation isn't going to fix the damn system."

I smile thinly. "You're right. Meditation isn't about fixing the system; it's about finding clarity within yourself. But let's talk about the system since it's clearly on your mind."

Dan's eyes narrow. "Damn right it is. I worked my ass off for forty years, and what do I have to show for it? My pension's gone, my healthcare costs are through the roof, and my kids can't afford to buy a house."

"Your anger is justified," I say evenly. "The deregulation of industries under Reagan—banking, media, and manufacturing—set the stage for this. Corporations were given free rein to prioritize profits over their workers. Pensions were replaced with 401(k)s, which employees paid for and are subject to market volatility. Healthcare benefits were slashed. And housing? That's a whole other conversation about speculative markets and corporate greed."

Dan's face reddens. "So, what are we supposed to do? Just roll over and take it?"

"No," I say firmly. "We fight back by understanding the system and refusing to play by its rules. Meditation helps you see clearly, to recognize the lies we've been sold. The American Dream isn't dead, but it's been stolen. Our job is to take it back."

Dan leans back, his arms still crossed but his scowl less pronounced. "You've got a lot of opinions for a meditation teacher."

I chuckle. "Meditation isn't about escaping reality. It's about facing it head-on, with clarity and courage."

By the end of the day, I'm drained. The sessions have been emotionally charged, each conversation peeling back layers of pain and frustration. As I sit in the empty meditation hall, the weight of the participants' struggles settles over me.

I close my eyes, taking a deep breath. Inhale. Exhale. The system is rigged, but the fight isn't over. After the last meeting of the day, I will step into my office and shut the door. Then pull the ledger from the locked drawer—handwritten entries, line after line, cross-checked with the latest fax from the Cayman account manager.

The numbers don't lie. They never do. But they do whisper hope.

Six hundred eighty-two thousand, two hundred fifty-three. And forty-seven cents.

I'm short.

And not just short of the millions. I'm short of time. If I don't clear seven figures and keep it clean, the IRS starts sniffing. The foundation begins to leak. The contractors start asking real questions.

Worse than that—if I fall below the threshold, I fall back into the middle. The dull ache of being average. Of being just another man working late for a pension that won't come, trying to stretch life into weekends and waiting for the market to crash.

The whole point of the structure was to escape gravity. But here I am, still close enough to feel its pull.

I left Texas because I refused to be cheated again. But if I don't crack the ceiling now—if I don't keep what I've learned to make—I'm no different from the rest of them. I'm just wearing better clothes while drowning slower.

That voice, the doom—it doesn't come during strategy meetings. It comes in the quiet. In the hollow spaces after the retreat ends, when the tea is cold and the cushion still warm. That's when it shows up. The anarchist. The saboteur hiding inside the architect.

Managing the system is undesirable to him. He wants to dissolve it. He wants to turn every signed compliance form into ash. Aiming to distribute encrypted bank records to all American homeless encampments, he plans to add the whispered instruction, "Take what you need". It was always yours.

And yet—I never let him out.

Because clarity says: meditate.

And control says: optimize.

But the anarchist says: burn.

That's the war inside me.

I'm the man who teaches breathwork to seekers on day one, then codes a new offshore routing protocol the next. I preach non-attachment and hoard financial firewalls like relics from a dying empire. I tell these people to let go, to breathe, to witness the flicker of thought—but I won't even let go of my own illusion of invincibility. Because clarity is beautiful ... but it doesn't pay for the abbey. Control does.

Even so, somewhere in the middle of that contradiction, something in me screams: It's all a scam. The structure is the prison. The system isn't broken—it's working exactly as designed.

The anarchist doesn't always whisper. Sometimes, he howls. Like just now—when I saw Dan's red face clenching with fury. A tiny part of me, uncoiling like a snake, wanted to lean in close and say it out loud:

Don't meditate it away, Dan. Smash something. Walk into your nearest Chase Bank and piss on the carpet. Hack the local government's servers and donate the mayor's slush fund to a homeless shelter. Set the rules on fire.

The words trembled at the back of my throat like a prayer I didn't believe I could say aloud. My hand twitched toward my mouth, like it might tear itself free, like the anarchist wanted to grab the mic and spit the real sermon.

But I caught it. I caught it because I am still addicted—to appearances, to order, to the dream that maybe I can outfox the prison instead of blowing it open.

Another day. Another war fought silently.

I don't want to be remembered for outsmarting the machine.

I want to be the ghost that short-circuits it.

But you can't wiretap that confession. You can't write it on a grant proposal. You can't say it aloud in a room full of yogis lighting candles for global peace.

So I fold it up. Like a map I'm not allowed to follow.

I sit there, legs aching, palms open, the candlelight flickering against the Buddha statue at the front of the room.

And I wonder—if I stop needing to win, would I still need to fight?

Or would I finally let it burn?

I stay seated on the floor, the wood hard against my hips, the candlelight thin and flickering like a signal trying to reach a ship already sinking.

I could burn it all. I could walk into the retreat's accounting office tomorrow, strip the ledgers bare, and wire the funds into offshore shells no one could trace.

It would be so easy.

The mechanisms I've built—the anonymous trusts, the layered corporations, the ghost accounts—were never meant for protection alone. They were weapons, forged out of anger, disguised as strategy. Each one a concealed blade. Each one a silent scream against a rigged game that demanded I play nicely while they fixed the scorecards.

Survival in the grip of a harsh winter taught me to build these tools. A desire for wealth taught me to sharpen them.

But clarity—clarity tells me one truth that control can't drown out: If I use them, if I really use them—not just to survive, not just to outmaneuver, but to attack—the life I've built will implode.

The abbey. The retreat centers. Corporate shells wrapped in spiritual missions. All of it.

They'd trace it back, eventually. They always do.

The machine doesn't fear rebellion—it feeds on it.

I lower my head into my hands, elbows pressing into my knees.

It isn't the fear of prison that stops me. It's the fear of irrelevance.

Build or burn. Live wealthy, or die honest.

I lift my head slowly, hands falling to my sides like empty flags of surrender

"Shall we go?" Teresa asks as she and Ana Lorena enter my office. "We have to pick up supplies for tomorrow and I need us to run by the house to get my contact solution."

"I asked Ken!" Ana Lorena says to Teresa. She looks like a detective who has uncovered the last clue to the mystery. "It's not like anything we had thought."

"His eye... oh my gawd tell me," Teresa says.

"It got infected when he was nine. The small village in China where he was born couldn't afford the medicine to fight the infection."

"Oh that is so sad," Teresa says.

"Is that what he told you?" I ask. "They couldn't afford the medicine?"

"Those weren't his exact words but the context of it was, yeah, they didn't have the right medication to save the eye."

With my head nodding sideways. "Sort of a rip off on the whole story, if you ask me. It wasn't that they couldn't afford the medication. He grew up in China. A communist country. They don't buy medicine they acquire the medicines the village needs from the centralized medical center. The issue was that when he was infected, the United States had imposed sanctions on China and communist countries in general that prevented them access to the chemicals and medications that would have saved Ken's eye.

"Like all communities in China, when a person needs help the entire population helps. They petitioned the government for the medications. When there was none, they petitioned the government for help. It was through that effort the Chinese became aware of Ken and found him to be above average intelligence. They sent him to the best schools, and he earned a degree in engineering from China's best university.

"He was an expert at ceramic microchip technology. However, Japan was the place for ceramic chip manufacturing. But the two countries had more hate for one another than cooperation. So Ken wasn't going to get an internship in Japan. But the Kyocera Corporation was working on a joint venture with the United States and they had a manufacturing plant here, in San Diego. China sent Ken here so he could learn everything about the technology from Kyocera.

"Life is filled with odd happenstance and serendipity, and wouldn't you be surprised to find Lama Sundra Jhinpa and Ken Kuang crossing paths? They did. Turns out Ken has a pretty sharp mind for finance, too, and he was helping the foundation with their investments. Anyway, the longer story about Ken's glass eye, I think, is more profound."

"Sanctions are more cruel than the evil people who make them," Teresa says. "Here he is working in the country that cared nothing about him."

"This country cares about no one and nothing unless you are rich, I say."

"That story is as twisted as yours," Ana Lorena says. Her hand reaches for mine and she holds my hand tight.

"Refresh my memory again about what happened at Bell Helicopter that caused you to leave Texas," Ana Lorena says. "Wasn't it something to do with the company taking money out of your paycheck? Something like that, right?"

I blink. For a second, the cedar-scented meditation hall is gone, replaced by a hot Texas tarmac and the sterile hum of fluorescent lights in a break room no one had cleaned in weeks.

~~~
~~~

Chapter 2: Yellow Tie Confessions
Net worth $240

A dozen bicycles lined the side of the building outside the engineering office, their kickstands bracing them like sentries. Each bore the marks of the late 1960s—chrome fenders catching the sunlight, wide handlebars adorned with rusting steel bells, and faded chain covers painted in muted greens and blues. There were no handbrakes or gears, just sturdy single-speed chains, coaster brakes, and weathered leather seats perched atop sturdy steel frames. They stood like relics of another world, ghosted in chrome and saddle stink—ancient in this modern day and age, even in 1988, when jet noise and space shuttle launches were the currency of progress. The surrounding air held the smell of sun-cooked rubber, old chain grease, and that sourness of leather after too many wet seasons. You couldn't inhale near them without tasting rust and memory.

After pulling one out, I lift the stand into place with the top of my right moc-toe loafer. Throw my leg over the seat and take off across the compound. Exploring the many buildings each morning has become the highlight of my day. Discovering the manufacturing industry.

The late May sun in Texas was already pushing the morning past comfort, pressing heat down like a hand on the back of your neck. The pavement shimmered near the compound's edges, and even the wind—when it stirred—carried a burnt tang of metal, dust, and ozone, as if the air itself was exhausted from weeks without rain. There wasn't a cloud in the sky, just a dull metallic glare off the rooftops, and the promise that by noon, the heat would turn mean.

The closer I rode to the prototype hangar, the more the air shifted—less sunlight and chain oil, more burnt polymer and chemical adhesives. When I slid off the bike near the large aircraft wing on the assembly rig, the smell was thick with epoxy and scorched carbon fiber, a synthetic pungency that clung to your sinuses. A headache in waiting. This wasn't the fresh bite of metalworking or the clean snap of aviation fuel—this was the scent of pushing the envelope too fast. Mistakes, you could smell them.

Right before I get to the prototype assembly, I see the foreman standing in the main aisle. I slow my pace and come to a stop beside him. His hands on his hips and he watches as the assembly-line workers leave their station. He looks over at me and nods.

"Mornin'. Y'all out fer a ride, or ya got somethin' fur me?"

"I'm making my way to the flight line."

"Takin' the long way round then."

"What are we watching?" I ask.

"You mus be new hare. Never seen you afore. An dis here is the worker's union at its finest. Ya know what I mean?" He looks me over with a more discerning glance.

"My name is Mark. I've been here about five weeks now."

"According to labor agreement terms. These employees are entitled to a fifteen-minute break. Now dat break don't actually start up till theys down at the end of the buildin where the break room be. How long ya figure it would take you to walk down to that break room from hare?

"Well. Let me see." I say as I lean to my right for a good look at the far side of the building. "Not more than a minute, I'd say."

The workers took six minutes, as they often stopped to converse in depth periodically. Even those who aren't involved in the conversation stop. The group moves as a hive.

"See dat ryche dare be reason nuff fer why I never gonna be in dat union." Says the guy working in the subassembly area directly across the aisle from the prototype area in a thick Texas accent.

He set down his rivet gun and walks over to join us.

"Hell of a meanderin' mob. Typical lazy union workers. Hey, I'm Danny." He says, extending me a hand.

"My name's Mark."

"Hoo wee! Listen to da accent on him." He says to the foreman.

"He's green as a garter snake too." The foreman says through a restrained laugh.

He is right, of course; I am green. My thoughts flash to my recent onboarding sessions as a new employee. I have been on the job for five weeks, and I spent the first week in orientation. As an engineer at Bell Helicopter, I had to join the professional employee's union. However, assembly line and manufacturing workers have the option not to join their union. Like Danny, they can be scabs.

Of course, Danny is shunned for his choice. The workers have nothing to do with him and ignore him.

"Dey are all ta same," Danny says. "As a foreman over at GD for five years I had sumpin like two dozen infractions from dat union. Five years of my life all fur not cuza dem.

"They shut me out, man. Union guys used to sneak epoxy into my coffee mug. Bitterest thing you'll ever taste—like drinking melted plastic. Couldn't get the flavor out for days. Burned into my teeth. Dose guys tore up my locker. Called me a traitor right to my face in front of my supervisor. One time, someone greased the ladder I was on. Fell twelve feet. Broke two ribs." Danny smirked bitterly. "I'm still here. Because unlike them, I know how to work with this skin. I know what this wing needs. And I'm not gonna beg for a union card to prove it."

He must have been fired. I thought.

"Now the fifteen-minute break begins," the foreman says.

I look down the aisle to see the workers sitting in the break room.

"Two years workin' direct on the main assembly line," Danny says while we watch the workers on their break. "They hired me on here to work in sub-assembly. What a waste of my talents. They should have put on this prototype assembly line. But the union said not unless I join dem.

"Look at the shit mess dese hare workers made of their first wing! By myself I could have built the entire wing in half da time it took fourteen of dem."

I look over at the first wing that sits on the tractor-trailer. I remember last week when I rode through here, it was late. All the workers had gone home, and I had parked the bike and wandered around the wing. The wing is the first V-22 Osprey of six protos.

As I looked it over I saw there were dozens of red cards tagged over the wing. After reading a few, I was able to detect the workers' struggle with the aircraft's new carbon-fiber skin. It has ten times the strength of Kevlar, is undetectable by radar, has half the weight of aluminum, but if it breaks, it shatters like fiberglass. It requires a high level of skill these workers did not yet have.

"There are a shit ton of damages on wing one," I say. "I was looking it over one evening last week. Most of the damages seem avoidable from what I read on the reports."

"Hell ya got dat right," Danny says. "I have experience on this black skin and could show dem how to drill it right. Frickin' union bullshit."

This Danny is working overtime to impress me that he's got skills and experience.

"There ain't nothin' I can do to move you onto the line, Danny," the foreman says. "You know the union has already rejected the chit. Unless you join the union, and you should. There's no way to get you out of subs.

"There are always lots of mistakes and rework tags on the first several prototypes. There's not nuttin' different. Wing one has some tragic errors, but what has me bugged like a porch light at midnight is how far behind the schedule be. We got wing two to load into the fixture. And upper management wants to get wing three staged.

"Hell on wheels, I don't have two people to start number three."

"Could be an experiment on the assembly process," I say. "I remember talking to the engineers at McDonald Douglass and they told me they had to work around military specifications by designating an engineering experiment on the assembly process. They told me it helped them get schedules back in line."

The foreman spun on his heels to face me. "You say your name was Mark, right?"

"My name is Mark. Yes."

"Mine is Gil." His hand shot out like a gunslinger. "You willing to take on Wing Three as an engineering experiment?" He didn't release his firm handshake. As Gil's grip tightened around mine, my mouth went dry. I swallowed and tasted copper—something sharp and metallic. Like the breath you hold just before blood spills. This wasn't pride. It was something else. Something closer to consequence.

"I will, but I'm unsure how to go about the paperwork."

"The paperwork is on me," Gil says. "You shore ya wanna take dis on? I mean, this is shit hot if'n ya do. Management is all up in my face with this fifteen million dollar bonus from the military if we can get wings two and three out for tests on schedule."

I feel heat across my neck and circle to my face. Uncertain what I'm in for. I nod and glance at Danny. He's expressionless. As I nodded, something twisted under my ribs. I should have felt proud—getting the nod from a foreman, taking the lead on a prototype wing. But all I felt was watched. Like I'd just volunteered for a position in someone else's game, and the rules were still being written.

"What do you say, Danny? Do you want to take on Wing Three with me? Just the two of us?"

"In a big way," He says. "Hell, sign me up, cowboy."

"Here they come," Gil says as he nods toward the break room.

My attention turns to the workers as they head back up the aisle. The pace is a little slower and they spread out more. Not as many conversations now.

"Better get on back over to work, Danny," Gil says. "I'll send the paperwork off to Lawrence," his eyes big as jiffy pop on the stove. "We'll see where this goes."

"Thanks, Gil," I say as I push off and pedal my way past the workers and out the bay doors. Nothing could help me set aside a haunting feeling. I know I've set off a domino. My senses are all tingling, and a visceral awareness. It feels like being catapulted off an aircraft carrier on rough seas—one violent, unrelenting thrust into the unknown. The deck disappears beneath you, the horizon rushes closer, and every nerve burns with the raw knowledge that there's no turning back. I'm airborne, unstable, but undeniably alive, hurtling into a moment that will change everything.

As I glide past the break room, something makes me glance toward the far end of the building. A man I haven't seen before is standing just outside the stairwell to the mezzanine offices—tan jacket, mirrored sunglasses, a little too still. He's not dressed like management or floor crew, and he's not carrying anything. No clipboard. No radio. Just standing there, watching. He's nobody but he creeped me out.

I keep pedaling. I don't want to look again, but I feel it—burning in that spot between my shoulder blades. It's not paranoia. It's training. I've felt it before. Libya, '86. When you know someone has you in their sights, you don't have to see them—you just feel it.

I cross the sun line and hit the pavement, breathing harder than I should. Something's started. Something I can't name yet. But I've been launched before. You don't mistake it.

My legs pumped harder, as if I could outpace the feeling chewing up my back. I knew better.

Control, that was the illusion. The briefing rooms on the Coral Sea moving towards Libya were full of it: maps and missions, polished certainty—and yet every time you lifted off, there was a bullet waiting somewhere you couldn't chart. A heat signature you never saw.

Same here. I thought climbing Wing Three would be the way up the ladder out of mediocrity. But now I saw it for what it was: not a ladder, a noose. The only question was how long they'd let me climb before they yanked it tight.

I kept my head down, steering the bike toward the parking lot, feeling the sweat break free from my temples. The hard truth was kicking my teeth in: You don't control the climb. You only control the grip. Crossing the sun line again, I hit the pavement, heat pouring off it in waves that distorted the bay doors behind me. My legs pumped harder than needed, trying to outrun something baked into the air. Even the sky looked taut—too blue, too clean.

Every time it comes to a life-changing event, it's always a bizarre sensation. Like when I left the Navy and moved to Texas, all the while fear and tension tried to freeze me in place. I didn't know what I was doing the first time I took flight and every living molecule inside me was screaming don't do it. Or the first time I got a contract to build condos with no clue how to do that either. Just like the decision to leave home at fifteen to avoid murder. Sort of Nike moments; just do it.

The day was nearly over when I got back to the Vortex Room to grab my keys and head home. A message on my desk. 'Come see me immediately.' Signed by the VP of engineering, TJ Lawrence.

"Have a seat, Mark," Mr. Lawrence says as he slides back from his desk a few inches. "I had an idea about you when I met you. See, what I know is you are an all-star player. There's not a doubt in my mind, son. You have the talent and the brains. The only question I have to determine is what position. Are you my quarterback, maybe my wideout? See, I need time to figure out where to put you on the team."

"Spares isn't working out for me, Mr. Lawrence," I say. "I know you said everyone starts in spares."

Before I could continue, he slapped the desk with a loud crack. The slap rang in my skull, and something sour crept up my throat—acid and nerves. A taste I remembered from mission briefings that went sideways. This wasn't a promotion. It was a warning, and I could taste it.

"That's my call, boy!" He shouts. "This is my department and my decision. You don't run downstairs and out to the assembly plants, making arrangements with the line foreman without checking with me! That move of yours today was beyond explosive. You have no idea what's going on with this new contract, with the military. This is a political quagmire, and you stepped both feet into a pile of horseshit.

"You know what happens to smart guys who make their own moves without reading the room?" Lawrence leaned forward, eyes sharp as rivets. "They get reassigned to places like Amarillo. They work twelve-hour days on projects that never see daylight. And no one returns their calls. You remember Lenny Doyle? Yeah, exactly. You won't find his name on any directory anymore."

He leaned back. "I'm not saying you're out. I'm saying you're being watched now. You ever hear of being blackballed, Mark? It doesn't happen with memos. It happens with silence. With 'he's not a good fit' whispered during budget reviews. You don't get fired. You get erased."

~~~

Helicopter wings that swivel are not a new concept, but in every previous attempt, the projects failed. Many men dies in the attempts. The transition from a helicopter for takeoff and landing to twin-en-
~~~

gine aircraft for transport has been a dream the V22 will fulfill. Danny and I jumped into wing three with different goals and a common objective. He was everything he had boasted about. He knew assembly and he could read blueprints like a veteran engineer. Our combined builder skills and intuitive insight brought us together quickly and with ease.

The days flew past and the tension was building. The union was fighting back hard. They wrote objections when Danny and I failed to take breaks. Then they filed complaints when we would stay an hour longer after the shift. The work on wing two was falling behind despite their fourteen-to-two favor.

Our first red card came on a Monday. It was the start of week four in the assembly. We had a titanium bracket that was used to attach the wing to the fuselage. Well, it's probably the one thing in the world nobody wants to have failed. For example, the wing falling off at twelve thousand feet would not be good.

"Damn it to hell and back!" Danny shouted as he threw the reamer to the floor. The high-strength steel reamer rang out like a church bell as it bounced a few times before coming to rest on the concrete.

"Hey, man," I scolded as I climbed out of the wing. "What is the problem? Are you alright?" I was thinking he had hurt himself.

His face was red, and his head shook from side to side as he paced between his toolbox and the assembly jig. He said, "I should have waited for your double-check on the alignment. I'm sorry, Mark. I truly destroyed that fitting." He pointed up at the top of the wing.

In a panic, I race up the ladder. The drill motor was locked in place and a pile of metal shavings from the hole he has drilled were still hot.

"I see nothing out of place, Danny. What am I missing?"

"Look inside. From underneath."

With a flashlight in my left hand and a mirror in my right, I position the mirror underneath. When the mirror was in place, I could see the hole he had drilled. It showed me the figure eight. It should have been a perfect circle, but the reamer had gone through at a slight angle, causing the now misaligned hole. There is no way to put a titanium bolt through a crooked hole.

"Call quality control over," I say. We'll have to send this one to Stress for a workaround."

Danny kicked at the concrete with the heel of his roach-killer-toe cowboy boots. He turned toward the QA desk across the aisle and marched off.

After grabbing the vacuum hose, I cleaned the area of the shavings, careful not to disturb the drill jig. Then I recovered the reamer Danny has tossed and set it beside the jig. When the QA representative arrived, he was less than cordial. He was a union man and, of course, Danny still refuses to give up his signature to join.

"Y'all ain't supposed to touch anythin' before I sees what be and do a report."

"Nothing is touched. I cleaned up the area so you can see it clearly. File a grievance if you have to, but nothing has been moved."

He mumbles and inspects the job. Making notes and drawing a diagram. Then, after several minutes, he says, "This is probably the most expensive fixture on the entire aircraft. Likely ain't any spares for these. Could take months to get a replacement."

I hear the workers from the other wing laugh, and as I turn to look, they scramble to get back to work.

"I'll request they pull the one from wing four from inventory stores," I say. "I don't think the damage will scrap this fixture, though. It's not as bad as all that."

"You mus be sniffin' glue, boy," he says as he mock-laughs while climbing off the assembly fixture. "This is a critical connection fitting. Not somethin' no one is gonna sign off on."

"There is an easy fix for this," I say to Danny. "I have an idea. Come see it and tell me what you think."

Reluctant as a teenager who had just been told to take out the rubbish, he climbed up from the other side of the wing to meet me at the top. After I explained my idea of how to fix the misaligned hole, his eyes were wide and his spirits lifted.

"That's a shit-hot idea. With that sort of tool we could change a ton of rework hours and replacement costs. Hell, it could save this company millions in replacement parts."

"Serious?" I ask skeptical of the extent of the impact. "It seems like such a no-brainer tool design to me."

"You draft up the design," he says. "I'm going to go find some tool steel and start making the prototype. If I build it quick, we can prove its use on this error. Make sure you define the test and verification of the design."

Three days later, we had nine people on top of the assembly fix-ture. Three from Stress Engineering and two from Army contracts and specifications, two from quality control, and two from Bell Helicopter legal team. They each took turns looking at the tool Danny and I had designed and have positioned in place to clean up the misaligned hole in the fixture. Everyone seemed to be more excited about the new tool than disappointed in the red-card assembly error.

When we had all the approvals, Danny set up the reamer and turned the motor on. A minute later, the hole was repaired. Although the hole was now oversized, it was perpendicular and perfectly round. Stress had already procured the new bolt, albeit larger than the design called for. However, rather than weakening the fixture with an oversized hole, the math proved that the fixture was strengthened.

"You guys will get a bonus for creating a new tool," Gil said after all the observers had left. "There's a lot of upper brass talking about the two of you, and this is icing on the cupcake."

Just like Gil told us, there was a bonus for creating tools for the company. It took a week before Danny and I got our bonus check. But before that arrived, the two of us were part of a staged photograph where we acted like we were working on the wing. The photo would be front page of the company's monthly magazine. The article will mention us by name.

"Big day for you two," Gil says as he hands an envelope to Danny and another to me. "Don't spend it all in one place." He laughed as he walked away.

I ran my thumb under the flap and tore the envelope open. Before I could pull the check out, one of the union employees came up to me.

"That bonus was well deserved, man. You two are doing a hell of a job up here all by yourselves. Making the rest of us look like fools. Man, you got us beat by a month or more now."

"Thank you, brother," I say, extending my hand. "My name is Mark."

He grinned an unfriendly grin. "You need to thank the union for those checks, man. We fought management for everything you get. If not fur us, you would get nuttin' but a pat on the back from management. Y'all need to join up and do the right thing."

He strolled off. "Alright, you made a good point," I say.

"You need to get your partner to sign on."

"Hot shit man, take a look at this!" Danny says with excitement as he reads the check. "Is yours the same as mine?"

"Let me see." I pulled the check from the envelope and read $500.00. Danny craned his neck to look at my check.

"Hell yeah," he slaps me on my back. "I'll be going out to dinner this Friday." He danced some boot scootin' cowboy steps as he stuffed the check into his oversized wallet, which is linked to his belt with a long silver chain.

While I didn't show it, my reaction was a little different to the check. I had calculated that the new tool had initially saved the company over $30,000, and I had estimated the tool would save the company half a million dollars a year. Year after year. Danny and I had created two other tools and four new jigs. It was that fifteen-million-dollar bonus for getting wings two and three completed on schedule that had my attention. Though the $500 was a kick in the teeth from management, I held on to my optimism.

A few months later when the Military representatives voiced concerns that Wing Three was going to be completed before Wing Two. They requested a written explanation from manufacturing management. Management's response was to have Gil switch the union workers over to Wing Three and to put Danny and me on Wing Two.

Three weeks later, Wing Two was estimated to be completed seven weeks ahead of schedule, and Wing Three would be five weeks ahead. Problems arose. The buyers in materials were not ready for a quick completion, so the components for Wing Four would not be in inventory. This means a work stoppage on the assembly line. Management's answer to this was to send me to Philadelphia to head up the final assembly where the wing from Bell Helicopter would be attached to the fuselage from Boeing and the two engines that are supplied from Rolls Royce. They moved Danny to the Cobra assembly line, where he wanted to be in the first place. Union be damned, he still refused to sign on.

Philadelphia is an enormous city. It seems bigger than Dallas, Denver, and Seattle. Those were the only other big cities I had been to. From Manhattan to Virginia, it's all one continuous metropolis. Out west, where I came from, there are hundreds of miles of open space between the cities.

The Boeing assembly plant in Ridley Park was huge. Everyone seemed to be there to watch the V22 come together. Six months away from first flight. It would be aircraft number three that has the honor of testing the rotation of the wing and engines. Aircraft one and two would be used for static testing.

Overwhelmed by the media attention and the size of the plant, I was looking forward to my bonus check. My heart keen on my share of that fifteen million dollar bonus. I was heading to the cafeteria for lunch when two men in suits approached.

"You are from Bell Helicopter, right?" His New York eastern accent was thick. Nearly Italian sounding I thought.

"That's right. My name is Mark."

"Right, Mark. I thought so. My name is Griffin and this handsome fella with me is Henry. We are from Sikorsky in Stratford, Connecticut. We want to buy you lunch."

The old guy, Griffin, sits at the table with his chair pulled back, his legs crossed tight with the left knee over the right. He's formal and well-off, but not rich. Henry is my age, maybe older. Could be thirty. He doesn't look comfortable in a suit, and how he digs into his sandwich confirms he's, like me, born poor. He is probably an unfortunate product of the Reagan and Bush policies that are devastating the country's working class.

"How are they treating you over there at Bell, Mark?" Griffin starts between sips of a steaming cup of coffee. "I want to cut straight to it. We need a creative genius at Sikorsky. A guy like you could go a lot further working at a huge company like United Technologies."

While I chew on a bite of my toasted ham and cheese, I watch his eyes. He's sincere and impatient. I nod with a slight weave of my head.

"That's our parent company," Henry says while chewing and swallowing his meatball sub. He seems to be rushed. As if he's used to rushing through lunch.

"You should come work for us in our International Programs Division," Griffin says. "Henry here can fill you in. I want you to know we will double your salary, and I can get you a five-grand signing bonus. I have to go. It was nice meeting you, Mark." He rose and fast stepped out of the cafeteria.

"Don't worry about him," Henry says as he crumples the sandwich wrap and napkin for the waste can. "He's ready for retirement and, you know what I mean? Anyway, management wants us to recruit you for our International Programs."

"What exactly is that?"

"So we basically modify Black Hawks and the S-92 for foreign governments. You know what I mean? So we can't sell them the same aircraft we sell to our military, so we modify the products. It's intense work, and you get some overseas time. Right now, we are seeing a lot of new buyers. Japan, India, and Indo-Pacific, just to name a few. You know?"

"Cool shit," I say. "But there's one problem for me right now. See, Bell is getting a multimillion-dollar bonus for getting wings two and three out of assembly on schedule. I don't want to do anything that jeopardizes my cut. Otherwise, I would probably be interested."

"Oh hell no, Mark. I know you've only been in this military contractor business for a few years, so like you don't know it. Those bonuses go to the executives. A handful of fat cats at the top. They don't share that with guys like us. We're just minows and sweat labor. You know what I mean?"

A week later, I received a letter from Sikorsky offering me the position, a generous pay increase, and a ten-thousand-dollar sign on if I accepted within two weeks. The offer was substantial. They would pack and move all my personal property, including my car. For the first month, they put me in an all expenses paid stay at the Marriot Residence Hotel, and they bought my house in Texas at full value. I don't have to worry about selling it.

These were different times, and while offers like these used to be common, they are today becoming rare. Before 1981, corporations used their profits to attract talent and to invest in their employees. President Bush was changing the laws, though. The Republicans wanted to further deregulate corporate restrictions to give larger incentives to executives rather than provide for employees. They used Reagan's Hollywood-trained and experienced acting skills to push legislation that deregulated corporate benefits so that corporate profits no longer had to pay for employee medical and retirement pensions. Continuing the theft, President Bush and the wealthy aimed to create a country where ninety-nine percent of the population lived in desperation, while rewarding the elite one percent simply for their wealth.

Here I was working right at the end of the golden age of the American middle class and the beginning of the American oligarchy. I can only hope the American people will never elect a Hollywood-trained actor into politics again.

My last meeting with Mr. Lawrence was befitting of my awakening. I had thought my skills would lead to wealth, but now I realize the system is rigged. He had a lot to say about the system being out of his control, and how he had to comply with company policy and corporate standards. It was his gaslighting that I found most disturbing.

"This is unfair and most unfortunate, mister," he says. "You didn't give me a chance to fight for you. You could have come to me and told me you were unhappy. I could have made changes to your wages and benefits. Why didn't you come to talk to me before accepting their offer?"

My eyes were wide. Shocked at the idea that, in his mind, this was somehow my fault. "I saved this company's ass. No. That's not fair. Danny and I gave you our best and got your V22 contract out of the red and on schedule. I created three tools and four assembly jigs for the company and at a very light estimation, made an extra twenty-five million dollars of profits in the last year. You gave me two thousand five hundred dollars for the effort. That's .0001 percent of the profits derived from my work.

"So you wonder why you can't keep talent at this company and why these unions fight back so aggressively. You have a fairly narrow vision and a deep misunderstanding of people. I know you misjudged me. Do you think I work to get by or because that's what people in my caste are supposed to do? I believe in myself and my right to fair compensation for my skills, not to be bound by a corporate wage policy set to arbitrary brackets based on a job title.

As I exit the Vortex Room of the engineer's building, Danny was standing by the row of bicycles waiting.

He kicks at a loose bolt on the ground. "So that's it? You're leaving?"

I see the tractor pulling the V22 wing three towards the flight line. "Looks that way."

"Damn shame. We were on a hell of a roll. Management was startin' to sweat, you know? Thinkin' bout how much they'd have to pay us if they couldn't pretend we were just another couple of grunts."

"Yeah?" I couldn't help but grin at his use of the word grunts. "Well, they didn't have to pretend. They just had to write the checks small enough so we'd get the message."

"Five hundred bucks for a tool that'll save 'em millions," he scoffed. "Hell, that don't even buy a good set of boots."

"Look at that thing, Danny," I say as I nod at the V22. "The dream. A machine that can do it all—hover like a chopper, fly like a jet. The future of military aviation, right there. And yet, what's it doing?"

"Sittin' on its ass, waiting for some suit to sign a piece of paper," his forehead lined and eyes were wide.

"Exactly. Built to be free, designed to break every limitation we've known, but it's stuck. Every step forward, there's someone in a meeting, someone looking at a budget sheet, someone saying, 'Not yet.'"

"Kinda like us," Danny says, shaking his head.

"Exactly like us. We built the tools, solved their problems, got their schedule back on track. And what do we get? A photo in the company magazine and a check so small I had to hold it up to the light to see if it was real."

Danny leans back, stretching. "And you think Sikorsky's different?"

"I think they're at least offering me something closer to what I'm worth. Double my salary. A real bonus. Hell, they're even buying my house. I don't have to fight for every inch there.

"I'll tell you the truth, Danny. I think I know how this industry works. No matter where you go, there's always a brass ring just out of reach and some exec who thinks your hands belong in your pockets instead of on the money that makes them rich. But at least with this move, I'm getting my hands on something more than scraps."

We walked and talked for a long time. He told me about his date with the woman in procurement. It had been a long time coming, and it sounded like they got off to a good start. The nights came early in December, so we made our way to the parking lot.

"Goodbye, Danny."

"See you in the sky, brother."

Chapter 3: The Cost of Loyalty
Net worth $7,800

"How about a game, Eightball?" Grandpa always answers the phone like this when I call. You see, we played a lot of eight ball together and, well, he had 'dad' humor.

"Those were the best days," I say with a chuckle. "Did you get the V22 rollout video?"

"What a hoopla," he says with an air of reverence. "More brass and neckties than I could count. I saw the writeup they did about you and the photo on the cover of their company magazine."

"It is an impressive aircraft," I say. "They didn't want to pay me a fair share for what I gave them. You know. I'm too impatient maybe, but I don't want to 'die' rich, I want to 'live' rich.

"Not to go too far off topic, but do you remember when the new company I'm working for was sending a limousine to pick me up at Kennedy Airport? Well, it turns out that Connecticut Limo is a corporation that provides bus service out of Kennedy to Connecticut. A bus company, not a limo service," I laugh and then wait for him to laugh. He didn't, but he went deeper. He often changes his tone and demeanor when he dives below the surface to explain why and how things are.

"It's a cult of Hard Work," he says, "where the masses believe effort equals reward, and you have to shatter that illusion. In the big world universe, the mega antagonist you are going to face is Mankind's Fear of Chaos; humanity needs structure. Governments, banks, laws, and religious institutions exist because people are terrified of an unregulated world where true ambition is unchecked. This isn't you getting wealthy, it isn't just making money—you are tearing down the psychological safeguards of civilization. The Architect, as the Universe names it—a faceless entity representing the world's deep-seated need for order.

"Take care, kiddo. Here's your Grandma."

"Sorry," she says. "You know, since he's had all the strokes, he gets scattered like that. Don't listen to him. Tell me who are you dating now? Is she pretty? What am I saying ... all your girlfriends are pretty."

"You know, the new job is so different from anything I imagined I would ever do. Working in Japan, flying across the Pacific to South Korea, Guam, it's interesting work too. But no."

"No, what?" she asks.

"You asked me about a girlfriend. None right now. I'm too focused to go hunting for companionship."

"A man needs a woman in his life. She'll help you and share the burden with you. Your son lives in Las Vegas now."

"Oh, yeah?"

"About two months ago, I guess. They moved from Twentynine Palms to Nevada. He runs and competes in track and field racing in school. His picture was in the paper. I'm sending you a newspaper clipping from their local paper.

"There's some sad news about your sister, Caryl," her voice drops. "My gosh Mark. You knew she was living with a man down in Albuquerque, right?"

"Last time I spoke with your daughter, she told me the guy was slapping her around some. She made me promise to leave them alone. She said it was a life lesson Caryl needed to learn on her own."

"Sandra, your mother, she should have let you intervene," she says. "Hindsight is twenty-twenty. Anyway, they drove off Red Mountain Pass in the blizzard. The road was iced over. The rescue teams had to wait two months because of the avalanche danger. Once spring came, they were able to recover their bodies. It was just horrible, Mark."

"Listen, Grandma, I have to go."

"Take your time to understand the sorrow," she whispers. I can hear the tears in her voice. "And don't hurry it away. Emotions are nothing to fool around with."

"Thank you for keeping me up to speed on the family. It helps to know what little I can. There's a shop in town with a sale on a computer I need. Today is the last day of the sale, and they close in an hour. So I have to run."

"Call your mom sometime. Bye for now. We love you."

There is never any proven way to deal with death. I don't know what I was feeling. My sister was nine when I left home nearly sixteen years ago. This was so bizarre, but while I couldn't feel any grief, I knew we were all destined for life's end. At this time in my life, I have been living on my own longer than I lived at home. Poor sister. It must have been a frightening last moment.

In the silence of the hotel room, I imagined her face as a child—freckled, mischievous, forever nine in my mind. And then a flash of her body—broken, frozen, anonymous beneath Red Mountain snow. Not the image any brother should carry. That night I didn't drink. I didn't cry. I studied the new vulnerabilities in the ACH system. The price of never returning, I told myself, is this: Grief is a form of gravity. I chose velocity instead.

But even velocity has a cost. That night, I disassembled the emotion the way I'd debug a program—line by line, testing its logic. I told myself that sorrow was inefficient. It served no design. But somewhere beneath that calculation was an unprocessed truth I couldn't delete: I hadn't protected her. I hadn't even called. If control meant letting go of family to preserve the mission, then maybe clarity was just cowardice with a clever name.

I opened the folder I'd labeled "Bank Layering Models" and stared at the flowchart—Korea, Japan, Guam, Cayman. It looked like a schematic for escape. But from what? My father's grind, my sister's silence, the government's script?

No. It was worse.

I was running from being average. And that terrified me more than guilt.

Since I'm changing everything—jobs, state, career—it makes sense to start fresh with the banking schemes too. Rapid changes in the world, and new computer systems promise to upgrade banking from transaction-based ledgers, where deposits and withdrawals are recorded manually or in batch processes, to fully digitized records, moving money at the speed of a keystroke. Banks are rolling out Core Banking Systems (CBS) to handle real-time transactions, pushing toward Electronic Funds Transfers (EFTs) to reduce reliance on paper checks. The SWIFT network dominates global transfers, but domestic money movement is shifting to ACH (Automated Clearing House) transactions, allowing corporations and payroll systems to phase out physical banking altogether. Meanwhile, financial deregulation under Reagan has left gaps in the system, and those paying attention can see where the weaknesses are—banks are rushing to modernize, but security is playing catch-up. I stay on the path of educating myself through 2600 Magazine, which is in 1991 to hacking what The Anarchist Cookbook was to underground sabotage in 1971—essential reading on social engineering, phone phreaking, and wire fraud tactics. Bank security is still a joke; blue boxing can bypass long-distance fees, and war dialing can find unsecured modems linked to financial institutions. The real game isn't breaking into a vault—it's knowing where the data is and how to make it move. This isn't just about keeping up; it's about staying ahead, because the system is changing faster than anyone realizes, and those who understand it first will own it.

Seymour, Connecticut, just off the historic Naugatuck River, has a small house perfect for me. Two days after I arrived, I put in an offer to buy it. Fingers crossed. For now, I'm heading to downtown Seymour, where there is a PC Store that has the perfect new setup for me.

The artificial heat was bold as I entered the store. The floors are wet with melted snow and the footprints of previous customers. I kick the snow from my boots and step inside. Unmistakable smells of plastic and solder are near suffocating, the air humming with the low whine of CRT monitors lined against the walls. "The Future is Now," the banner reads, a gaudy splash of red and white above a display of machines that promise speed, power, and possibilities.

I run my hand across the cold plastic casing of the IBM PS/2 Model 80. A 25 MHz Intel 80386 processor—lightning fast for its time. I can almost hear the computations snapping to attention. It's got a 120MB hard drive, more storage than I know what to do with. Yet. The salesman, a slick-haired kid in a cheap blazer, prattles on about its advanced micro-channel architecture and how it "crushes" the limitations of the older ISA bus. I nod like I care.

Otherwise, I desperately want to use the Hayes Ultra 9600 baud modem sitting in a glass case behind the register. It is the key to dialing in, slipping past firewalls and into the quiet, digital sanctums where money moves before anyone knows it's gone.

And then there's the language. The future of programming, they say. A hybrid beast—Borland's Turbo C++—blending structured efficiency with the raw power of object-oriented design. It'll let me build something modular, something adaptable. A system that can hide itself in plain sight, rewriting its footprint as it goes.

While these are not the systems, mainstream media hype for the huge advertising budgets. I get my advice from my old trusted source called The Private Sector and Metal Shop Private. These are folks on the BBS that share key viruses, program hacks, and phreaking updates. They had lists that were coveted by CIA and FBI like the X.25

network access codes, which was an international data network, including, like the name says, access codes.

"How will you be paying?" the cashier says with a smug eastern-privileged tone of voice. "Let me guess, a personal check?"

I slap my platinum card down on the counter, watching the kid's eyes widen. "I'll take it all," I say, my voice even. The machine, the modem, the compiler.

When I got back to the hotel, there wasn't time to set up the new system. It can wait until I move into the new home.

A sleepless night ahead of the early morning meeting with the buyer, sales representative, and design engineer for the Japan program. My anxiety holds me tight and I have no time for much else. Sikorsky and this first project. My mind runs wild in many directions. It is all very exciting. Before I could sleep the morning arrives.

"You must have a receipt for each meal. Daily," Luz, the program's project manager, says. "Do not buy alcohol with your meals; the company does not reimburse for alcohol." She goes on and on about per diem expenses. The sales representative then stands and takes the last twenty minutes of the meeting explaining the contractual pieces.

"Their engineers will be in charge of the modifications. They will develop every design and process control. We are there to provide oversight and guidance."

"Can you clarify what oversight entails?" I ask.

"Our seats are together," he says. "On the flight over, I will explain the details. Most of these people aren't interested in engineering and we shouldn't bore them. Anymore than we want to listen to their explanations of what we can and cannot drink with our meals."

"Don't start with me, Greg Dillon," the project manager says, his half-smile undercut by the sharp edge in his voice.

He runs into my shoulder as he walks past, so taking the hint, I grab my notes and follow him out.

The first time I met the Japanese engineers, I could feel their quiet scrutiny. Not just of my expertise—of my presence, my intent. In their world, technical knowledge wasn't enough. Respect had to be earned, not assumed, and an outsider—especially an American flown in for oversight—was an unknown variable.

I played it carefully. Measured words, observant silence, patience. I knew better than to challenge their way of doing things outright. The project was ambitious—cutting-edge aerospace, a collaboration that merged precision manufacturing with military-grade innovation. Speed was what the Americans wanted, but Japan's focus is on perfection. Somewhere in between, reality had to take shape.

The engineers were sharp, disciplined, and meticulous to the point of obsession. I had to prove my worth, not just with numbers, but with time. So I watched. I learned their rhythm. I let them see I wasn't here to upend their methods—I was here to refine them.

Two weeks after arriving, the project manager called me out at the start of the morning meeting. Where every day the entire team reviewed the helicopter progress and prioritized the day for design engineers and production. Today he decided it was the right time to introduce me.

"Why you here?" he asked.

"I'm sorry. What?"

He repeated his question, forceful, in a thick accent, "Why you here?" Then motions for me to come to the front of the meeting room.

As I walked from the back of the room, "Before I tell you why I am here, I have two questions. First, why does everyone speak English? I thought that was going to be our biggest obstacle."

"This is the language of the computer age," Itsukiro says. "We must know English to learn computers from American capitalists."

"That is a very interesting phenomenon. Thank you, Itsukiro. My second question is, what the absolute fuck are you trying to do here?"

My voice is loud, my face red, and I can feel the anger boil. As I took a pointer stick from the hamper and directed everyone to the blueprint on the wall.

"This is a firewall. Did you see it?" A few nod, but many appear frozen in place.

"Yes. Good. So why are you running fuel and hydraulic lines through a firewall? Are you fucking insane? Do you want to kill everyone in this helicopter? For six days, I have watched you in this meeting, and not one person has questioned the design.

"That is why I am here. To stop you from murdering pilots and crews. This shit isn't going to get past me. You aren't going to make chicken soup with chicken shit.

"Thank you." I walked back to the rear of the meeting room while the team sprang into a chaotic exchange.

But while my days were spent ensuring the tolerances held, and the program stayed on track, my nights were spent thinking about something else entirely.

Because Japan wasn't just an engineering opportunity. It was the gateway I discovered on a layover in Seoul, an unexpected delay that left me with twelve hours to kill. I wasn't in the habit of wasting time.

At a bar near Itaewon, I met a man named Dennis, an ex-pat from Chicago who'd been living in Korea for years. He wasn't military, not anymore. He had the air of someone who had figured out how to make money move—and more importantly, how to keep it from being found.

"You work for an American company?" Dennis asked, swirling the whiskey in his glass.

"Defense contract. Engineering oversight," I said.

He smirked. "Sounds like the kind of job that pays well but doesn't let you keep much."

I raised an eyebrow. "And you know a way around that?"

He leaned in slightly. "You ever heard of nominee accounts?"

I shook my head.

"Korea's got banking laws that make it easy to move money without too many eyes on it," he said. "If you know the right people, you can set up an offshore entity in the Pacific—Guam, for starters. Then, if you structure it right, layer it through a corporate shell in Korea or Japan, then suddenly you've got an account that isn't tied directly to you."

I took a sip of my drink, letting the idea settle.

It made sense.

Japan was a bureaucratic nightmare for foreign banking, but Korea? It was fast, modern, and less rigid. And Guam—well, that was still U.S. territory, but with just enough leeway to work with.

Dennis shrugged, finishing his drink. "Just something to think about."

I was already thinking about it.

By the time I boarded my flight to Tokyo, I had a new plan forming. Engineering by day, strategy by night.

Back in Tokyo, I buried myself in the project. I kept my head down, made sure my work was flawless, methodical, unimpeachable.

I knew better than to draw attention.

During the day, I was the engineer. I met with the technicians, reviewed schematics, adjusted for tolerances that the Americans hadn't accounted for. The Japanese respected that. They saw I wasn't just some corporate oversight figure—I knew the machines as well as they did.

But at night, the genuine wealth building work began.

I started asking quiet questions. Banks that handled foreign accounts. Legal firms that specialize in corporate filings. I established a contact in Osaka who had worked for an oil company—he gave me a name in Seoul. That name led to a banker in Busan who knew how to structure a shell company.

I met with him in a back room of a hotel, the place where conversations weren't recorded and deals were made on paper, not computers.

"This company," he said, sliding the documents toward me. "It does not exist. It is a name. A set of numbers. A signature on the proper form."

"And the bank account?" I asked.

"That depends on how you structure it," he said. "A nominee director in Korea keeps your name off the paperwork. A secondary corporation in Japan gives it legitimacy. And Guam?" He smiled. "That's where the money moves."

I looked over the documents. It was clean. Almost too clean.

I signed.

By the end of the month, I had an offshore structure that didn't trace back to me.

And no one—not my company, not my colleagues, not the project—had the slightest idea.

~~~

Bizarre trends and sensationalism have combined in an epidemic of madness across the U.S. "What can I get you?" the nun on the other side of the pulpit asks. Her large breasts burst out of her modified habit, her painted face framed above her wimple. She can only hear me if I shout above the sound from the band playing in the choir stalls of this once Catholic church now operating as a nightclub. The pews, stained glass windows, altar, and plethora of life-sized statues of saints remain in place, including Jesus bleeding on the cross hanging above the barkeeper's shelves stacked with hundreds of bottles.

The air inside is humid and pungent with the smell of old incense, cheap cologne, and sweat—a layered stench of piety and partying. Somewhere beneath it all, a faint trace of mildew clings to the wooden pews and velvet kneelers like a warning.
~~~

"Doctor Pepper, please," I shout.

"That's it?" Her dark brown eyes raised in a disgusted judgment of my non-alcoholic request.

Moments later, she slides a tall, ice-filled chalice towards me, sweeping up my five-dollar bill with her left hand as she moves on to the next customer. I scan the scene. How would I find the contact in this loud, poorly lit, and crowded bar? He won't be on the dance floor, and I doubt he's sitting on a pew. Everyone else, I decided, was a candidate. A vague BBS message with six words: "Yellow Tie event, Boston Church Club 8 PM."

I look around, wondering if I have the wrong bar or perhaps the wrong day. I'm the only one wearing a yellow tie.

I take a sip. Syrupy. Synthetic. The medicinal bite of prune and cherry tries to pass as refreshment but sticks to the roof of my mouth like regret. It's a drink designed to fake joy, and here it is—served in a chalice beneath a bleeding Jesus.

As I look up at the iconic symbol, my thoughts run like a prayer. More than a raise is what I'm looking for. I don't want a seat at their goddamn table. I want my own table—in another house, on another street, in a city they've never heard of. A place where their rules don't apply. Where I'm not just another useful cog, but the axis they orbit.

"Jesus. You wore one," he says. "That's ... committed, man. But no, 'Yellow Tie' isn't about a tie. It's about caution. It's about keeping your mouth shut and your signal clean. You know, 'Yellow Tie'—like 'Tying Up Loose Ends'? The whole point is that if you had to ask, you weren't supposed to be here."

"So then, I should lose the tie?" I say, trying to be cool, calm, and collected.

His laugh lit up the bar, and his head bobbed in the direction that led the way to the side door. The air shifts as we pass through the door. Gone is the sweaty press of perfume and incense. Out here, the night smells of moss, wet stone, and the faint rot of fallen leaves.

Randal exhales, the warmth of his beer breath mixing with the icy breath of the crypts. It's not unpleasant, just ... honest. Out here, the stench of the church's contradictions has no place.

I tossed the tie into a shrub a few feet into the church graveyard. "Stupid of me to take it so literal," I say.

"Hell naw, man, I was dead sure it was you when I saw that beacon around your neck. But ya know, it will always stay just between us." His laugh was contagious, and I half expected he would wake the dead with it.

"This is all Oprah's fault." He took a long time to sip from his chalice.

Cautious to not slip on a racial slur, I struggle to ask the obvious question. After a long pause, he seized the opportunity to have a go at me.

"Are you scared to say something about her because she's black?" he asks.

"Why would I say something about her being black?"

"So then you don't want to say anything about Oprah because I'm black?" His eyes went wide, so all I could focus on was the whites and his matching bright teeth.

"Stop being so provocative, man. Shit. So explain what Oprah has to do with any of this," I say as I sit my chalice on a gravestone and shove my hands into my pockets, seeking warmth.

"It was your boy Reagan who deregulated the media. You know, making it okay for everyone to tell fibs on television. Truth is no longer a requirement. Next thing you know, we wake up to 24-hour cable news. All day long news instead of what's really happening, we now have CNN in answer to a new demand for constant programming. It took a year before they verged beyond straight news reporting to include analysis and commentary to fill time. Their success encouraged other networks to follow suit.

"Talk shows and personality-driven formats, you know. Shows like The Oprah Winfrey Show and The Jerry Springer Show shifted daytime television from scripted dramas and soap operas to opinion-heavy, personality-driven content. These shows are less about objective storytelling and more about engaging with polarizing or sensational topics. Striking at everyone's sensitivities and caused deeply divided public opinion. It sells advertising in the millions of dollars.

"Now here we are, coming up on a decade of deregulation, and the trend is causing bars to open up in abandoned churches where you can take drugs and get drunk in front of your gods. In a couple more years, my brother, these networks will adopt even worse content. A pivot toward more ideologically driven news coverage. No longer will the public have news based on facts that support truth. We will have opinion shows decorated as news hours and just like our politics, we'll treat everything like it's a sport where one side wins and the other loses. The only thing is, we all lost the last threads of freedom ten years ago."

This guy is as well-informed as anyone I have ever met. He's telling me my own thoughts with a familiar angst. Perhaps a colored angle is new.

"That isn't my boy," I say. "The politicians in this country are bought and paid for. Both sides are millionaires working for the mega-millionaires. Soon to be billionaires. And your girl, Oprah, is in collusion with the highest-paying advertisers. One thing you missed is the up-and-coming internet. If it becomes half as powerful as expected, it will provide instant access to breaking news, and audiences will become less reliant on traditional opinion and personality broadcasts. Networks will be forced to focus on opinion segments, which will be measured for success by viewers engaged for longer periods."

We are far from the church now. Deep inside, the graveyard's labyrinth of tombs and headstones. I stop and extend my hand. "I'm Mark."

"I'm Randal ." His grip was casual but committed. "So, you're into finance systems?" Randal asked, taking a slow sip from his glass.

"I'm into finding the gaps. The places the money falls through. Doesn't matter if it's a bank, a casino, or an insurance scheme—there's always a way in."

Randal chuckled, a rich sound that hinted at something deeper than mere amusement. "Funny. I think we see the world the same way. You ever work with S and Ls?"

I raised an eyebrow. "Savings and Loans? That industry is as dead as this graveyard. A devastation that is going to cost the public billions. A debt from Bush and Reagan policies. Which is why it's the perfect hunting ground," I say, leaning in. "They're transitioning to digital records, but the process is slow and uneven. Some banks still use only paper records, others use a mix of paper and digital records, and some are in a transitional state. You see what that means?"

Randal considered it. "It means ... discrepancies. Money that can exist in two places at once."

I grinned. "Exactly. Echo accounts. Money that's real in one system but not the other. Imagine a ledger that tells one bank there are thousands of dollars in an account, but the other side never debits it. That money still exists—digitally, at least—for just long enough to move it."

Randal exhaled slowly. "That's bold. No salami slicing, no skimming pennies. You're talking about full-scale synthetic money."

I nodded. "An Echo ledger. A money illusion that exists long enough to be leveraged into cash. It's not just theft. It's financial alchemy."

Randal leans back on a polished marble crypt, rolling the thought over in his head. It wasn't just viable—it was genius. "And how do we get the cash out before the illusion collapses?" My eyes gleamed.

"That's where you come in," he says.

"I've read about your expertise in system integrity. We don't just steal. We reinvest. Our goal isn't to drain accounts—we move the money so fast that no one notices they have been robbed until it's four countries away. I make sure the timing stays airtight. No loose ends."

Randal grinned. "I like it. Let's start small. A proof of concept."

I lifted my challis. "To the Echo Ledger."

Randal clinked his challis against it. "To making money out of thin air."

Randal and I spent two weeks refining the approach. He ran simulations, stress-tested the latency gaps between digital and paper systems, and built a script that could generate echo transactions. I reached out to my offshore contacts in South Korea and Japan, setting up a third corporate front that could receive and cycle the funds.

The first score was modest—$150,000 wired to a fabricated corporate account under the guise of a real estate investment firm in Seoul. Just enough to verify that the system lag would keep us under the radar. When the funds landed and the bank failed to register the anomaly in time, I knew we were onto something.

Randal leaned back, fingers tapping against his beer bottle. "We scale this, we're talking millions. Maybe tens of millions."

I nodded. "But we need to be disciplined. We don't get greedy. We don't leave patterns. Every hit needs to be unique."

"This is criminal bullshit, and federal bullshit too," he says.

"It's the same crap the politicians do every day, only they pass laws and regulations to disguise their crimes."

Randal smirked. "And you're sure you can keep this invisible?"

"That's what I do. Your expertise in S&L and me, I make the transactions so clean it becomes invisible."

Randal leaned back, his expression shifting—less amused now, more calculating.

"So. What's this project you mentioned in the email?"

I took a long breath. "Brunei."

His eyebrow arched slightly, curious but not impressed yet.

"I met the Sultan. He's a paradox. Conservative in public, radically pragmatic in private. Likes to talk theology in the morning and ask questions about synthetic yield curves by sundown."

Randal chuckled. "Royal schizophrenia."

"No. Royal insulation. He rules a population of less than half a million with full no cost healthcare, no taxes, state-sponsored housing and education—an Islamic monarchy wrapped in a socialist safety net. But that safety net is a mirage. They don't publish economic data for a reason. The state's balance sheet is increasingly off-books, and the oil reserves are ... aging."

"And you're the American lifeline."

"Something like that," I said. "They're packaging their sovereign family trust into four shells, each tied to a different initiative—climate innovation, Islamic education, women's equity, and of course, a halal biotech fund. All paper. All pristine. I do the money movement. They grant diplomatic courtesy. Everyone wins."

Randal exhaled slowly. "Offshore identities?"

"Already set. I had dinner with his nephew. He knew just enough to make my operation airtight. We'll run the KYC through Kuala Lumpur. Singapore legal team is clean and discreet. BVI holding company layered over a Liechtenstein Stiftung. We'll build the investment vehicles as philanthropic arms. Just enough truth to be convincing. Just enough fiction to be untouchable."

Randal grinned. "You always two steps past safe."

I raised my glass. "Safe's for pensioners."

He stayed quiet for a beat too long. Not the kind of pause that comes from wonder—but the kind that smells of calculation. I've seen it in boardrooms, casinos, and war rooms—men running the odds behind their eyes.

"You ever burn a partner before?" he asked. Casual, like he was asking about my last vacation.

"Not unless they asked for it. There's no safety net beneath either of us."

Randal gave me a slow nod, like that was good enough—for now.

That's when I knew he wasn't just testing the system. He was testing me.

He nodded, then glanced around the graveyard, like he was making sure the dead weren't listening in. Then he shifted gears.

"You realize, of course," he said, "that all this is fallout from the '90s expansion. Higher tax revenues gave municipalities an illusion of control. Suddenly, cities and states had leverage—they could borrow, build, inflate their own shadows. It was Reagan's long con bearing fruit."

I took another sip, waiting.

"Reagan didn't deregulate to create freedom," Randal said. "He deregulated to create plutocracy. Anything that stood between corporations and their executives—fair wages, environmental accountability, fiduciary ethics—it all became negotiable. He stripped the bones off the New Deal and handed the marrow to shareholders."

I laughed. "So the invisible hand got a manicure."

"No," he said. "It got a gold ring and a private jet. But the idea that corporations are people? That was born in Bush's evil scheme for making America rich and poor. Wealth cannot grow unconditionally unless you gut the middle. And those evil, wealth addicted people—they don't die. They multiply."

"Reagan didn't just deregulate, Mark. He broke the backs of the unions—took a sledgehammer to the last line of defense for working people. PATCO was just the opening shot. The moment he fired those air traffic controllers, every CEO in America got the green light. They slashed pensions, froze wages, turned benefits into optional perks.

"And when the blood dried, they shipped the jobs overseas—China, Mexico, Singapore, Korea. Anywhere someone would work for pennies and keep their mouths shut. They gutted entire cities like fish and called it efficiency. Left behind shopping malls and payday lenders where factories used to be.

"The middle class wasn't lost. It was sold. And the rich? They made it look like we were the problem—like we didn't work hard enough, hustle fast enough, believe big enough. That's the genius of it. They took everything, then sold us shame for dessert."

He glanced sideways at me.

I shrugged, "That's why the system can't be reformed. It was never broken. It was built this way, one politician after another. Bought and paid for. And now we're the parasites? Nah, man—we're the antibodies."

"Look at Detroit," he said. "Used to be the arsenal of democracy. Now it's a museum of promises that never made it past the factory gates. Entire blocks look like a war zone—gutted homes, stripped plants, schools without heat. And what did the suits do? They blamed the unions for wanting too much and called it the natural order of capitalism."

He tilted his chalice and took another sip.

"Indianapolis? Same playbook. Once they got NAFTA signed, they walked those manufacturing jobs right out the door and handed 'em to a twelve-year-old in a Mexico City sweatbox, and draft dodgers in Canada. Then they flooded the Midwest with payday loans, box stores, and fen-fen to keep folks quiet while the equity firms bought up the remains.

"And the kicker?" he added, voice low and bitter. "They convinced half the country to vote for the same bastards who lit the match."

I let the silence stretch.

Then I nodded. "Brunei gives us time. The U.S. gives us motive."

Randal smiled. "And we provide the means."

The warmth in Randal's voice cooled as we walked in silence past a row of crypts slicked with moss. I could hear the faint beat of the music leaking from the church walls behind us—like a memory trying to stay alive.

"You said not to leave patterns," Randal said at last.

"Right."

"Then that means no wives. No real estate. No kids in private school. No trust funds. No charity galas or second homes in the Berkshires. You ready for that?"

I stopped. The cold of the granite under my palm reminded me of the Texas soil I buried myself under, once. "Why do you think I came back to the East Coast?"

"Everyone comes here eventually," he said. "But not everyone makes peace with staying invisible."

He let the statement sit like a verdict.

"You think I need to be seen?"

"I think you need to be known," Randal said. "That's more dangerous."

I wanted to laugh. But it landed too close to bone. Randal hadn't asked for proof of funds. He was profiling my hunger. That's what he was testing.

"You got a lot to lose, Mark. That house in Seymour? That's a monument. You're building a future on secrets. Just make sure it doesn't turn into a tomb." I didn't answer because he was right.

My house wasn't just a symbol of reinvention—it was a vault of buried intent. Every wire running through those walls, every reinforced panel, kept control from slipping. I learned in Texas that remodeling a home provides a money laundering opportunity the IRS cannot touch.

But clarity? That was bleeding away, bit by bit, every time I justified the next move.

"If we get caught," I said, "we get buried under a prison."

Randal nodded, finally smiling again. "That's why we don't get caught."

But his tone had changed. He wasn't just my partner now. He was my mirror.

We clinked glasses again.

"To sovereign socialism," I said.

"To Reagan's ghost," he replied.

Chapter 4: Fathers of the Future
Net worth $18,000

Who buys five Black Hawk helicopters, not for war, but for pleasure? Who takes a machine built for the brutal efficiency of battle and transforms it into a floating palace?

I step inside the first of them, a craft reborn, its cavernous interior shedding every trace of its military past. The cockpit, once a stark arena of dials and switches, is now a sanctuary of bird's-eye maple, its swirling golden grain polished to a mirror sheen. Deer-skin leather, so supple that my fingers sink into it, wraps the seats—no longer rigid slabs of survival. A scent lingers in the air, something rich, something decadent: aged scotch, rare spices, the quiet exhalation of obscene wealth.

Further inside, the fuselage stretches into a chamber of hedonistic design. A wet bar gleams under a gold-plated fixture, stocked with crystal decanters filled with centuries-old spirits. The dark luster of the Makassar ebony shelves drinks in the light. Opposite, a cinema screen retracts from the ceiling with the whisper of a well-oiled mechanism, revealing a row of silk-clad recliners facing a state-of-the-art projection system. It is a fortress of indulgence, soundproofed with aerospace-grade insulation, ensuring that not even the four mighty rotor blades can disturb the sanctity of its luxury.

Beneath it all, the mechanical heart of the beast has not been forgotten. The engines have been tuned, reworked, and optimized—not for war, but for speed, efficiency, silence. The ride is unnaturally smooth, gliding through turbulence with the ease of a yacht over still water. A military beast transformed into a god's chariot.

And the man behind it? The Sultan of Brunei. A ruler of unfathomable fortune, a monarch whose treasury outshines entire nations. Brunei, a tiny kingdom flush with oil wealth, where golden-domed palaces rise from manicured gardens, where excess is not a privilege but a birthright.

Five Black Hawks, stripped of their war paint, gilded in extravagance, all for one man. Because when your wealth has no limits, neither does your vision of comfort.

Yet beyond the Sultan's golden gates, another Brunei exists. In the villages nestled against lush rainforests, life is a contrast of fortune. Here, the oil wealth trickles down in government subsidies, free housing, healthcare, and education, but the grand opulence seen in the Sultan's palaces remains a distant dream for most. The streets are quiet, the people polite, content yet aware of the unseen walls between them and their ruler's riches.

At the bustling Gadong Market, merchants trade fresh seafood and woven textiles under the glow of hanging lanterns. Elders sip thick, sweet tea, recounting stories of a time before the kingdom's wealth flourished. There are no visible signs of poverty—Brunei's citizens do not suffer as in other nations—but neither do they live in luxury. The Sultan's fortune belongs to him alone, while the nation survives on his generosity.

Even as Black Hawks glide overhead, transformed into flying mansions, the people of Brunei continue with their quiet, measured lives, neither destitute nor lavish. Here, wealth is a force of nature—seen, felt, but never truly shared.

I like it here. People are not worried about providing for their lives and not over-stressed because at any minute they can lose their income, go bankrupt, and become lost in a system that all but devours them. No one treats them like corporate commodities.

Flying here requires a layover in Hong Kong. So, using the time to my advantage, I hired a lawyer. Started a corporation, applied for a business bank account, and a residency identification with a name change. Eight weeks expedited. Lawyers are expensive and hard to find with these specializations.

The Sultan's car pulls into the circular drive outside. Soft hues of a retreating sun paint the sky, as the air is thick with jasmine and fresh rain. The car—a custom Rolls-Royce, black as onyx with gold filigree along the trim—glides to a perfect stop, as if choreographed. The driver steps out first, a tall man in a crisp white uniform, and moves to open the rear door.

There is no hesitation, no fumbling. The Sultan waits, poised, until the door is fully open before emerging. He does not simply step out; he unfurls. One foot touches the ground first, lightly, as if testing the earth. Then, with a fluid motion, he rises, his robes of ivory silk cascading around him. His every movement is deliberate, unhurried, as though time itself waits for his command.

His presence is magnetic, effortless. The fabric of his attire whispers against the air, a seamless blend of tradition and modern elegance. Gold-threaded embroidery runs along the cuffs and collar, subtle yet unmistakably regal. He walks with a grace that suggests he has never known uncertainty, each step measured, neither rushed nor sluggish.

The meeting room awaits. As the Sultan opens the door, the air from outside rushes in—humid, thick with the fragrance of tropical orchids, damp earth, and the distant brine of the South China Sea. The scent of polished mahogany and frankincense lingers within, mingling with the outside world, a collision of nature and refinement. Instinctively, the staff falls silent as he enters, an unspoken recognition of his authority. The Sultan takes his seat at the front of the room, steepling his fingers, his gaze unwavering. Outside, the world moves on, but within these walls, the Sultan concentrates power and wealth.

Twenty minutes later, I burst out of the meeting at full speed. I don't stop running until I'm inside my room at the lodge. My breath is rapid as I wait for an answer on the other end of the phone. "Come on. Come on, answer!" I say to the ringtone.

"Projects, this is Trevor," his voice cracks into the receiver.

"Why the fuck didn't you tell me this contract is a shit show?" I say as my heavy breathing and exasperation collide.

"Mark?" Trevor asks.

"Bloody Christ on a spear, man. I sat in a meeting for twenty minutes while one of the wealthiest people on Earth tore me a new ass in the most polite, perhaps respectful manner. He is such a nice man. But shit hit the fan!"

"Take it easy, Mark," he says. "We've been dealing with this shortage and delays for a while. It's under control."

"Shove that 'take it easy' up your cherry ass. The Sultan is meeting with the team from Aerospatiale right now. He told me that if we don't have ship 2 to him in three months, he would cancel the order for the other three."

"The supplier is struggling with a new commutator with its ceramic core. It's a specialty motor the Sultan insisted on. No other manufacturer makes these ceramic parts. Even Aerospatiale would have to use the same supplier."

"Where's the supplier?" I ask.

"They are in Lexington."

"Get me a flight to Lexington and let the supplier know I am on my way."

"What are you doing?" Trevor's voice changes as he asks, moving from curiosity to anger as he spoke the four words.

"Saving your ass! Send me the details and I will pick up the ticket at the airport. I want a rental car in Lexington."

The phone was silent for a moment. "I'll see you at the airport," Trevor says. "We'll go to the manufacturer together."

Furious and confused, I throw my clothes into my Samsonite carry-on bag. The lodge concierge calls for a cab to take me to the airport. I've never been so humiliated ... and I can't get my thoughts straight. But I know one thing is for certain: I need this contract.

The connection through Hong Kong is critical to my enterprise, and I need two months to set up my corporation and banking and three months from then to get my Hong Kong residency identification.

Having the South Korean business and bank is a start, but this company and the one I have in Gibraltar will get me and Randal right. He sets the loans in motion, and I move the money between corporations. Randal uses his access to the banking software to advance loans with funds that didn't exist. It all falls back on the S&L. The paper trail eventually catches up, and the ledger reveals the horror. The banks have been making loans with money they don't have. Shit hits the fan and they scramble in five directions. Two of those directly affect me. First, they investigate how they overspent the budget and implement corrective actions to prevent recurrence. I cannot use that S&L again. Second, they contact my business, the company they lent the money to, and request a return of the funds. I, of course, have a handful of international receipts from other businesses where the money has already been spent. It cannot be recovered.

For years, I told myself I wasn't like the others—not just another fraud with a suit and a pitch. I believed I was smarter. Faster. That I could learn how to slip through the cracks in the machine because I understood how it worked better than the filthy conservatives and their wealthy backers who built it. I knew which dials to turn, which hands to grease, and where to vanish if things went sideways. But now, standing in that quiet hotel room with my Samsonite half-zipped and my mind fractured into twenty directions, I felt it—the thing I'd refused to name.

I wasn't untouchable. I was hollow.

Not because I was losing the contract—that could be replaced. Not because the new ID was not ready—I could easily have gotten around that. But because somewhere along the way, I'd stopped being a man building something and become a man hiding from collapse. Every corporation I registered, every offshore account, every midnight call with Randal, wasn't about freedom anymore. It was about covering my tracks, so no one could see how terrified I am to be average.

That was the veritable war: not the banks, not the Sultan, not the auditors. The war was in my chest, between the calm clarity of admitting I'd built a sandcastle... and the gnawing urge to keep pretending it was marble. Inside the airport I look in my wallet and notice the missing ID.

It's in the drawer in the room back at the palace hotel!

The flash hits my thoughts and its heat fills my entire being.

I left my Korean ID in the room!

A wave of panic stirred the memory in Seoul—the way the clerk at the South Korean bank handed me the ledger and bowed, no questions asked. I remember the exhilaration of inventing new selves on legal paper. Clarence Williams in Seoul. Lindsey Brem in Kyoto. All variations of a single illusion: that I could stay ahead of the fall if I just moved fast enough. But the fall wasn't coming from behind me. It was inside me, waiting.

And what scared me most wasn't getting caught. It was waking up one day and realizing there was no "me" left to catch—just paper, signatures, and obligations I could no longer explain.

The Sultan never runs. He doesn't need to. He is the center of his own gravity. I am not. I am a man orbiting wealth, trying not to burn up on reentry.

And now, with one document forgotten, a five-country relay of forged legality unraveling around me, and a Gulfstream on the tarmac waiting to carry me deeper into the lie, I had to decide: admit I'm no different than the suckers I swore I'd never be—or sprint faster into the abyss and pray the landing doesn't break me.

The private Gulfstream IV from Brunei was going to be ready in an hour. One airline on and off of the island. The Sultan's airline was taking me to Hong Kong, where I was picking up a direct flight to

Gibraltar. The email from Trevor was long. I skimmed through it to understand the flight details. Gibraltar to Heathrow. A three-hour layover and then a long flight to Kennedy. This time, a five-hour layover and then a flight to Lexington.

When the crew came to take my Samsonite, my heart was in my throat. I'm exposed and heading for prison ... I can't take a cab back to the lodge. I'll miss my connection in Hong Kong.

In that moment, I understood something I hadn't let myself admit—not in Connecticut, not in Seoul, not even inside that floating Black Hawk casino in the sky. No matter how far I ran, how many layers of shell companies and offshore accounts I created, I was still one slip away from ruin. The Sultan? He was the storm. I was just a man holding a kite in the wind, pretending I could fly.

And what scared me most wasn't prison—it was that maybe, just maybe, I'd already lost the only thing that kept me from being average: the illusion that I had it under control.

As he takes the bag from my icy hand, he says, "Ten minutes to boarding, sir."

Nodding and looking around in a panic. "Is there a phone?"

"A phone, sir? Yes. There is one." He points to a wall near the exit doors.

"Give me a few minutes," I say. "It's an emergency call. Okay?"

"We can no wait, sir. The pilot is make over schedules. Sorry."

Pay phone. I search through my pockets for a coin. My heart thumps in my ears, and my head pounds with pain. I'm too young for a stroke. There. I pull a token from my left pocket.

"Palace Lodge. How can we serve you?" The receptionist asks.

"Hello," I say as calm as I can, "This is Mark. The project engineer from Sikorsky. I just left the palace about thirty minutes ago."

"Yes, Mark. Of course. What can I help you with?"

"I left a few items in the drawer next to the bed. Can you put those items in a safe for me until I get back?"

"Oh my goodness, sir. Do you want me to have the driver bring them to you? I take it you are at the airport."

"There is no time. See, the flight is going in a minute. I will be back here in three weeks, and I can get them."

"Hold on a minute." She says.

Every second feels like an hour. The silence on the phone hangs in the air like the end of my life as a free man. My thoughts raced as I imagined trying to explain to Randal why he's going to prison. Say goodbye to his wife and sons because I was too stupid to protect my end of the business.

"Hello, sir," she says, "are you there?"

"Yes. I'm here!"

"The register shows you are back in three weeks. So we will keep the room locked until you return. I hope that will be okay."

"That is fabulous!"

The crewman waves for me to tell me it is time to board the airplane. Outside, on the tarmac behind him, I can see the boarding ladder is being pulled up and the door is closing on the plane.

"Goodbye," I say as I slam the receiver down and run for the plane. Begrudgingly, the crew lowers the boarding ladder and lets me onboard.

The air in Lexington was colder than I expected, sharp and gray, like the feel of weather meant to slap sense into a man. The rental car was waiting at the curb. Trevor was already in the passenger seat, holding a manila folder as if it contained a map to salvation. He didn't speak when I opened the door. Just handed me the folder and waited for me to read.

I skimmed the first page. Delays. Ceramic fracture during testing. A revised production estimate: six months.

"This is a death sentence," I said.

"They're a niche supplier," Trevor muttered. "No one else builds commutators to these specs, let alone with ceramic cores. The Sultan wanted a whisper-quiet glide with military-grade torque. This was the only way."

"You should've said something before we promised delivery."

"You should've asked."

The silence that followed was the kind that corrodes partnerships. We drove the rest of the way to the facility in tension so thick I could feel my molars grind.

The supplier was a squat red-brick building tucked behind an auto body shop, with a sun-faded sign that simply read: CRYOTEX SYSTEMS. Inside, it smelled like burnt ozone and metal filings. The floor manager, a balding engineer in his sixties named Denny, met us at the front office with a nod and a limp handshake.

"You here to yell?" he asked, his voice gravel-soaked.

"I'm here to understand," I said. "Because in three months, if we don't deliver, I lose a contract worth more than your entire annual output."

Denny's laugh was bitter and short. "Son, I've got six prototypes shattered under stress testing and a machinist in ICU from a blown housing seal. You think I care about your contract?"

That was it. The illusion snapped. No amount of money, offshore registrations, forged receipts, or poetic engineering reports could control this. A man named Denny, wearing a shirt with a grease stain shaped like a gun, had more power over my future than I did. This wasn't about brilliance. Cleverness wasn't the issue here. This was about materials science and bone-weary laborers trying to invent a miracle on deadline.

I looked at Trevor. "We're not flying back tonight."

"We're not?" he asks.

"No. We're going to find out if Denny and his team are heroes, liars, or about to bankrupt us all."

~~~
~~~

The IRS building squats on High Street like a gray, nearly windowless warning, a monument to everything I don't understand about government power. It's nondescript in the way only federal buildings manage—concrete, security cameras, tinted glass that lets them see me while I see nothing. I know they're watching.

The street hums with Hartford's midday traffic, but it feels distant, as if I'm hearing it through water. A delivery truck rattles past. A woman in a business suit, strides toward the entrance with the confidence of someone who knows she belongs here. I don't.

The air is thick with the scent of fresh rain, which sinks into the pavement and leaves everything slick and shining. Puddles gather along the curb, reflecting the sky in fractured, shifting pieces. The trees lining the street, young and bright with new spring leaves, shake in the breeze, their wet branches trembling as if they, too, are waiting for judgment.

The sidewalk beneath my feet might as well be quicksand. The weight of history presses down—not just mine, but every name ever dragged through this place, every small business owner who thought they were playing the game right until they weren't. Capone didn't go down for murder or racketeering. He went down for bad bookkeeping. So did more than a few men smarter than me.

The IRS lobby smells like damp carpet and paperwork. Rain followed me in, clinging to my jacket, dripping from my sleeves onto the tile. Fluorescent lights buzz overhead, washing everything in a colorless haze. A few people sit on stiff plastic chairs along the wall, staring into the void, waiting for whatever verdict the government has in store.

I step up to the directory, a beige metal cabinet with a sheet of names behind plastic, and trace my finger down the list. The black ink on the paper shows my auditor's name; the paper looks like it hasn't been updated in years. Fourth floor, room one.

Decades of use cracked the up arrow and yellowed the elevator buttons. I press it and hear the cables groan above. The doors open to an empty cube lined with brushed aluminum panels, scratched and scuffed like they've seen one too many briefcases, swung too hard. I step inside, press four, and watch the numbers flicker.

The ride is slow. A single ad for a government savings bond program curls at the edges behind a plastic cover. Someone scratched a circled capital A into the metal panel beneath it—rebellion in its smallest, most meaningless form.

The fourth floor is quiet. No receptionist, no small talk, just the indistinct murmur of voices behind closed doors. Room 1 is at the end of the hall, the frosted glass panel on the door bearing the auditor's last name in block lettering.

I knock once and step inside.

His office is minimalist to the point of sterility—gray metal desk, a filing cabinet, a government-issue rotary phone in faded beige. No decorations, no personal touches, just a single framed certificate on the wall, the kind that lets you know he's trained to pick apart your financial life and find what you did wrong.

He looks up from a thin manila file, my name stamped across the front. His expression is unreadable, but I already know how this is going to go.

"Take a seat."

I do. The chair is hard. Unforgiving. Just like everything else in this place.

The IRS auditor flips through the paperwork, pausing just long enough to let the silence stretch, let it settle into something heavy. The sound of paper shifting against paper is the only thing breaking the stillness, a slow, deliberate rhythm, like a countdown. He's not just going through numbers—he's sorting through my life, looking for cracks, waiting for me to flinch.

He doesn't look at me when he speaks.

"Your bookkeeping is a mess." Another pause. He flicks the edge of a stapled receipt with his finger, like it's evidence in a case I didn't realize I was on trial for. Then, finally, he lifts his eyes, flat and unimpressed.

"Flying jets in the Navy doesn't excuse you from showing respect for the USA."

The words land with a thud—not just for what they mean, but for how he says them. Like I've insulted the very idea of America by existing outside of its approved structures. Like discipline, sacrifice, and skill mean nothing unless they fit neatly into the right government-issued box.

The envelope falls from his hand and lands on the desk between us. I recognize my handiwork from three years previous when I readied that envelope to send my yearly tax return; I penned over the IN on the send to and above them at a slight angle I wrote a capital E. Changing the pre-addressed envelope inscription from "Internal Revenue Department" to "Eternal Revenue Department."

So that's what this is all about. The IRS doesn't have a sense of humor. I'm partly relieved. Stupid of me to take a shot at them. A psychiatrist would claim it was a textbook case of a criminal's act for self sabotage. As if. They want to believe every crook wants to get caught.

He doesn't stop.

"I see you have an engineering degree." He thumbs through another page, barely glancing at it. "You should have stuck to that—you're not qualified to run a business."

And there it is.

I don't move. I let nothing show. But something inside me shifts, a pull in my chest, a split-second flash of heat. Though I often doubt my abilities, the shell game each of us plays in our incriminations and self loathing, the imposter syndrome per se. I recall a memory from a time long ago as a young boy of eight years old. Following the daily strapping from the stepfather, mother said to me, "I know it's not your fault. You're just a follower. Not the leader." Her words, like the auditor's words, reinforce my determination to succeed.

He wears a thick gold wedding band. Expensive. His fifty-dollar haircut and a two hundred dollar Italian shirt and tie. He's from money. It must be nice to have everything handed to you from birth. No meritocracy for this silver spoon baby. He didn't earn this job at the IRS. His daddy's connections paved a clear path.

"You owe the IRS fifteen thousand dollars. That includes penalties. I suppose you are going to want to make payments?" He looks at me for the first time since I came in. I nod. "You will receive the payment vouchers in the mail in about two weeks.

That was it. I left the building, trying hard to keep my cool. The culture on the East Coast is very different. Hard for me to adjust. When someone calls you out like he just did in Colorado, I would have smashed him in the eye. But here, everyone talks and bullies like it is natural.

I crossed the street without remembering how I got from one curb to the other. For a second, I wasn't Mark—I was just mass. Bone and nerves on autopilot. I glanced at my reflection in a darkened window and didn't recognize the man staring back. If I had walked straight into traffic, I don't think I'd have flinched. Not out of despair—out of indifference. That's how it starts, I thought. Not with a bang, but with bureaucracy. A slow death by form 1099.

Twenty minutes later, I'm walking into the bar to meet Randal. My nerves are still rattled.

I find Randal at the phone booth inside the bar. Standing tall in his pressed navy colored suit, the sharp cut of his jacket making his thin frame look even leaner. He's a black man with smooth, angular features, a sharp jawline, and eyes that scan the room like he's always half a step ahead of whatever's coming. His tie is knotted tight, perfectly centered, the detail that says everything about how he moves through the world—controlled, precise, deliberate.

But right now, that composure is cracking. He holds up a finger to both request my patience and to wait for him.

His voice is low, clipped, just enough edge to tell me he's fighting with someone on the other end of the line. I don't need to hear her words to know it's his wife. He shifts his leather briefcase from one hand to the other, runs a hand over his clean-shaven head, exhaling slow, measured, like he's trying not to let frustration seep through.

"—it's not the school," he says, jaw tight. "I don't want to pull them out. You think moving them somewhere else fixes this?" A pause. His fingers tap against the briefcase. "No. We don't rock the boat, not over this."

He listens. His lips press together, his eyes narrowing slightly. Whatever she's saying isn't sitting well with him.

"I'm not saying I don't care. I'm saying we don't need to turn this into a thing. Let's talk when I get home."

He ends the call, exhales through his nose, then finally looks at me, forcing out a smile that doesn't quite reach his eyes.

"Sorry about that."

I shake my head. "No need."

He gestures toward the phone with two fingers like he's mentally moving past the argument already. "Whiskey first?"

We grab our drinks and settle at a small table by the window, the rain still misting against the glass outside.

"The idea of God irritates me," his intention abrupt like he's in mid thought. "Not just the word, but everything it implies—power, judgment, the weight of control disguised as salvation. Christianity, especially, gnaws at me. Probably because that's the one they drowned me in, pulled me under with, held me captive beneath until belief was supposed to be the only thing keeping me alive. Except I never really believed. Not in the way they wanted me to.

"I was coerced. Indoctrinated. And, eventually, unsaved.

"If there was a God, I think I would call it something else. Maybe fate. Though fate feels too scripted, too neat. Maybe karma, but karma is too restrictive. It relies on causality, and causality is only part of the equation. The duality of existence runs deeper than mere cause and effect."

"Karma is tidy." I take control of the conversation. "It assumes balance, that what goes out must return in kind. But I've seen too much to believe that's all there is. I've watched people who deserved ruin walk away untouched. I've watched the kindest souls get obliterated. If karma was all there was, everything would feel like an equation, but it doesn't. It feels messier. Unwritten.

"And the more I examine causality, the more it leads me somewhere else—to a realization I can't ignore. Chance.

"Chance unsettles karma, what bends fate into something unrecognizable. It's the near-miss that should have been fatal. The once-in-a-lifetime encounter that shifts the course of everything. It's that moment when causality and randomness collide, merge, and then separate again. If God exists, maybe it isn't a being, or even a force, but that transition itself—the exact moment where the predictable and the impossible meet.

"And maybe that's why no other name quite fits. Maybe the only honest way to describe it is simply I am. Not a promise. Not a command. Just existence itself, untethered from meaning. And maybe that's enough."

Randal was grooving with my soap-box. "Aletheia," he says. Then when he saw my raw surprise at his word. "That's a Greek word for 'unveiling' or 'truth' In The Greek society it's more of a reminder that truth is not fixed—it is revealed through the constant interplay of cause and randomness, through what happens and what almost happened."

"The Buddhist find nirvana is between the duality," I say. "Nothing is—like between the exhale and inhale. There's a place where there is neither."

"Truth, but not the absolute kind." Randal lights his cigarette and takes a long draw. He talks as he exhales a bluish fog. "Not the kind written in stone or dictated from a pulpit. Unveiling. Aletheia isn't a god that demands worship or obedience. It doesn't judge. It doesn't punish. It simply reveals—pulling back the curtain between cause and chance, showing the intersection where fate stumbles into accident, where inevitability wavers and something unexpected takes its place.

"Aletheia is not merciful, but it is honest. It does not intervene, but it exposes. It does not control, but it forces you to see.

"Maybe that's why people cling to smaller gods, ones with rules and punishments and rewards. Aletheia doesn't offer comfort. Just understanding. Just the raw mechanics of the universe—causality colliding with randomness, shaping a reality that is both predictable and unknowable."

"Good to know I'm not the only philosopher in our enterprise. No promises. No meaning beyond what you choose to see. Just the unveiling.

"Aletheia is."

Randal pulls his belt free from the loops and snaps it taut between his hands. "People always think a belt's a good way to go, but it's bullshit," he says, rolling the strap between his fingers. "Think about it. You ever really consider what happens when someone tries to hang themselves with one of these?"

I shift in my seat. "That's too morbid of a topic, don't you think?"

Randal smirks, threading the belt through his hands. "Nobody's saying it ain't. That's not the point." He lifts the buckle, tapping it against the table. "But alright, if you wanna take the moral high ground, let's go there. If suicide by belt is too dark, as you say, then tell me—why do so many movies and books use it? Over and over. Nobody boycotts the director. Nobody refuses to publish the novel."

I sigh. "Okay, okay. So maybe it's not black-label morbid. What's your point?"

"My point," he says, stretching the belt again, "is that if a guy is at the point of looping this around his neck, you think he just came up with that on the spot? Hell no. He's been over the whole damn roster—pills, the bridge jump, gun under the chin, gun in the mouth, gun to the temple. This belt? This ain't Plan A."

I rub my jaw. "Alright, so what? Maybe it's all he has."

Randal lifts a brow. "Sure. So let's walk through it. Jail scene, right? Guard forgets to take the guy's belt. Not saying women don't off themselves too, but in jail? You and I both know it's a hundred-to-one men to women. So the guy slides the belt off, loops it over the bars, pulls it tight around his neck." He grips both ends, tugging hard for emphasis. "Now what?"

I shrug. "Now he chokes out."

"Nope." Randal shakes his head. "Problem is, the belt ain't got holes that far up the strap. He can't fasten the prong into the tongue. So what's he gonna do? Hold it tight till he blacks out?"

I nod. "If he's desperate enough, yeah."

Randal clicks his tongue. "Nah, man. Ain't how it works. You know as well as I do—the animal instinct kicks in. Mind and body don't go out easy. No matter how much a guy thinks he wants to die, survival instinct overrides the ego. His fingers will claw at the strap, legs will thrash for footing. Maybe he even passes out, but the second his grip weakens, boom—he's free. And if that doesn't happen? His arms are gonna fail before his brain does. There's no way around it."

I watch him let the belt go slack in his hands. "So you're saying it's impossible to hang yourself with a trouser belt?"

Randal smirks. "I'm saying it's cinematic." He tosses the belt onto the table, the buckle clanking against the wood. "Looks good in movies. Reads well in a book. But in real life?" He leans back, crossing his arms. "People don't just let go."

I exhale through my nose. "Jesus, man."

"What?" His smirk widens. "Too morbid for you?"

I shake my head, rubbing my face. "Nah. I just don't know what's worse—that you're right or that you actually sat down and thought this through."

Randal laughs. "Like I said—nobody's saying it ain't morbid."

Randal exhales, rubbing his jaw like he's weighing whether to humor me or throw the conversation out with last week's trash.

"There is a deeper lesson in this dark story," I say, leaning forward, tapping a finger against the belt buckle on the table. "Are you familiar with the Self—uppercase S—and the self, lowercase?"

Randal slides his arms out of his coat, shrugs. "No, man. What's the point?"

"There's the everyday me, myself, and I. The lowercase self. The one caught in existence, moving through routines, believing in the tangible, but unaware of its own nature. Then there's the True Self—uppercase S. The one that observes, that watches the lowercase self from a distance. The one that knows nothing is as it seems, yet isn't anything else either."

Randal lets out a low chuckle. "Far out, Mark. That sounds like some trippy shit straight out of the Far East. Let's spark up a joint and trip on it." His laugh drips with sarcasm.

I shake my head. "Look, man, all I'm saying is, when someone doesn't get Tao or Zen, when all this talk about discovering the true Self just sounds like abstract poetry, the idea of suicide by trouser belt—that is a doorway."

Randal snorts. "A doorway to what? The morgue?"

"A path to clarity."

His face shifts. The sarcasm doesn't drop entirely, but something flickers underneath. A curiosity. A thread of intrigue he doesn't want to acknowledge. He leans back, studies me like he's trying to decide if I'm full of shit or if there's something worth hearing.

"Shit," he says finally. "Alright. I'm all ears, my brother. Enlighten me, baby."

I gesture toward the belt, still coiled on the table. "That moment—when a man pulls the strap around the bars, when he tightens the leather, when he presses his throat into his own will ... who is making that choice? Not the lowercase self. The lowercase self is the one that's suffering, the one that wants to escape, the one that believes in endings."

Randal watches me, silent now.

"But the one watching it all unfold ... the one beyond suffering, the one that sees it all for what it is? That is the True Self. The witness. The presence beneath the noise." I let the words settle between us. "And if you learn to stay with that Self in every moment, if you let go of the lowercase illusion, then all is right. Even in death."

Randal rubs his chin, staring at the belt. His fingers twitch slightly, like they want to pick it up. Like they want to test the theory.

Then he exhales sharply and shakes his head. "Damn, man," he mutters. "It's the yellow tie man all over again. You really took this whole 'too morbid' thing and ran with it."

I grin. "I'm just saying. If you're gonna think about death, might as well do it right."

Six hours later, with the pen in my right hand resting on the empty page of my diary. I write over the date and replace it with the word—every day. Below, I skip two lines and pen: Me versus the mega antagonist, God (Or the Concept of Divine Judgment). If money is the ultimate power, then God, morality, and the fear of eternal consequence become the last chains that keep people from pursuing it at all costs. The protagonist rejects all spiritual limitations—they are their own god.

Metaphorical Representation: The Final Tax Collector represents the debt that cannot be escaped, including judgment, death, and the price of playing god.

Dear Diary,—my inability to find an easier, quicker way to wealth. The only way to get there and stay out of jail is through a full-time job as a smokescreen. Unable to buy off lawmakers, I cannot manipulate the system to suit my needs. I don't have the wealth to swindle the media to spin my narrative. I am alone against them.

Chapter 5: The Forgotten Passport

Net worth $39,800

The phone rested between my ear and shoulder as I pop the stay-tab on a Dr Pepper. The pour is slow and the sound of the carbon dioxide against the ice cubes produces a refreshing smell.

"The first time I met the monks, I didn't know what I was looking for. I still don't.

"The temple breathed like burnt sandalwood and something older, something weightless, like the air had forgotten how to carry the weight of urgency. The walls were bare, unadorned, as if anything extra would be an insult to the space itself.

A monk sat before me, head shaved, robe draped over one shoulder in that effortless way that suggested either absolute stillness or a lifetime of discipline.

Though it makes me uncomfortable as I feel like a simp. My cheeks and neck are hot. I asked the only question I could think of. "What is Buddhism?"

"The monk studied me. He didn't answer right away. Instead, he let the silence stretch, let it fill the space between us like he was waiting to see what I would do with it. When he finally spoke, his voice was calm, unhurried."

"Who is asking?"

I frowned. "I am."

"Who is 'I'?"

A trick question. I could already feel the setup, the slow unraveling of identity like a thread someone was about to pull. I leaned forward slightly. "Me. The person sitting in front of you."

The monk smiled. "And if you were standing?"

I exhaled sharply through my throat. "Still me."

"And if you were asleep?"

I hesitated. "I suppose, still me."

The monk nodded, folding his hands in his lap. "Then if you are always 'you'—whether sitting, standing, or sleeping—why do you believe you must ask what Buddhism is? Why not simply experience it?"

I glanced at the open space around us, the simplicity of it all, the way the world outside had already faded.

Experience it? I was processing his words and as I opened my mouth to respond, but her voice cut in over the phone.

"And did you?"

I tilt my head slightly. "Did I what?"

"Experience it. Or did you just collect the words, label them and store them away, and move on like you always do?"

The conversation fades away in haste as the doorbell rings five times.

The voice I know too well. A voice that hasn't softened over time on the other end of the phone call asks, "is that the doorbell?"

"Yes. Someone wants my attention. Can you hold on a second, mom?"

"Absolutely, honey. I'll wait."

After I sip my Doctor Pepper, I set the glass next to the phone and go to open the door.

"Certified mail," the postman says. "Sign here." He hands me the invoice.

The invoice shows me it is the paperwork from the United Technologies Incorporated patent office. I sign the sheet and exchanged it for the large envelope he pulls free from his leather mail sack.

I set it down beside my half-empty Dr Pepper, condensation pooling on the glass.

"You still with me?"

"Of course." Her voice is smooth, but there's something under it. Not concern, not exactly—curiosity wrapped in restraint. "Is everything okay?"

I hesitate, just for a second. A second too long.

"You tell me," she continues. "Certified mail usually means one of two things: bad news, or something you've been waiting on for a long time."

I exhale through my nose, tapping a finger against the envelope. "Maybe both."

A beat of silence. Then she shifts. I can hear it in her breath, in the slight change in her tone—the motherly instinct that flickers between detachment and investment, like she's debating whether to press or let it go.

"You never answered my question," she says.

I rub my temple. "Which one?"

"Did you experience it? Or did you just collect the words?"

I stare at the envelope, its edges crisp, untouched. A government-issued confirmation of something I started but haven't yet finished.

The monk's words still linger, thin as smoke, weightless but impossible to ignore.

Who is asking?

I roll my shoulders, stretching out the tension. "I don't know."

Another pause. Then her voice shifts again, a note of something familiar creeping in.

"Ah," she says, "now that ... that's an honest answer. How did these monks come into your life? Are you working with a Chinese contract these days?"

A cliche or a stereotype. Most people think Chinese are Buddhists, but most Chinese are Taoists.

"When they took me away from Sikorsky to work at the corporate offices in Hartford, United Technologies, UTC for short, part of the compensation package they gave me included a paid master's degree from Boston University. The campus at B.U. is crawling with monks, and seeing them on campus got my curiosity up."

"Wow, a free ride at B.U. That is quite a comp!"

"There are eight of us enrolled in this corporate sponsored program. The first day was intense. I mean, out of sight, cool. We went to a large classroom with maybe, I don't know, I didn't count, but probably twenty other new students. The Dean of Graduate Studies gave us a welcome speech that was remarkable. Told us we were the future leaders of enterprise. That our minds will lead and shape the world for centuries to come. Through our efforts and contributions to humanity, people will live in a prosperous, healthy, and fulfilling life.

"I was gobsmacked. I remember thinking, this is how wealthy people treat students. How different from any other school I ever went to where the first day introduction was little more than a roll call and just to reply 'here' when you heard your name. The only time I met the dean at my undergraduate university was at the end of my second year and only because I hadn't paid for the third."

The cold glass in my left hand catches my attention as the condensation causes it to slip from my grip. I steady it with a quick reaction, then take a mouthful of the peppery fruit soda. My mind recalls a private meeting with the dean later that day following that welcome message at B.U. His assistant found me in the hallway and escorted me to the dean's office.

"Let the dean know Mark is here." He said to the secretary. "Have a seat Mark. Dean Stevenson will be right with you." She said. Five minutes later, she told me to go in.

The door closes behind me with a soft, deliberate click, sealing me into a space that was never designed for people like me.

Dean Stevenson's office isn't just an office—it's a monument to power. It's the kind of room meant to impress, intimidate, and remind you exactly where you stand.

A massive mahogany desk dominates the space, polished to a mirror shine, reflecting the light from a floor-to-ceiling window that overlooks the city skyline. The walls lined with shelves of leather-bound books, titles in Latin and French, first editions that have probably never been opened but exist to send a message—this is where legacy lives, where generational wealth has been distilled into mahogany and gold.

A Persian rug, deep red and intricately woven, softens the sound of my steps as I cross the room. The air carries a faint scent of expensive cigars and aged leather, a scent that feels curated, cultivated over years, the way dynasties curate their image.

Dean Stevenson sits behind his desk, leaning back in a custom-tailored navy blue suit so precise it moves like a second skin. The monogrammed cuffs, the subtle pinstripe that only wealth can afford—everything about him is measured, controlled. His watch gleams under the soft light, something Swiss, something worth more than my car. His hands, well-manicured, barely lined despite his age, rest lightly on the desk as if he has never lifted anything heavier than a pen in his life.

His eyes land on me with polite disinterest. He doesn't offer his hand. Doesn't stand. Just flicks his gaze over me like he's already calculated my worth and found it wanting and lacking.

"Mark." He says my name the way a man might acknowledge a clerk ringing up his purchase—an afterthought, something transactional. "Have a seat."

I sit. The chair is just uncomfortable enough to remind me that this isn't my space, my world.

He steeples his fingers, measuring me in a silence that is deliberate, weaponized. Then he exhales through his throat, a quiet sigh of expected disappointment.

"We don't typically see applicants from your background excelling here." His voice is smooth, cultivated, the practiced tone men like him have perfected over decades. "Perhaps you should lower your expectations. For your own benefit."

And there it is.

The words settle between us, no different than the IRS auditor's smug assessment. The way power wraps itself in different disguises but always delivers the same message to the born poor and less fortunate—you don't belong here.

The IRS uses legalese, the dean uses prestige and privilege, but both serve as reminders to men like me that the system was not built to benefit us.

The difference is, the IRS expects a check. The Dean? He expects an apology for me even trying.

He leans back in his chair, waiting for me to fold. Waiting for me to request to be released from the program, to admit I made a mistake.

I don't.

I let the silence stretch, mirroring his own game back at him. The weight of the room, the generations of men like him who have sat behind desks like this, thinking their words are enough to shape the course of another man's life.

I let him wait.

And when I finally speak, my voice is even, controlled.

"That's an interesting perspective."

The first flicker of surprise crosses his face. He wasn't expecting that. He was expecting submission. Deference. A quiet exit.

But I'm not giving him the satisfaction.

Because the thing about men like Dean Stevenson is they don't expect you to recognize the game.

But I do. And I play to win.

"Where did you go, sweetheart? You went quiet on me." Her voice in my ear stops my flashback of the memory. "Do you enjoy the university?"

"Yes. The workload is brutal, and the level of learning is challenging. I have to study a lot."

"What are you reading these days? I mean, besides college requirements. Do you have time for reading?"

"A great recent novel, Rising Sun by Michael Crichton. What are you reading, mom?"

"Just finished a masterpiece of a novel that chronicles the journey of Ayla and Jondalar as they traverse the Ice Age in Europe, offering a vivid portrayal of the challenges and landscapes of the time. The writer, Auel's meticulous research and storytelling resonate. It's called The Plains of Passage by Jean M. Auel. If you like historical novels, get that one."

I finish the last of the Dr Pepper and swallow with a loud exhale and a burp. "Sorry about that." I chuckle, but she was less than impressed. "My workers are pulling into the drive and I need to go now."

"It was nice to hear from you," she says. "Stay away from the monks. It is all Satan's doing. Pray to Jesus for guidance."

"I miss Grandpa. We also had good conversations about life and he kept me sane. Anyway, bye."

"Bye then. I love you, Mark."

After setting the crew to work on the restoration projects at my house, I settle into a folding chair and the folding table with my computer on it. The glow of my IBM 386 a CRT haze over the desk, the hum of the processor barely noticeable over the steady rain tapping against the window. My fingers hover over the keyboard, half-written notes flickering on the CRT monitor, the outline of something big—something elegant in its deception.

The BBS scrolls in real time, new messages lighting up like a coded conversation unfolding in the background. Somewhere out there, men like me are feeding the system, pushing limits, cracking open the structures the government wants to keep locked down.

The Hacker Quarterly lies open beside me, this quarter's issue breaking down the vulnerabilities in telecom billing systems—exactly the kind of inspiration I need.

I take a slow sip of flat Dr Pepper left from last night, mind sorting through the moving pieces. The pieces that, when put together, build a machine that looks like business but runs like crime.

Step One: The Front–A Telecom Company That Doesn't Exist

I type out the foundation of the con, line by line, watching it take shape: Shell Company in the Cayman Islands I pull the BBS thread with a list of law firms specializing in offshore incorporations. Easy to set up, harder to track.

Fake Licensing Agreements A few doctored documents from a "partner" in Hong Kong, a few telecom connections fabricated with just enough legitimacy to fool the system.

Call Resale Network Prepaid phone cards sold through shady distributors targeting immigrant-heavy neighborhoods.

I exhale, fingers flexing over the keyboard. This part is the simple part.

Step Two: Generating Dirty Money

The Hacker Quarterly article outlines the basics of PBX hacking, but I already know it well enough to work without the guide. Hijack an unused corporate PBX, reroute calls, fake traffic logs.

Stolen Credit Cards Buy Our Prepaid Cards. We create revenue out of thin air. Looped Calls Between International Carriers → We generate artificial call volume, charge telecom providers for it.

Billing Fraud Through Layered Routing → Each call hits at least four different networks before disappearing into a loop of nothingness.

The screen blips. A BBS post from a known phreaker confirms something I suspected—the clearinghouses are months behind in reconciling traffic records. That gives me time.

Step Three: Laundering the Profits

I lean back, cracking my knuckles, eyes scanning the plan taking form. This isn't just about moving money. This is about war. Me against them.

Inter-carrier payments funnel to offshore accounts → Looks like corporate cash flow. Shell company "consulting firms" invoice for fake infrastructure costs → creates paper legitimacy. Payouts routed through casinos, real estate, and gold markets → untouchable.

Me against the government.

Me against the Mega Antagonist.

This isn't crime—it's playing the game the way they do. They rig the rules, they own the referees, and they control who gets to win. But this? This is learning the code of their world and rewriting it for myself.

I save the file. Encrypted. Hidden in a buried directory.

The scam is ready. The pieces are in place.

A whisper echoes in the silence of the room, not from the BBS or the fan whir of the computer, but from somewhere deeper—older.

"Who is asking?"

The monk's voice again. Except it's not memory this time—it's presence.

I stare at the high resolution glow of the monitor. My finger hovers over the Enter key like it's a trigger.

"You came here for clarity," the monk says, voice threading through the dim office like incense smoke. "Not control."

I don't turn. I don't need to. The monk isn't there.

"You asked what Buddhism is," the voice continues. "And now you make something that can only end in shadow."

My breath slows. The moment stretches, taut with a choice I already made.

"Who is asking?" the monk repeats, softer this time, as if the question isn't meant to be answered—but lived.

The only thing left is to press enter. Run the program.

~~~

The air smells like cut grass and cooling asphalt, the last traces of summer warmth fading into the pavement. A jet rumbles overhead, distant but unmistakable, cutting across the evening sky. Somewhere across the park, a siren wails and fades, swallowed by the city's rhythm.

The ball thunks off the backboard, catching just enough of the rim to spin out. Miss.

"That's an H-O-R."

"Damn," Randal mutters, jogging to grab the rebound. He dribbles back, slow and deliberate, taking his time. The sun is low, the sky fading into deeper blue, that perfect stretch of summer evening where the air still holds the day's warmth, but the heat has gone.

I roll my shoulders, stretching out the ache from the past week. Another flight. Another hotel. Another contract that should've been gold but turned to rust.

Randal fakes right, spins left, and banks the shot clean off the backboard.

"You hear back on the Brunei contract?" he asks, wiping his hands on his shorts.

I shake my head. "Nothing official. Entire projects in limbo until we work out their supply issues."

Randal sighs, dribbling between his legs, eyes on the pavement. "And the Chinese deal?"

I catch the ball, spinning it between my palms. Then I look at him.

"See what you have to understand, Randal—when I said I played basketball when I was younger, I meant ten or eleven years old. Pee Wee League basketball."
~~~

I dribble the ball between my legs. Lose control. Chase it. Dribble with both hands like some kid who just learned what a basketball is.

"It was nothing skillful, no coaching. See, I had one spot on the court that I ran to, and there I would wait for someone to throw me the ball. I never missed. I could hit that shot with my eyes closed. But I never learned to play defense. Never knew how to dribble the ball or pass to other players."

I mimic his fake right, spin left, and then nail the shot.

His eyes pop wide. "That right there is the spot. I still got it, baby."

I chase after the ball, fire it to him, and exhale audible, ujjayi breath through my nose, stretching my arms overhead before stepping toward the three-point line. I signal him for the ball.

"When I got back to Brunei, the Korean documents were still in my room. The Hong Kong corporation paperwork was a mess. If the lawyer can't push it through by the end of the month, it's dead in the water."

Randal nods, like he already expected that answer. He pivots and launches a shot from the top of the key—it bounces twice off the rim before sinking.

"That's the game."

I run a hand over my face, shaking my head. "You callin' it?"

He grabs the ball, tucks it under his arm. "Yeah, man. That's enough."

I know what's coming. I can see it in the way he wipes the sweat from his forehead, the way his body shifts, weight on one foot like he's debating if he wants to say it. He bounce-passes the ball.

"We gotta drop the S&L game," he finally says. "All of 'em are failing nationwide. FDIC is eating them up, and it's only getting worse. We keep playing in that arena, we're gonna get burned."

I roll the ball between my hands, bouncing it once, twice, thinking.

"I need two more loans. What if we just process two more and then we are out?"

Randal lets out a slow breath. "Mark, man—"

"I don't have my new thing up yet." I meet his eyes. "Two more. Then I'm out."

His jaw tightens, but he nods. That's the thing about Randal. He knows when to push and he knows when to let me run my play.

He gestures at me to pass him the ball. I do. He spins it once in his hands, then smirks.

"You still loving it in Detroit?"

The air is thick, humid with the lingering stillness of the day, but cooling fast. The sound of cicadas hums in the trees, blending with the distant murmur of a jet cutting low over the city. Somewhere a car alarm chirps twice, resets, like a warning. Or a reminder.

I laugh, shaking my head, but there's no humor in it. Just exhaustion buried under the need to keep moving.

"I don't know. I built them something—a system, a process, a way to take chaos and turn it into gold. UTC got everything. Lean production, slashed costs, record-breaking efficiency."

Randal bounces the ball once, the sound sharp against the pavement. Waiting. Watching. The way he does when he knows there's more coming.

We start walking toward the parking lot, the court behind us now just a place we burned through conversation.

"The suppliers?" I continue. "They got efficiency. The executives?" I let out a scant breath, shaking my head. "They got obscene bonuses, penthouses, stock options that turned them into gods."

"And you?"

I catch the ball when he passes it back, hold it against my hip, rolling it under my palm. The texture of worn leather beneath my fingers.

"A plaque," I say. "A recent assignment. Sleeping on dirty hotel mattresses, eating shit food, flying to places I don't care about." I spin the ball again, let it drop, watch it settle like the weight of it means something.

"Not a raise. Not a bonus. Not even a goddamn handshake that meant something."

Randal scoffs. "Yeah. That sounds about right."

"Reagan ripped the cap off executive pay, and the sharks continue to feed like never before. Profits soared, wages stayed the same, and the company rode my work to heights I'd never touch. Before the media giants forced public opinion to hate unions, my efforts could have been shared with all the employees and not just hoarded by a dozen filthy rich, power hungry Republicans."

We stop at the edge of the lot, the pavement still warm underfoot, heat radiating from the hoods of the parked cars.

I nod toward the Cadillac parked under the sodium lights, the paint deep and glossy, the reflection of the streetlights stretching across the curves of the hood like silk.

"This yours?" I ask, tilting my head. "Is this a Cadillac Allanté?"

Randal grins, but only a little. "Smooth as cream cheese, baby." He lifts his hand when I move toward it. "Don't lean on it."

I smirk. "Man, look at you. Fancy as hell."

He shrugs. "Had to splurge a little. Wife loves the hell outta this machine."

I let my fingers graze the door handle. The smell of new car leather flashes, and images of money linger.

"So I left. Transferred to UTC Automotive, packed my life into a box, and headed to Detroit."

Randal nods. "Where the Big Three are crumbling, and you are supposed to save 'em."

I snort. "No. I'm not that kind of miracle worker. Mexico, Honduras, Guatemala—factories humming, workers sweating, margins getting tighter while the execs get fatter."

Randal exhales, slow, measured. "And still—no million-dollar payday for you."

I toss the ball into the air, catch it, hold it against my hip like something that still belongs to me.

"Nope."

The streetlights flicker on, stretching shadows across the cracked pavement. Randal leans against the fence, looking at me like he's trying to figure out if I'm still hungry or just too stubborn to quit.

"So this Caddy is what ... sixty grand, thereabouts?"

"If you gonna be nosey," he says, stepping in closer. The car gleams behind him. "It was a bit more after the stereo upgrade."

I let out a short laugh. "Upgrade? It comes with a Bose system. What the hell else—" I stop myself, hold up a hand.

"Bit expensive for a small-time bank corporation's computer systems guy. And, crimson red metallic is like a beacon. Screams out—Look at me!"

Randal doesn't blink.

"We cool, Mark. Nobody's watching me. You're the guy washing the laundry."

I shake my head, but the unease sticks to me like humidity before a storm.

I look at the Cadillac again. The way the streetlights catch the curves, the way the night presses in, thick and unmoving.

"But it wasn't all bad," I say. "Detroit."

Randal unlocks the car, slides into the low leather seat. "Sounds like my boy is growing up." He smirks. "You got you a girlfriend? I mean, shit, that's great news if it is."

He snaps the seatbelt into place, then glances up at me.

I chuckle, nodding toward the car. "Is there enough room in there for you and the ball?"

He snatches it from my hands, tosses it onto the passenger seat. "Send me the loan information. I'll be back next month. Graduation day at B.U. You still coming, right?"

"Wouldn't miss it."

I watch as he pulls away, taillights glowing red before disappearing into the dark. I follow not long after, heading from Boston back to Connecticut, the road slipping beneath me in a blur.

My thoughts aren't here, not really. My hands work the wheel, shifting, accelerating, changing lanes, but my mind?

Teresa.

Detroit.

The Dearborn office. My first day. My thoughts follow the memory.

I take a slow breath. The air is different there. The memory shifts beneath my skin, pulling me back to the beginning.

The Division Chief of Quality Assurance stands with his hands clasped behind his back, chin lifted just enough to let me know who's in charge. His suit is a little too crisp, the kind of man who starches his shirts like he's pressing authority into the fabric.

"This is your team," he says, gesturing toward the two women standing beside him.

The first one—Camille.

Dressed to be seen. Short skirt, high heels, sparkling jewelry that catches the fluorescent light like bait. Fake nails, fake eyelashes, face masked under twenty dollars of careful deception. She smells like a department store perfume counter, the scent thick, practiced, weaponized.

I don't trust women like this. Not in business. Not in life.

Then—Teresa.

The smile makes me look closer. Not polite, not forced. Real. And the way it reaches her eyes? Like she means it.

A shift.

A small one, but undeniable. Something shakes loose in me, something I haven't acknowledged in years.

"This is it?" I ask, scanning the room. "Three of us? I had five at UTC."

The Division Chief tilts his head, amused but firm. "Just the two of you on the road." He nods toward Teresa. "You two will travel. I share Camille."

Camille crosses her arms, shifting her weight onto one hip like she's heard this speech a hundred times.

"She stays here in Dearborn," he continues. "She'll manage meetings, book your travel, handle anything you need. Pay your bills, feed your cat, wash your laundry."

Then he laughs, like it's all some kind of joke.

Camille gives a slow, unimpressed blink.

"I don't do laundry," she says.

Teresa and I work nonstop for weeks, fine-tuning the roadshow, preparing to take my patented process to the automobile industry suppliers around the world.

I'm selling liberation—a way to free them from wasted manufacturing time, losses on failed products, and buried profits hidden deep in inefficiencies.This is a service I developed for suppliers that resulted from saving the commutator supplier for Brunei.

Teresa is green.

Never been to one of my events.

Zero engineering experience.

But she's smart.

I don't waste time explaining things twice. I don't have to. She listens, asks the right questions, stays sharp.

But the office is another story.

Camille and Teresa have some kind of unspoken alliance, a secret language of smirks and side glances I never fully grasp. And me? I'm the target. The new guy.

Post-it notes on my desk with fake meeting times.

My office phone rerouted to HR as a prank.

A memo changed from "Process Improvement Plan" to "Profit Implosion Plan" before I sent it out.

I don't laugh.

Three weeks in, I finally crack.

"Dinner," I say, half a demand, half a challenge.

Teresa tilts her head. "Are you asking me out?"

"Yes," I say, like I'm negotiating a contract.

She smiles. "Okay."

And just like that, something shifts again. But it was after the third date when we no longer wondered. There's a line you cross when a woman stops being a date and starts being your weakness. I crossed it blind.

We go to see Alexander Zonjic. A solid, smooth jazz show, perfect for the night, the mood, the rhythm of whatever this is developing between us.

Then—surprise.

On piano? The one and only, Bob James.

I glance at Teresa, and she's already looking at me.

"You knew?" I ask.

She shakes her head. "No. But I was hoping."

We both love jazz. Not just as music, but as language.

The night turns into a sophisticated conversation, layered like a jazz arrangement itself.

"New York jazz—tight, complex, syncopated. Down to the Bone rides that line, disciplined, intricate.

"Los Angeles? Warmer, moodier, looser. The Rippingtons."

"New York jazz keeps you on edge," Teresa says, twirling the stem of her wineglass. "Like you're walking a tightrope."

"And L A?" I ask.

She smiles. "Like you've already fallen, but the landing is soft."

We sit there, letting the music settle in our bones, the conversation moving in that effortless way that means this isn't just another date.

It's something else.

Something worth remembering.

The, next evening.

The scent of garlic and roasted meat lingers in Teresa's house, the low glow of candles warming the space. It's our fourth date, and I expected a cozy dinner—not a full shift in how I see her.

I glance around. The furniture? Classic, well-chosen.

The kitchen? Stocked, lived-in, real.

The house itself? Hers. At age 26 and single, it is almost unheard of.

I set down my glass of wine, impressed despite myself.

"You own this place?" I ask, letting my eyes drift across the framed art, the solid wood dining table that looks like it's seen genuine conversation.

She smiles, a little proud, but not boastful. "My dad held my hand," she admits. "But he's not the type to do things for me. He's my life coach."

That stops me.

"Your dad?" I repeat, setting my fork down. "You mean he's active in your life? Helps you? Like, actually involved?"

She tilts her head, reading my reaction. She notices everything.

"Yeah," she says simply. "He's not just my dad—he's my foundation."

I sit with that for a second, chewing on the thought as much as the food. It doesn't compute. Fathers don't do that. Not in my world.

Before I could stop myself, I say, "I need to meet this guy."

She studies me for a beat, then grins. "Sunday. Family day."

Sunday comes, and I find myself standing in the middle of an empire of noise, laughter, and impossible warmth.

Papa Bertrand.

Mama Bertrand.

Nine children.

Eight spouses.

Fifteen grandchildren.

I am gobsmacked.

The chaos should be overwhelming—a tornado of voices, tiny hands tugging at sleeves, plates clinking, chairs scraping, everyone talking over each other. But somehow, it isn't.

Because right in the center of it all, Papa and Mama Bertrand are jubilant. Not stressed. Not irritated. Radiant. As if every single one of their children and grandchildren is the most valuable life in the universe.

Papa Bertrand, in his late seventies, but built like he never lost a fight—not against age, not against life, not against anything. Broad chest, thick forearms, hands that still look strong enough to fix whatever needs fixing.

His skin is a pale tone, sun-worn but not fragile, a face shaped by time, but not overtaken by it. His nose? Big, prominent, like it was carved to fit only him. Same with his ears—large, slightly disproportionate, giving him a kind of wise, old-world charm.

His hair—what's left of it—is white, combed back from his forehead, clean but not fussy. His neatly trimmed silver beard, the kind that doesn't hide his expressions but frames them—a permanent fixture on a man who speaks with more than just words.

He wears a white linen shirt, unbuttoned at the collar, sleeves rolled up, like he's always ready to get to work, even if the only work left is listening, teaching, knowing. His watch is old, worn, the leather strap molded to his wrist from decades of wear.

I take it in, watching the effortless way love is distributed like air in this house. No competition. No favorites. Just presence. Attention.

I overhear bits of conversation Papa Bertrand has with his sons, his daughters, his in-laws. He isn't just making small talk—he's engaged. Fully invested in whatever they say.

He tells one son, "You need to stop thinking about the job and think about the career."

He tells a daughter, "That idea of yours? It's not crazy. It just needs patience."

He lifts his grandkids onto his lap, tells them stories as if they are the only people in the room.

This man isn't just a father. He's a force.

And then, after lunch, his attention turns to me.

"Come," he says, already walking toward the back of the house.

I glance at Teresa and she smiles. "Go."

So I follow.

We step outside, into the quiet shade of a massive oak tree, where the noise fades but the warmth lingers. He doesn't rush to speak, just breathes in the day, waiting.

Then, finally, he says, "So, Mark. Tell me who you are. Not what do you do or where are you from? Who are you?"

I stare at him for a second, caught in a moment I didn't see coming.

I open my mouth, but nothing useful comes out. Not CEO. Not engineer. Not even survivor. All those roles feel borrowed.

"I'm—" I pause. "I'm trying to be someone who doesn't need to lie to himself to be able to sleep at night."

He doesn't nod. Doesn't blink.

"You don't get there by running faster," Papa Bertrand says. "You get there by stopping long enough to see what's chasing you."

I say nothing. But inside, something gives way. Like the air's changed pressure, and I hadn't noticed until now.

Chapter 6: Shadows at the Club
Net worth $230,000

The air is thick with the scent of pine and hot earth, the midday sun pressing down in lazy waves. The trees here are tall, ancient, their shadows stretching long across the narrow path. In the distance, Lake Huron shimmers under a sky so blue it feels impossible.

I inhale deep, taking it all in. This place is untouched in a way cities never are.

"I can see why you live here," I say, watching the water shift, the wind rippling across its surface.

Beside me, Papa Bertrand chuckles, that low, effortless Jeff Bridges kind of laugh—like everything's already been figured out, and the joke's on me for taking so long to catch up.

"Yeah, it's nice," he says. "Summers are short here in Sault Ste. Marie, but beautiful."

Then, before I can steer the conversation anywhere else, he cuts me off at the pass.

"First thing that pops into your mind."

I glance at him. "What?"

"First thing. Don't analyze. Don't calculate. Just say it." He side-eyes me. "And stop changing the subject."

I exhale, smirking. "Nobody's judging me?"

He grins. "Well, not completely true." He kicks at a pine cone, watching it tumble down the path.

"Teresa's four brothers are in shock."

"In shock because she's dating a bald man?"

"Maybe a bit of this, that, and the other thing." He shrugs. "But mostly? You're the first white man she's ever dated. Far as I know."

I don't flinch, just nod. I figured as much. But he's not looking for a reaction—he's watching, weighing, seeing how I carry that truth.

Then his gaze shifts back to the trees, back to the path ahead.

"But what drives you?"

I don't even hesitate. "That's easy. I'm looking for wealth."

Papa Bertrand stops walking.

Not suddenly, not for effect. He just lets my words settle, lets them weigh the air. He then nods once, as if that's exactly what he expected me to say.

"The American Dream," he says, exhaling like he's already lived the full spectrum of it. "The greatest myth ever sold. That wealth should be aspirational but never fully attainable. That you should chase it your whole life—but never actually reach it."

I watch as he kicks a small stone off the trail, sending it skidding into the brush.

"You ever notice how the moment a man breaks through that ceiling, he stops being celebrated?" he continues. "The working class worships the hustle. They love the struggle. But the second you leave them behind? You're the villain, cheating the system."

I nod. I've seen it. The rags-to-riches stories people love—only if the man keeps one foot in the mud. If he climbs too high? He's an enemy.

"They call it the dream that keeps people playing the game," he says, watching a group of retirees sip iced tea on a porch ahead. "But it's not a dream—it's a leash. The promise of wealth is what keeps people working themselves to death, hoping the scraps will one day become a feast."

A couple of kids ride past us on their bikes, streamers fluttering from the handlebars. Their laughter cuts through the weight of the conversation, but neither of us looks away from the trail.

"My grandfather used to tell me about the Dream Keepers," I say, adjusting my pace to match his. "A silent force that makes sure people play the game—but never win."

He tilts his head, curious.

"They set the rules," I continue. "They tell you how hard work pays off, how saving money leads to wealth, how loyalty to a company will one day give you security. But it's a rigged system. The Dream Keepers make sure you never get close enough to see behind the curtain."

Papa Bertrand lets out a dry chuckle. "And here you are, breaking the game."

"That's the plan," I say, smirking. "Me versus the Mega Antagonist."

We turn a corner, passing a row of homes tucked between the trees. Neatly trimmed lawns. Hammocks swaying in the breeze. Families grilling, laughing, living. A postcard version of retirement.

I gesture toward them. "Look at these people. They worked their whole lives, followed the rules, saved their money. And now? This is it. This is the big reward. Sunday barbecues and grandchildren visiting twice a year."

Papa Bertrand raises a brow. "And you think that's not enough?"

"I think wealth is political power. The ability to leave an empire, rewrite history, outlive your body."

He considers that. "You think wealth makes a man immortal?"

I exhale. "Maybe. Or maybe it just gives him the illusion of permanence."

We stop near a bench overlooking the lake. The water flickered gold and silver sparklets under the late afternoon sun in mid-July.

"You ever think about what happens to your empire when you're gone?" he asks.

I lean against the back of the bench, arms crossed. "Yeah."

"And?"

I smirk. "That's why I plan to live forever."

He laughs, deep and full. Shakes his head.

"You ever hear about the Oblivion Banker?" he asks.

I frown. "The what?"

"The final collector." He stretches his legs, resting his arms over the back of the bench. "Doesn't matter how much you own, how big your empire gets, how many people remember your name. Eternity always comes to collect."

I turn that over in my head, watching the lake shift in the wind.

"Think about all the kings, the emperors, the tycoons," he continues. "They built palaces, industries, nations. And where are they now?" He shrugs. "Gone. Erased. Nothing but footnotes."

"So you're saying none of it matters?"

He shakes his head. "I'm saying it only matters while you're here. And once you're gone? The Oblivion Banker comes knocking."

The wind shifts, rustling the branches above us. The lake stays the same.

My empire dies with me.

It's a thought I don't like. Who would I leave it to if I built a golden palace? My son ... the thought feels like a dead end.

I stand up, stretch, shoving my hands into my pockets. "Well, guess I'd better spend it all before I go."

Papa Bertrand laughs again. "Now that's the first smart thing you've said."

We head back toward the house.

I feel Teresa's eyes on me before I see her.

And I wonder if she's watching the way something in me just changed.

We're almost back to the house, the distant chatter of the family gathering pulling us forward. But Papa Bertrand isn't done with me yet.

"Are you a Buddhist?" he asks.

I glance at him. The question doesn't feel random.

"I've explored Buddhism," I say, rolling my shoulders, loosening the tension I didn't realize I was carrying. "The last couple of years with a serious curiosity."

He nods. "I can tell."

That caught me off guard. "Oh yeah?"

He smirks, that knowing look of a man who's seen more than he lets on.

"Me too," he says. "But I'm also something else."

I tilt my head, waiting.

"You need to meet Teresa's friend," he says. "Archbishop Timothy Negrapolis of the Greek Orthodox Church."

"Archbishop?" The shift feels sudden and very unexpected. I don't know what the difference is between a bishop and an archbishop. I wish I had an encyclopedia or knew someone who does.

I glance at him as we step onto the porch. "Why?"

Papa Bertrand pauses at the door, hand on the knob, looking at me the way he did before.

Like he already knows what's coming next.

"Because Buddhism will give you peace, Mark. But Timothy? He'll make you wrestle with it."

And then, just like that, the door swings open.

"We're going to be late, slowpoke," Teresa says as we come through the door. She hooks her arm around mine, and we make our way to the front door and out to my car. Papa Bertrand's words play over in my mind. I feel content. Someone to replace those deep conversations I've missed since Grandpa's passing.

The freeway stretches ahead, dark asphalt humming under the tires, the glow of the dashboard casting soft blue light over Teresa's face. She's got one hand on the armrest, the other lazily tapping a rhythm against her thigh. The silence between us is comfortable but charged, like she's letting me settle before she goes in.

Finally, she exhales. "That must have been overwhelming for you. Are you okay?"

I keep my eyes on the road, shaking my head slightly. "You have a family like something I thought only existed in TV fantasies."

She snorts, turning in her seat to face me fully. "Your family is the bizarre one." The sharpness in her voice isn't mean, just direct, slicing through the bullshit like a scalpel.

Then she tilts her head, lifting an eyebrow. "Talk about Mommy Dearest or Bastard Out of Carolina. Jesus, Mark—your childhood sounds like the kind of backstory a villain gets in a gritty indie film."

I let out a dry chuckle. "Oh yeah? What would you call it?"

She leans back, grinning. "Hmm. 'How to Raise a Socially Maladjusted Finance Bro in Ten Easy Steps.'"

I give her a side-eye. "Finance bro? That's offensive."

She holds up a finger. "I said socially maladjusted finance bro. The maladjusted part is key. You're like if Gordon Gekko had existential dread and a secret passion for ethical loopholes."

I exhale through my nose, shaking my head. "I don't even know where to start with that."

She points at me dramatically. "See? That's the maladjustment. A normal guy would say, 'Shut up, Teresa,' or 'That's bullshit,' but you? You analyze it like I just presented an algorithm that might have a flaw."

I smirk. "You're really enjoying this, huh?"

"Oh, beyond." She stretches, then adds, "You're not used to being around people who actually like each other. Admit it."

"Tell me about the basement under your house. Why is that door padlocked and why do you go schizophrenic when I want to go down there?"

She waits a moment, Elvin Bishop plays Travelin Shoes from my CD and she waits until it finishes. Then shuts the stereo off.

"Hey!?" I protest. "That next one is one of my favorites. Juke Joint Jump."

She tilts her head, eyes bright with the kind of conviction that makes you question your own opinions.

"His story in That Little Ugly Thing is better," she says, tapping her fingers against her knee. "Juke Joint Jump is fun, but it's trying too hard—all energy, no bite." She flicks her gaze toward me, like she's daring me to argue. "Little Ugly Thing is Bishop at his best—gritty, funny, a little unhinged, like he's halfway through a bottle of something strong and telling a story that only gets better the longer he talks. Juke Joint is a party song; Little Ugly Thing is a whole damn personality."

She leans in, eyebrow raised. "You don't want to hear about the basement? You want to hear Mr. Bishop sing?"

I smirk, shaking my head. "Tell me about the great mystery that is your basement. And speaking of Bishop, your dad says I should meet your friend the Archbishop."

Teresa lets out a slow, dramatic breath. "The basement," she says, staring at the road ahead like she's seeing something truly apocalyptic.

"The basement is a haunted, hellish quagmire filled with the excrement of the devil and his ten thousand minions."

I glance at her, amused. "Hell's excrement?"

She holds up a finger. "Ten days. Ten. Days. After I signed the papers and locked myself into a soul-crushing mortgage, I will be paying off until I'm nearly sixty. The sewer backed up."

I blink. "That's unfortunate. Grime and punishment, soiled by fate, even."

She turns to me. "Unfortunate? Mark, it's not funny. I didn't know that tree roots had swallowed the sewer pipe that connects my house to the street. Meanwhile, I'm flushing my tampons by the dozens—"

I groan, holding up a hand. "Spare me the details—"

"No, no. You need to hear this," she says, grinning like she enjoys my discomfort. "One night, at four in the morning, I woke up to hell itself creeping into my nostrils. Flashlight in hand, half-asleep, I stumble through the house, trying to find the source of this ungodly stench."

I can't help but smirk. "And?"

She shudders. "And I found it. The basement. Two feet deep in sewer water. Just … stewing. None can enter that." She shakes her head like she's recalling a true war story. "The lock is the only thing standing between us and Armageddon."

I let out a low whistle. "Damn."

She nods, dead serious. "Exactly. Everything down there is destroyed. Books, photo albums, things I thought mattered—until they didn't."

I smirk. "So you just locked the gates to hell and moved on?"

She shrugs. "What else could I do? Besides, it's just stuff."

Then, like it's the most natural thing in the world, she says:

"As for the Archbishop of the Greek Orthodox Church, I was dating his driver for a few years. Bishop Timothy wanted me to marry the Greek and move to Greece. Even after I broke things off, the Bishop and I had become good friends. We still are."

I stare at her, waiting for the punchline.

She leans toward me, voice playful, but there's a glint in her eye.

"I'm taking him clubbing later. Do you want to come along?"

I pause, completely thrown. "You take him clubbing?"

Her laugh spills into the car, light and unexpected, like a rush of air in a closed-off space. It makes me feel something I haven't in a long, long time.

She grins. "He calls it clubbing. It's a real super secret, though. Nobody can know the Archbishop is out in the nightclubs of South Detroit."

I shake my head, half in disbelief. "Teresa. Do you hear your-self?"

She gives me a slow, knowing nod. "Oh, I know exactly what I'm saying."

But my mind is elsewhere now.

I haven't touched my telecommunications project in days. I still haven't finished the script. If it doesn't get sent soon, it won't send me a dime.

The loans from Randal have stopped.

And Boston—something's off. I need to fly out and figure out why everything's stalling there.

The new contract starts in a week. Teresa and I have six weeks of travel ahead—across the country, Mexico, Costa Rica. No time for a night out with a clubbing archbishop.

But then she looks at me.

"Well?" she asks, tilting her head. "Come with me. Meet the wise and holy archbishop."

Five hours later we arrive at the gates of the Archdiocese, slipping in under the cover of darkness, the city lights casting long shadows across the old stone walls. The gate guard sees Teresa first and his face brightens.

"Miss Bertrand," he greets, his voice warm but professional.

She grins. "How's the night treating you, Nikos?"

He waves a hand. "Better now that you're bringing trouble." His eyes flick to me, weighing, assessing. Not suspicion—just calcula-tion.

Teresa gestures casually in my direction. "This is Mark."

Nikos looks at me for a beat too long, memorizes me, then nods once—slow, deliberate. I nod back. Something unspoken settles be-tween us.

"If you ever need parking downtown," he says, "the church lot is open to you."

It's not a paltry offer. Not just a free space for my car—it's a recognition. A quiet welcome. The first step inside something bigger.

I don't say thank you. I just nod again. Another man's acknowledgment, another silent agreement.

Teresa drives us through the lot, past the cathedral's towering silhouette, parking near a side entrance to the Archbishop's residence. The multistory stone house looms over us, its stained-glass windows casting muted colors onto the wet pavement.

We step out, moving along the side of the building, past a line of old hedges, until we reach a noticeably large door.

She doesn't knock. Just pushes it open, and we step into a dimly lit hallway, short and narrow, lined with dark wood.

Then I see him. He stands at the far end of the corridor, his posture straight, his hands clasped together, the heavy folds of his black cassock draped over his broad frame. His high, ornate kalimavkion—the cylindrical black hat—marks his authority before he even speaks.

He doesn't react immediately to our presence, just flicks his gaze toward us, lifts a hand. A silent command: Stay back. Stay quiet.

His attention is on the two older women standing in front of him.

They clutch their hands tightly to their chests, fingers knotted together as if holding on for dear life. Their voices murmur in urgent Greek, words flowing fast, rich with pleading, sorrow, desperation.

Archbishop Timothy listens. He does not interrupt. His expression is unreadable—serene but firm, empathetic but unmoving.

I can't tell if he's offering comfort or giving them a decision they don't want to hear.

But whatever this is, it's serious.

I glance at Teresa, but she doesn't move, doesn't speak, just watches.

The two women leave, their murmured Greek trailing into the quiet hush of the hallway. Archbishop Timothy lifts a hand—one more minute—before disappearing through a heavy wooden door.

The second he's gone, Teresa's fingers brush my arm, a slow, absentminded movement that turns intentional as her fingertips slide down to my hand.

I turn my palm open, and she follows, threading her fingers between mine.

It's not just a touch. It's an acknowledgment. A confirmation. A little electric pulse of something neither of us has put into words yet.

I shift closer, just enough for my breath to graze her cheek.

"Want to make out at the diocese?" I murmur, lips hovering a fraction of an inch from hers.

Before she could answer—

"Okay, guys. I'm ready."

Archbishop Timothy's voice cuts in from right behind me.

I jolt forward, straight up into the air like I just got caught passing notes in church.

Teresa grins but steps back, her fingers slipping from mine like she hadn't just been holding them.

I exhale sharply, recovering.

Timothy smiles—not unkind, not judging, but definitely amused.

"You must be Mark," he says, extending his hand. "Call me Timothy, please."

I shake it, nodding, still feeling like a kid caught in the back pew whispering during Mass.

Before I can say something intelligent—

"Let's get going," Teresa cuts in, all business. "Or we'll never get a table. It's getting late."

I ride in the back, watching and listening to the two of them talk up front like old friends.

They slip into conversation seamlessly, trading stories, teasing each other, laughing at inside jokes that tell me this isn't just a passing acquaintance—this is genuine friendship.

Timothy isn't stiff, isn't weighed down by the formality of his title. He's relaxed, engaged, even cracks a few jokes that make Teresa roll her eyes.

But what catches my attention is the fact that somewhere between the Archdiocese and the car, he's completely transformed.

Gone is the heavy cassock, the tall hat, the unmistakable presence of an archbishop. Instead, he's wearing dark jeans, a crisp bolo, and what I swear are Italian leather shoes. And to top it off? A silk Italian fedora, tilted just enough to suggest he knows exactly what he's doing.

I exhale slowly. This man is no rookie to the night scene.

For someone who just spent twenty minutes counseling women on some crisis in another language, he looks like he's been doing wardrobe changes in church parking lots for years.

And me?

I lean back against the seat. It's 8:40PM and I'm watching the city lights bleed together, the freeway pulling us deeper into the heart of South Detroit, toward a jazz club, toward whatever the hell this night is turning into.

Then—my pager buzzes. Again.

I pull it out, glance at the glowing red numbers. Same sequence. Whoever this is, they've been trying to reach me for the last hour, paging repeatedly.

I rub my jaw, letting it sit in my palm, the tiny screen demanding attention. Later, a few drinks into the evening with the band playing old school New Orleans jazz, and at 11:35 PM, my pager beckons again.

Teresa and Timothy are engrossed in their conversation, laughing about some story I missed. The night moves forward, rolling me along with it, but my head is somewhere else.

Because someone is desperate to talk to me. I cannot ignore it any longer.

~~~

"You've Got Mail."

The robotic chime from my America Online inbox cuts through the silence, sterile and routine, but tonight, it feels like a gavel slamming down on an unseen verdict.

I click immediately, my fingers tense against the mouse. The open mail icon flickers, the familiar lag of dial-up dragging out the wait.

How the hell did we ever do business before email?

The world feels faster now, more connected, but this—this glacial loading screen, this endless wait for text to crawl across the screen—it's unbearable.

I skim a Hacker Quarterly article while I wait. E-Trade. A new stock trading platform. Buying and selling stocks over the internet? It sounds like something out of science fiction. But then again, so did my life eight years ago.

The Final Report from South Korea. The email finally loads. My eyes move fast, scanning for the details that matter—the numbers, the confirmations, the damage.

South Korean Attorney.

Corporations closed.

Bank accounts shut down.

Fees paid.

Remaining balances transferred to Hong Kong.

Three companies.
~~~

I exhale slowly, cross-checking the amounts against my journal entry—the one labeled "In Case of Emergency." My escape plan.

The clock on the shelf reads 2:22 AM. Eight hours until the law office in Dearborn opens. Eight hours before I could start picking through the wreckage of two years of work, now wiped out like it never existed.

Randal. I sensed something was wrong when the loans stopped processing. But I didn't expect this.

Randal is gone. Fine. He played his part—and he got sloppy. That won't be me. I've already moved the data, scrubbed the trails, mirrored the ledgers across five jurisdictions. They think cutting him down collapses the structure. But I am the structure now. What I've built—it doesn't rely on loyalty or friendship. It runs on leverage, recursion, and my capacity to think six moves ahead. I don't stop at the loss of Randal. I upgrade him.

My eyes closed. What were the last words I said to him?

"You can't call me. Never again. Don't worry about a lawyer. I'll send one. Your wife and kids will be alright. I don't have a lot of money but it should ... Listen, man. I will take care of them with what I have."

Then—the sound of plastic slamming against metal. The payphone receiver hits the cradle. A full stop. A cut connection.

Randal is gone. Locked up. Indicted. The Feds moving in on everything tied to the S&L industry. One last transfer of money for his family to survive, and I close accounts and scrub until zero traceability.

I should be grateful. I'm mostly insulated—I saw the storm coming and shut it all down before it could take me with it. But the cost?

Everything.

Two years of work.

Gone.

Randal.

Gone.

Hong Kong and South Korea.

Gone.

I stare at the screen, at the last few words of the email, at the finality of it all. I am free from jail.

I lean forward, pressing my palms into my temples. My body feels heavy, drained, like it's shutting down piece by piece. I can't sleep. I can't think. I reach for my daily journal, flipping to the last entry from three nights ago. The last moment before everything changed.

Before I became something else.

Diary entry—Teresa isn't just smart—she's sharp, the sort of sharp that doesn't need to announce itself. She listens before she speaks, but when she does, it lands. Not loud, not aggressive—just dead-on accurate.

She grew up at the bottom of a family of nine, where survival meant wit, timing, and knowing when to strike. A childhood of older siblings toughened her up, taught her how to throw words like punches and how to take a hit without losing her grin.

That smile. My heart craves.

It isn't the polite kind, the socially approved version. It's big, takes over her entire face, a full-tilt, unfiltered expression that defies hesitation. When Teresa smiles, it's all-in or nothing.

Her square jaw gives her an edge, something solid, something that keeps her from looking too soft. But then there are her eyes—dark brown, deep, impossible to ignore. They hold things back, but only just.

She's thin, light on her feet, always moving, like she's got too much energy to sit still unless she forces herself to. Not well-endowed, but she never cared, and nobody who knows her does either.

She spends as much time outdoors as possible, resulting in a sun-streaked olive complexion. A runner, a swimmer, anything that keeps her body in motion, because motion is control.

And control is everything.

Because when she slips—when the balance between diet, exercise, and her own brain chemistry tilts the wrong way—it gets dark. It doesn't happen often, not anymore, but when it does, it comes in like fog, thick and inescapable. The energy drains, the world dulls, and suddenly, she's under the weight of it.

But she fights.

She's learned how. She sticks to her routine like a religion, because it is one—a faith in movement, in rhythm, in keeping the world at bay through sheer will. The manic swings are cruel. And when she's good—when she's superb—she's a force.

A practical joker with a predator's sense of timing. She'll let you walk into your own downfall, let you say something stupid, then let the silence hang just long enough before she strikes.

She's not mean. But she's relentless. And when she laughs—really laughs—it's loud, full, the kind that demands other people join in.

Teresa isn't safe.

She isn't easy.

She isn't for everyone.

But if she lets you in, if she chooses you—you are chosen. And that means something.

I don't remember falling asleep.

One minute, I'm staring at the last entry in my daily journal, the ink barely dry on words written by someone who thought he still had control. The next—

The phone rings.

Loud. Sharp. Cutting through the stillness like a warning shot.

My body jerks upright, breath catching in my throat. For a second, I don't know where I am, what time it is, what world I woke up in. The dull blue glow of my computer screen still hums in the dark. The clock—8:46 AM.

Shit. I'm late.

I grab the receiver, my voice still rough from sleep. "Yeah?"

Teresa.

"Jesus, Mark, are you okay?" Her voice is tight, a little breathless, like she's been pacing. "You were supposed to be at work an hour ago. I was about to come over."

I rub my eyes, forcing my mind to catch up. Last night. The club. The pager. The call. The fucking email.

"I'm fine," I say, but my voice doesn't sound fine.

"You left the jazz club in such a rush. Then this morning, you just don't show up. No call, no nothing." She exhales, frustrated. "What's going on?"

My thoughts are a mess, colliding into each other. Setting up the trust for Randal's legal defense, figuring out how to keep his wife and kids above water, dealing with my anger, the raw disappointment of losing everything I'd built over the last two years.

"I've got to go to my lawyer," I say. "I won't be in today."

She goes quiet for a second. I can feel her reading between the lines. Then, soft but pointed—

"Is it your son?"

I blink, caught off guard. That's not where I expected this to go. Where is she getting these ideas?

"Or the IRS?" she presses. "I saw the audit letter on your table. You're being audited?"

My jaw tightens. I glance at the letter, still sitting where I left it. Bold, red-stamped bureaucracy staring back at me. One more goddamn fire waiting to burn me down.

"Three years in a row of being audited over something I did five years ago. It's no big deal. We can talk later. I can't be late for the lawyer. See you Wednesday."

There was a time was when I felt loss and despair I would call Grandpa and we would discuss the philosophy of human folly. I consider calling Papa Bertrand, and on my return from the lawyer's office, I do. No answer. He's probably at his bowling league. But before I go home, I decide to go to the diocese for a talk with Archbishop Timothy.

The rain comes down in sheets, hammering the windshield like it's trying to break through. The wipers can't keep up. Visibility is near zero, but I know the way. I know the route by muscle memory—past the faded brick storefronts, the closed diners with neon signs flickering in protest, past the empty lots and forgotten factories that were once the heart of Michigan and American industry.

I pull into the archdiocese's parking lot. The headlights catching rain swirling in the air like mist from a broken dam. The iron gate stands half-shrouded in the storm, its sharp black bars rising like the teeth of some unseen beast.

Nikos is in the guard booth, barely visible through the rain-streaked glass. He steps out, trench coat collar up, water dripping from his nose.

"Bit rainy for a social visit," he says, scowling as I roll the window down.

I nod toward the lot. "Is Bishop Timothy in?"

"Yeah." Nikos eyes me for a second, then steps back and waves me through. No questions, no hesitation. Another unspoken acknowledgment.

The place is quiet. The storm rumbles against the stone walls, the scent of wax, incense, and damp wood filling the air.

I find Timothy in his study, standing by the massive oak desk, flipping through a book like he has all the time in the world. The cassock is gone—he's in a black sweater, dark slacks, barefoot, like some Greek philosopher lost in thought.

I don't wait. I drop my duster onto a chair, soaking wet, water pooling beneath me.

"You ever think about how the Orthodox Church—hell, all organized religion—has spent centuries selling people on the afterlife while letting them suffer in this one?"

He doesn't even flinch.

"That's how you want to start this?" he asks, voice calm, like I just asked him about the weather.

"I'm past small talk."

Timothy closes the book, finally looking at me. "Alright, then. Let's hear it."

I step forward, hands on his desk. "Your church—your entire institution—has more power, more money, more influence than entire nations. And what do you do with it? You hoard it. You build monasteries, you collect gold artifacts, you whisper prayers over centuries-old manuscripts while people are out there starving."

Timothy's expression doesn't change.

"You watched what Reagan did. You witnessed his gutting of the working class, dismantling of unions, and deregulation of industries, turning cities like Detroit into graveyards. You could have fought back. Your power could have been used to help people.

"And you think we didn't?" he asks.

"No," I snap. "I know you didn't."

Timothy picks up his drink, swirling it slowly. "And what should we have done, Mark? Marched on Washington? Thrown our cassocks into the fire and declare war on capitalism?"

"Yes!" I say without hesitation.

Timothy laughs, short and sharp.

"Then we wouldn't be the Church. We'd be just another political faction."

"You already are," I fire back. "You just refuse to admit it. No different from the wealthy. You live in an opulent home. Everything is done for you. Cooks, housekeepers, and stately mansions."

He leans against the desk, observing me. "You think the Orthodox Church has power in America?"

"You could," I say. "You just chose not to. Afraid they might begin to tax religions."

Timothy sighs, rubbing his temple. "You don't get it. The Orthodox Church isn't the Vatican. We don't own global banks, we don't own stock in oil companies. You're mistaking us for the Mormons and the Baptists. We don't sit on piles of gold while peasants bow at our feet. That's the Catholics." He leans forward, his voice dropping.

"We survive."

I scoff. "That's convenient."

He lifts a brow. "Is it?"

"You expect me to believe that the Orthodox Church, the same institution that's been around for two thousand years, is just scraping by?"

"Survival isn't just about money, Mark. It's about power. And power isn't always about resistance."

I stare at him. "That's a cop-out."

"No, it's reality." He takes a slow sip of his drink. "You think Reagan broke this country on his own? He was a symptom. Not the disease."

"Then why didn't you fight?" I press. "You could have lobbied against corporate takeovers. You could have pushed back against financial deregulation. You could have helped unions, fought for workers' rights—actually made a difference. Instead, you let America rot."

Timothy leans back, arms crossed. He's not smiling anymore.

"You want to know the truth?" he asks.

I lift my chin. "Always."

"The Church didn't fight," he says, "because America didn't want to be saved."

Silence.

The storm rages outside, rattling the windows.

I exhale sharply, shaking my head. "Bullshit."

Timothy shrugs. "You don't fix a house when the owners keep tearing it down. The American people sold their souls to the market. They put stock brokers on pedestals and let the rich convince them that trickle-down economics would make them kings. They made their choice."

I grip the edge of the desk, knuckles white. "People don't get choices when the deck is stacked against them. People don't have choices when Wall Street owns the government and Reagan hands the keys over to corporations. That's why you should have fought."

Timothy exhales, rubbing his jaw.

"Alright," he says. "Give me your solution. What should we have done?"

"You want a list?" I fire back, my voice rising like I've been waiting my whole life for someone to ask. "Fine. You want to know what the Church should've done instead of lighting candles and counting coins?"

I take a step closer, fists clenched.

"You should've backed the unions. Every single one. Marched with the workers instead of praying for them from a balcony. You should've fought for living wages, real pensions, paid family leave—basic human dignity—not just in encyclicals but in the goddamn streets."

I pace, heat building in my chest.

"You should've broken the banks' kneecaps before they sold this country's future for short-term gain. Reinstated regulations, created community credit, taxed the hell out of the gamblers who call themselves brokers—redirected that blood money into schools, housing, and hospitals."

I jab my finger at the desk like it's a war map.

"You could've helped build a real safety net—universal healthcare, homes people could afford, teachers who didn't have to drive taxis on weekends. You could've led the charge on climate while we still had a planet to save—solar, wind, mass conservation—hell, even a national tree-planting campaign. But you sat still."

I stop, breathing hard, chest heaving.

"You could've broken the monopolies. Split the tech empires, cut off corporate lobbying at the knees. Pushed for co-ops, profit-sharing, anything that gave people a damn stake in their own survival."

Timothy's watching me now. Really watching.

I lower my voice, but there's a fury in it still.

"You could've invested in the future instead of hoarding the past. Public schools, retraining programs, real infrastructure—not ribbon-cutting bullshit, but jobs that meant something. Transit. Water. Broadband. Dignity."

I lean over the desk, knuckles white.

"You could've fought for democracy—for elections that weren't bought, for housing that wasn't a luxury, for justice and judges that didn't come with a price tag. You could've told the rich their profit margins don't outweigh a child's hunger. But you didn't. And because you were quiet, the wealthy felt they had your blessing to take it all."

Silence now. The storm still rages outside, but in here, it's quiet.

I straighten, looking him dead in the eye.

"You had two thousand years to choose people over power."

When I finish, he exhales, nodding slightly.

"That's quite a long and well-rehearsed list," he says.

"No shit."

He leans forward, resting his elbows on the desk.

"And you think the Church hasn't been doing that? Not in the U.S., no. But in the third world? Every single one of those initiatives? We're already there."

I shake my head. "That's not an answer."

Timothy's voice drops, quieter now. "It's the only answer that matters."

I grab my duster from the chair. "Thanks for the talk. I look forward to more."

"My door is always open, Mark."

But I'm already out the door before he can finish the sentence.

I should feel exhausted, drained. Instead, I feel wired—agitated but strangely clear-headed. The world is still a rigged game, the powerful still own everything, but somehow, I walk out of there feeling a little more certain. Humanity isn't lost, though the wealthy and conservatives continue to sell it off in pieces.

I slide into my car, buckle the seatbelt. Click. Then, like a jolt to the spine, my brain slams back into crisis mode.

The telecom business deposits. They're set to hit those just-closed South Korean accounts tomorrow. A death sentence. The red flags will trip alarms in every federal watchdog building across the globe, the banks will notify the feds, and by the time I wake up, I could be sitting in a holding cell.

I have hours, maybe less, to fix the code.

I gun the engine, tearing out of the parking lot. Every red light, every slow driver, feels like an enemy. What the hell are all these people doing out here after nine on a stormy Sunday night?

I mentally rewrite the scripts, running through every critical fix. If I miss one subroutine, one misplaced account entry, I might not make it to the end of the week as a free man.

Teresa's car is in my driveway.

I slow down, gripping the wheel.

Shit.

No time for this.

I pull up beside her car, kill the engine. Maybe she's asleep in front of the TV. If I'm quiet, if I slip in through the back, I can get to my computer without her knowing I'm home.

I twist the key into the lock, easing the door open—

Click. The kitchen lights flood on.

"Why are you sneaking into your own house?" Teresa's voice is half amusement, half suspicion.

I blink, caught mid-step. "Thought you'd be asleep watching 'In Living Color.'"

She leans against the counter, arms crossed, watching me like a cat who just caught a mouse.

I sigh, return her kiss, the warmth grounding me for a fraction of a second.

"I have fires to put out," I tell her, already angling toward the hallway. "I need half an hour in my computer room."

She tilts her head. "Want me to make coffee?"

"That's nice, but no. We have an early flight, and I need at least some sleep."

She bites her lip, watching me. Something shifts in her expression—soft but calculated, like she's waiting for the right moment to speak.

"There's something I need to tell you," she says finally. "And something really, really, really important I want to ask."

I rub my temples. "Teresa, can it wait? I have to put this fire out."

She ignores that. Instead, she grabs my hand, tugging at my fingers, playing with them until she pulls too hard and I flinch.

"Don't be such a baby," she teases, but there's an edge to it.

I sigh. "Fine. You're not letting this go, are you?"

She beams. That damn smile. The dimples. The wide, blinking eyes.

"When we come back in six weeks," she starts, "Bishop Timothy is taking me and my mom to Greece for two weeks. It's been planned forever, and I have to go."

I exhale, relieved it's something simple. "Okay. Do you want me to watch your house or—"

She hesitates. That's when I see it.

The nerves. The way her eyes flick away, looking for something stable.

I narrow my gaze. "What is it?"

She takes a breath. "How do you know Timothy again?"

I blink. "What?"

She shifts. "Why would he take us to Greece? I feel like I should explain."

"Teresa, I really don't have time for a long—"

"I was engaged," she blurts.

The words slam through me like a punch.

"Excuse me?"

She winces, holds up a hand. "To his acolyte. For two years. We broke up when he, uh ... turned out to be selling heroin to my sister."

Everything inside me freezes.

"You were engaged," I say flatly.

"Yep."

"To a guy who worked for the Archbishop."

"Correct."

"And he was selling heroin."

"To my sister, yes."

I rub my face. "Jesus Christ, Teresa."

She shrugs like this is just another fact, like she's telling me what she had for dinner. "I broke up with him, obviously. But Timothy had already planned for Mom and me to go to Greece after the wedding. And, well, we still want to go."

I sit down in the nearest chair. I don't even know what to say.

She laughs at my expression, that dangerous, teasing smile returning.

"Now you know my little skeletons."

I shake my head. "How did all of this fall apart?"

She waves a hand. "That's a long story."

"No, no, no, I don't have time. Just—ask me your question, and then I have to work."

She tilts her head, suddenly bashful.

"Okay," she drawls.

Then—

"Do you want to move in with me?"

~~~

The morning air is thick with wet earth and roasted coffee, a fragrance that belongs nowhere but here, in Costa Rica.

I sit beneath the shade of a sprawling almendro tree, its gnarled roots breaking through the sidewalk, its wide canopy filtering the early golden sunlight. The coffee bar is nothing more than a weathered wooden stall, tucked between a pharmacy and a souvenir shop, the kind that sells carved toucans and cheap cigars to tourists who think they're getting something authentic.

But the coffee is real. People who understand that good things shouldn't be rushed grew the beans in the highlands, roasted them yesterday, and brewed the coffee patiently.

Across from me, a monk sits serene and contained, his ochre robe perfectly draped over one shoulder, the other exposed to the humid morning air. His face is smooth but aged, his eyes carrying the type of depth that makes a man feel like a child just by meeting them.

He stirs his coffee slowly, watching the swirling foam as if it holds some great universal truth.
~~~

"Many leaders," he says, his Vietnamese accent thick but measured, "they want to talk about peace, but only when it costs nothing of them."

I nod, listening.

We've been here for over an hour, discussing his recent trip to Geneva, where he met with World Congress officials to talk about funding retreats—places for healing, for awareness, for silence in a world that never stops speaking.

"They like the idea," he continues, tilting his head, a faint smile on his lips. "But they dislike the practice. They dislike what silence brings."

I sip my coffee. It's strong, cortado, nearly black, no sugar.

"What does silence bring?" I ask.

He looks up at me, and for a moment, I feel completely transparent.

"Truth."

The street is coming alive—vendors setting up fruit carts, shopkeepers sweeping their doorsteps, the distant sound of motorcycles threading through the narrow undefined dirt streets.

A stray dog noses through a discarded newspaper, then trots away as a passing bus belches out a thick cloud of diesel exhaust.

Beyond the buildings, beyond the asphalt and the cafes, the jungle twentyfour hours a day sounds of howler monkey, Toucan, and unknown critters scream and sing, but at this time of day the insects and their scratching sounds are waking up.

The low hum of insects, the chatter of parrots, the occasional monkey call cutting through the morning. It feels like the edge of civilization, where the wild and the modern world rub shoulders but never quite belong to each other.

I glance at the post office. The metal door shutter is rolling up.

Time to go.

I turn back to the monk, setting my cup down.

"I'd love to stay longer, but I have business to take care of," I say.

He nods, as if he already knew I'd say that.

"Business," he says, amused. "The suffering you choose for yourself."

I half-smile. "Something like that."

He reaches into the folds of his robe, pulls out a small, delicate business card, and hands it to me with both hands, the way a man might present something sacred.

I stare at the delicate print of the card, aware of the thinness of the paper, feeling the fragility between my fingertips. Plum Village. A place dedicated entirely to silence, contemplation, and truth—words so far removed from my reality, they feel alien, almost absurd.

Yet, something deep and unnameable stirs within me—a quiet rebellion against the sterile security of numbers, identities, and accounts. A sudden memory strikes with visceral clarity: my stepfather sitting at the kitchen table in our modest home, hunched over tax papers, the yellow overhead lamp throwing shadows across his exhausted face. He was average—painfully, relentlessly average—always at the mercy of bills, mortgages, and the mundane suffocation of predictability.

And I remember his funeral. How ordinary it was. How quickly the world carried on without him.

My chest tightens, my fingers clenching involuntarily around the monk's card. This isn't just about wealth. It never was. It's about escaping the suffocating ordinariness that swallowed my stepfather whole, leaving nothing behind but a gravestone no one visits.

I glance back at the monk, his eyes still steady, patient, infinitely knowing.

"Do you think it's really possible?" My voice betrays more vulnerability than intended.

He tilts his head slightly. "What?"

"To stop running. To ever feel truly safe."

A long pause hangs between us, filled only with the sounds of the two worlds waking up, oblivious to our conversation.

He smiles softly, understanding. "Only when you realize that safety is not something you find out there," he gestures vaguely toward the bustling street, "but in here." His palm rests gently over his heart. "Then you stop running."

I feel myself nodding, a silent acknowledgment of a truth I'm not yet ready to fully embrace.

Not yet.

I stand. The chair moves backwards, scraping brutally against concrete. I tuck the card deeper into my pocket, as if burying evidence of a crime.

"Thank you," I murmur.

As I turn away, stepping into the swirl of life that awaits—money, power, anonymity—the monk's words cling stubbornly to my thoughts, whispered echoes promising an uncomfortable reckoning to come.

The post office air is stale, thick with the scent of old paper, ink, and humidity trapped in aging walls. The place is quiet, just the occasional rustle of letters, the soft murmurs of clerks behind the counter, the distant hum of a ceiling fan struggling against the heat.

I make my way to my personal mailbox. I feel the cold, smooth lock; its brass numbers are worn from use. I twist the key, the mechanism clicking into place.

Inside, a small package awaits.

I reach in, pulling out the small leather satchel, its worn edges softened from years of handling. I take the one from my shoulder, roll it tight, and replace the one I took by shoving it inside.

Then, I unzip the satchel, my fingers brushing against smooth cardstock.

I pull out a Costa Rican passport and an identification card.

My photo. A new name.

Alejandro Cortez.

I run my thumb over the raised lettering, the embossed seal, the crisp plastic of the ID.

It's real. Better than real.

With the ID in my wallet, the passport in my front pocket. I lock the box. I don't look back.

I step out into the heat of San José, the air thick with diesel, coffee, and the sweet, overripe scent of crushed fruit from a vendor cart nearby.

A yellow taxi idles at the curb, the driver lounging inside, arm hanging out the open window, his fingers lazily tapping the door. The car is old, a 1974 E series Toyota Corolla with faded paint and a cracked dashboard, but it still hums with life, the engine purring with the type of durability that only exists in places where cars outlast governments.

I raise a hand.

The driver straightens, flicks a burnt cigarette onto the pavement, and waves me over.

I slid into the backseat, the vinyl cracked, warm from the sun, catching slightly on my skin.

"Yo quiero ir a el Aeropuerto Internacional de Juan Santamaría," I say.

The driver nods, his dark eyes flicking to me in the rearview. A silent study.

He's older, maybe late fifties, his face lined from years behind the wheel, his shirt open at the collar, revealing a gold chain nestled in a mat of dark chest hair. A thick scar runs down his left forearm, jagged and faded.

He shifts into gear, and the taxi lurches forward, rolling into the tangled rhythm of San José traffic.

The city is alive, chaotic and unbothered. Buses spew black smoke, motorcycles weave through impossible gaps, street vendors balance trays of empanadas and cold beer, shouting their prices over the honking and Spanish radio chatter.

The driver plays Boleros through a tinny car speaker; the music crackling with age, heavy with longing.

We pass market stalls bursting with bananas and papayas, a church with its doors open wide, the smell of yesterday's rain mixed with today's humidity steaming off the pavement as we cut through a neighborhood where laundry flutters on balconies, strung like flags of everyday survival.

He doesn't ask me questions.

I don't offer answers.

At one point, he fishes a cigarette from his pocket, lighting it with a flick of his gold lighter, taking a slow drag before cracking the window.

"You going long or just passing through?" he asks finally, voice low, conversational.

"Just passing through."

He nods, like he's heard that before. In silence, the ten minutes goes past.

Juan Santamaría airport isn't big, but it's busy. Inside, the air-conditioning hits like a wall, the scent of disinfectant and fast food mixing with jet fuel. Departure screens, blinking red and green, line the walls, announcing the flow of people into and out of the country.

I step up to the ticket counter, my fingers resting lightly on the passport in my pocket.

The agent, a young woman with dark, tired eyes, glances up with a rehearsed smile.

"¿Destino?"

"Panama City."

"¿Ida y vuelta?"

"One way."

Her gaze flicks up the slightest hesitation, but then she nods, fingers clacking over the keyboard.

She prints the ticket, slides it across the counter.

"Buen viaje, Señor Cortez."

By 10 AM, I'm in Panama City.

The airport hums with movement, a crowd thick with travelers, businessmen, and locals weaving through the terminals with the efficiency of people who know the drill. The smell of coffee, sweat, and industrial air-conditioning fills the space, mixing with the muted scent of jet fuel drifting in from the tarmac.

Announcements in rapid Spanish, then repeated in crisp English, echo over the speakers, cutting through the chatter of tourists haggling over duty-free rum and businessmen barking into phones. I keep my head down, moving through the flow of bodies, out the exit doors, into the thick Panamanian heat.

Outside, the sun is bright and ruthless, throwing long shadows from palm trees onto the pavement. The air smells of concrete warming in the sun, grilled meat from a food cart, and the faint salt of the Pacific carried inland on the wind.

I don't take a taxi.

Instead, I step onto a local bus, the sort that rattles and groans but never stops running, packed with commuters who barely notice another face in the crowd.

The bus driver wears aviators, his arm draped lazily over the wheel as he navigates the chaotic traffic. Salsa music blasts from a tinny speaker, all treble—no bass, filling the space between conversations in Spanish, Creole, and English.

The passengers are a mix of shopkeepers, laborers, students, and expats. A woman in a bright red dress fans herself with a folded newspaper. Two men in suits argue over something in low, clipped

Spanish. A kid in a basketball jersey bounces his leg, staring out the window, lost in thought.

I lean back in the seat, feeling the vibration of the old engine beneath me.

Panama speaks every language. The accent is distinct—a blend of Caribbean rhythm and Latin sharpness, but nearly everyone here understands English.

I listen, picking up fragments of conversations. Talk of business, of government policies, of money moving through the banking system, of ships waiting to cross the canal.

It all flows through Panama.

The money. The products. The people.

Everything moves here, changes hands here.

Just like I'm about to.

The building is old, yellowed by time and humidity. Ceiling fans spin lazily, doing little against the heat.

I walk to my personal box, twisting the key, the metal cold against my fingers.

Inside—another small leather satchel.

I reach in, pull it out, unzip it.

I take my Costa Rican passport and ID, roll them tight, shove them into the bag slung over my shoulder.

Then I pull out the new ones.

Name: Rafael Montenegro.

The photo is mine. But the name, the history, the details—none of it belongs to the man I was an hour ago.

I slide the ID into my wallet, the passport into my front pocket.

Then I lock the box and walk away.

The terminal is louder now, the late morning rush pressing in from all sides. People argue over luggage fees, stand in long lines for overpriced food, check their watches like it will change their boarding time.

I head straight to the ticket counter.

The woman behind the desk is middle-aged, her uniform crisp, her nails painted a bright coral. She barely glances at me as she types.

"¿Destino?"

"Cayman."

"¿Solo ida?"

"One way."

She hesitates for a fraction of a second, just like the last one. The Panama ID and name and my American accent gives them pause. It's always a one-way ticket. I don't want to be in a rush to leave.

Her fingers clack against the keyboard.

"Next flight leaves in a half hour. Prop plane, small aircraft."

I nod. "That's fine."

She prints the ticket, slides it across the counter.

"Buen viaje, Señor Montenegro."

The plane is small, barely room for twenty passengers. The type of aircraft that makes even seasoned travellers hesitate.

The hum of the engines vibrates through the metal fuselage, and the air smells like heat, old upholstery, and aviation fuel.

I settle into my seat, watching the ground crew move methodically across the tarmac.

The propellers whine to life, a low, hungry growl that builds into a roar.

Outside, the airport is just another point of departure.

The city, just another place I left behind.

The wheels lift off the ground, and I feel the familiar pull—not just of gravity, but of movement itself.

As I settle into my seat, the hum of the propellers and vibration of the engines seep into my body. It's steady, a rhythmic pulse, like sitting in one of those massage chairs in a mall, the ones that shake your bones but leaves you feeling just loose enough to breathe again.

The window glass is warm against my temple, the blue Caribbean stretching below, a vast nothingness broken only by the occasional smudge of an island.

But my mind isn't here. I'm thinking about a couple of months ago in San José—the first time Teresa and I ran a two-week training event for an automotive supplier. A company that builds interior door panels and dashboards for Ford Motor Company.

Teresa was running the afternoon session, holding court like she was born for it, effortlessly keeping executives and engineers engaged. Me? I had an appointment to keep.

San José—the immigration attorney

The attorney's office was small but sharp, tucked into an upper-class neighborhood downtown. The furniture was sleek, all dark wood and polished glass. A single air conditioning unit rattled above us, struggling against the thick Costa Rican heat.

He was friendly, confident, full of energy, the confidence of a man who had been doing this long enough to know exactly how to sell it.

"The relationship between the U.S. and Costa Rica is close," he told me, leaning forward, fingers clasped like he was about to tell me a secret.

"Reciprocity between the two is absolute. No immunity. Everything you do is transparent and shared with the U.S.—including the IRS, CIA, and even the FBI."

He let that sit for a moment, watching my face.

Then he smiled.

"Here's what I do for you."

His hands spread, palms up, like he was offering me the whole damn world on a gold tray.

"For a onetime fee of seven hundred dollars, you can become a Costa Rican citizen. Full identification. Full passport. Completely legal."

I nodded, waiting. That wasn't enough.

He grinned, seeing that I already understood.

"But that alone isn't where you should stop," he continued, his voice smooth, effortless. "That's too easy to track down. Mark flies in from the States. Mark flies back from Costa Rica. Everything matches. Too clean."

His grin widened.

"But for an additional four hundred dollars, you can get a name change."

He sat back, letting the words sink in.

"You will become a ghost to the paper trail. Your U.S. records? They won't reflect anything but normal travel. But with your Costa Rican passport and ID? You can go anywhere in the world, and the U.S. has no way of knowing."

He tapped the desk, a slow, deliberate motion.

"This is how you disappear, my friend. Not by hiding. By blending."

Back to the present—above the Caribbean. The engines drone on, steady, soothing. The stewardess smiles, polished and professional, as she hands me a cold can of Dr. Pepper.

I nod in thanks, pull the stay-tab, and the sharp hiss of carbonation escapes into the stale cabin air. The familiar scent hits me instantly—that spiced cherry, artificial sweetness, a smell that drags my memory back in time. I take a long drink, letting the cold burn my throat, and suddenly—

I'm not in the sky over the Caribbean anymore. I'm back in Panama City. It was the first time I flew under a different name. The first time I looked at a boarding pass and saw someone who wasn't supposed to exist.

Alejandro Cortez.

I'd repeat it in my head until it felt real. Panama was just a layover, but the real reason I was there was for a meeting. A corporate attorney, but not like the one in Costa Rica.

No.

This man played in a different league.

His office wasn't just wealthy—it was meticulously curated. The type of place that reeks of control. Marble floors, deep leather chairs, and a view of the bay that stretched endlessly beyond the glass walls. The waiting area looked like a luxury watch commercial come to life.

Men in tailored Brioni suits, their Rolexes flashing under soft lighting. Women in high-end designer dresses, the brands that cost more than my first new car.

This wasn't a lawyer's office. This was a gatekeeper's throne room. If you had the money, you didn't just set up a business. You set up a system.

A web of untraceable accounts, blind trusts, and offshore corporations.

You built fortresses out of paperwork, and once inside, nothing could touch you.

The lawyer had a smooth voice that let you know he'd done this a thousand times.

"In Panama," he told me, "we do not have clients. We have architects of wealth. You are not simply opening a company. You are creating a vault. A system that exists outside of governments, outside of taxation, outside of reach."

I sat back, taking it all in.

This was the game.

This was genuine power.

A country could collapse. A bank could fail. A government could change overnight.

But a well-built offshore structure? That was eternal. As long as the right people got paid. And that's when I knew—

If I spent the money and time upfront, this would withstand anything life threw my way.

I blink, the plane hums around me. The Dr. Pepper is still cold in my hand. A stewardess walks past, adjusting a tray, the scent of pressurized air and cheap cologne filling the space.

The Cayman Islands are waiting.

And my next move is already in motion.

By 7:30 PM, I'm back in San José, Costa Rica, sitting at a table in a private dining room of an upscale restaurant, the space that corporate executives love—dim lighting, leather-backed chairs, servers in crisp uniforms who glide in and out like ghosts.

The air is thick with the scent of grilled steak, fresh ceviche, and the faintest trace of cigar smoke drifting in from the outdoor terrace.

Across from me, Teresa sits with her arms crossed, her expression unreadable as her fork sits idly on a plate of arroz con mariscos.

Three executives from the manufacturing company, beside her. They ignore the woman running their training program; they drink scotch, laugh, and talk amongst themselves, oblivious to her visible frustration.

I swirl the ice in my glass, taking a sip of my whiskey.

"How was the day, Teresa?" I ask, keeping my voice neutral.

She sighs, then leans back against the chair, shaking her head.

"I know I say it every time," she says, voice low but sharp, "but I don't think we have a chance at success with this team."

Chapter 7: The Bluff

Net worth $115

The stage lights hit hard, bright and hot like interrogation lamps, but I've stood under worse.

Before me, a sea of three thousand business owners, execs, and consultants—all buttoned up and wired tight, the practitioners who measure value in decimal points and net margins. Speaking in acronyms as if they are a language. Words like EBITDA and ROI.

Behind me, two towering LED screens loop my brand—"Lean Precision™: Profits Through Efficiency"—while IEEE banners line the walls, all navy blue, white serif letters, austere and corporate as a government agency.

My hands are steady. My voice, tuned like a jazz saxophone, lilting in and out of stories, numbers, laughter, punchlines, and pressure points.

I own them.

"We saved a textile firm in Honduras $6.2 million in eight months. A plastics manufacturer in St. Louis cut costs by 38% while increasing throughput. And last year? A wire harness assembly plant in Guatemala took our model and doubled their market share in 14 months."

Laughter bursts from the crowd at the well-timed jab I make about consultants who charge a fortune just to tell you what's already broken.

Even the suits in the first row smirk.

I pace the stage deliberately, rolling up the sleeves of my tailored shirt just enough to look like I work—not just talk.

I deliver the ending line. Sharp. Clean. A closer.

"You don't need more money. You need less waste."

Applause erupts—but it's brisk. Clipped. Mechanical. I nod, offer a modest smile, bow slightly, and exit stage left. I expect the buzz. The flood. The chase.

Usually, I can't make it to the damn snack table before I'm mobbed by business owners, VPs, and tech directors.

But today?

Nothing.

A few handshakes. A nod. One half-interested request for a business card from a guy who smells like tobacco and spilled gin.

I shake another hand. It's lukewarm. The grip is there, but the intention's gone. They're moving around me, not toward me. Cold. Too cold. My gut twitches. Not nerves. Instinct.

Ritz Carlton in Naples Florida.

The suite is a monument to luxury.

Top floor. View of the gulf.

Marble counters, plush Turkish robes, a bed that feels like it could cure depression.

The air outside is thick with a gulf breeze, and the sound of the surf brushing the shore is slow, hypnotic.

I should feel like a king.

But, I feel exposed.

I pour a drink. Neat. Let it bite.

Somewhere below, champagne flows, connections are made, partnerships forged.

But no one's knocking on my door.

No one's calling my room.

Nearly two years now they pay me $5,000 for a high power thirty minutes of speaking. Several events a year to a room full of power players.

And now? Radio silence.

I turn from the window and stare down at the slick stack of business cards in my briefcase.

I've never walked away from an event like this without at least two six-figure deals.

Tonight? Not even a hint.

Something's wrong.

The suite smells faintly of citrus and money—some clever trick of the Ritz housekeeping department—but I'm too restless to enjoy it. Teresa's out shopping, chasing high-end sandals or a linen wrap she doesn't need. We've got dinner with the IEEE chairman tonight, and I'm supposed to be relaxing, enjoying the rewards of success.

But the ocean feels too slow, too still.

The silence in this room is louder than applause.

So I pick up the phone and dial the number that grounds me.

She answers on the second ring.

"Well, there's my millionaire grandson."

I smile. "Not quite, Grandma. Not today."

She doesn't catch the edge in my voice.

Instead, she launches into a winding monologue about my son and his mother, how they've moved to Las Vegas, and how my boy—smart as ever—is still wearing those ridiculous trousers that fall off his backside.

"You'd think gravity would teach him a lesson," she says. "But no, he walks around hitching them up like he's auditioning for a prison fashion show."

I laugh, not because it's funny, but because I need to.

Then her voice shifts.

"There's something else."

A pause.

Long. Hesitant.

"It's your sister."

My stomach tenses. "What happened?"

"She tried to kill herself."

The words drop like cinder blocks. No ceremony, no warning.

I sit down slowly on the edge of the bed.

"What? When?"

"Last week. She took a bottle of pills. They found her slumped over the toilet. She's in the ICU now. Liver and spleen—both shot, but the doctors think she'll live."

"Jesus, Grandma."

And then, because it's Grandma and she tells everything like a pulp novel, she keeps going—voice low, steady, just enough judgment baked in to feel Catholic.

"You know how it started? Bears."

"What?"

"Stuffed bears. Not real ones. Those Beary & Friends things. They sell 'em on the Home Shopping Channel. She'd watch it every night—every damn night—and buy them. First, it was one or two. Then a dozen. Then hundreds. Then thousands."

"You're serious."

"Serious as a foreclosure notice. She maxed out every credit card, mortgaged the house twice, ruined her husband's credit, and when the bank finally kicked them out, she stored the bears in a rental unit. Seven of them. Seven storage units. Full of goddamn bears."

I run a hand over my face, the weight of it building.

"Then came the divorce. The court took the kids. Husband laid it all out for the judge—receipts, bank statements, photos of her passed out on the sofa surrounded by beady little eyes and bows and button noses. Said she'd order six at a time, talk to them like they were real."

I picture it. My sister, surrounded by mountains of soft, manu-factured affection, slowly replacing the human kind she lost.

"Why didn't anyone tell me?"

"Because you've been living out of a suitcase, Mark." Her voice softens. "You call when you can. But no one really knows where you are half the time. Central America? Boston? Detroit? You're always chasing the next contract."

She lets that sink in, and I don't fight her on it.

I tell her about the last two years. The travel. The hotels. The same twenty entrees on every menu, the stiff pillows, the too-early wake-ups and too-late flights.

"I'm gone six weeks at a time. Back for two, then gone again." I exhale. "And today was the first time I got the cold shoulder. Three thousand business owners in that room, Grandma. I gave them gold. But they weren't buying. Not even shaking hands."

She doesn't respond immediately.

When she does, her voice is soft but steady.

"Maybe they weren't cold. Maybe they just weren't your people."

"They paid me five grand for thirty minutes. And put me in a suite for three nights."

"Doesn't mean they want your soul, sweetheart. Just your math."

That hits harder than it should.

"So what now?" she asks.

I look at the clock. Teresa will be back soon. The IEEE dinner will be more posing, more small talk, more polished shoes and power games.

"I'm not sure. But, I need to get ready for my dinner meeting."

After Grandma hangs up, I sit staring into the polished reflection of the empty suite's coffee table, suddenly aware of how similar my sister's compulsions are to mine. Bears for her; contracts for me—each collection a desperate attempt to fill a void we refuse to name.

Without thinking, I open my laptop and pull up my financial statements, account balances, contracts, and client lists. Numbers scroll past—figures that once meant validation, security, triumph. But tonight, they blur into something else. Stacks of bears, useless and hollow, piling up in rented rooms. My chest tightens.

I click to open my recent email archive, skimming past messages that read more like obituaries than business correspondence. "Regret to inform you … termination due to new market pressures … necessary restructuring…"

Then an unfamiliar email catches my eye. Subject line: "Lean Precision™: A different approach." Curious, I click.

"Dear Mark,

"I watched your presentation today. You don't know me, and I didn't approach you afterward—I saw the crowd drift, saw your confusion. The thing is, I understand why. But hear me out. I run a workers' cooperative in San Antonio—small scale, but growing. We adopted your Lean Precision™ principles, not to squeeze margins, but to empower employees. Profits soared, yes—but so did wages, healthcare, retirement. We proved it could work, and we think you'd be interested.

"Maybe it's not the clients you lost today. Maybe it's the better kind of clients you've been courting. If you're interested in another way—call me.

"Yours sincerely,

"Enrique Delgado."

A worker cooperative. I blink at the screen, the concept alien yet exhilarating. My heart quickens with something I haven't felt in months—possibility.

Maybe Grandma's right. Bears or contracts, obsession is obsession. But maybe obsession, guided differently, becomes purpose. But now it's time for dinner.

The private dining room is all quiet opulence—white linen, golden sconces, a chilled stillness behind thick drapes. Outside, the gulf breeze rolls in off the water, but in here, the air is too cool, too polite, like everything's being watched.

I swirl my scotch, waiting for the moment that always comes—the slip, the offhand comment, the clue.

"The internet hacking," says the wife of the IEEE chairman, her voice that crisp, well-bred tone cultivated in elite circles and exclusive clubs. She lifts her glass of white wine delicately, swirling it as if decoding the future in its pale depths. "It's becoming a form of industrial espionage that even the FBI isn't prepared for. Did you read The Journal today? Companies are leaking personal data like sieves. I mean, I don't want my bank throwing around my information like Mardi Gras beads."

Her husband lets out a snorting laugh. "It's your Macy's account you're afraid someone will uncover. They could pay off the national debt with what you spend in a month on handbags and makeup."

She shoots him a look that would freeze a furnace.

Teresa doesn't miss a beat. She leans forward, calm, sharp.

"No one in their right mind would use a credit card over the Internet." Her tone is clinical. "There's no encryption, no firewall worth a damn, and nothing stopping your entire life from ending up on a Russian server farm. The web isn't a marketplace. It's a minefield."

Silence falls over the table like fog.

For a moment.

Then forks return to plates. The clink of cutlery. A laugh too loud from one executive on the far side of the restaurant.

But the energy is drained.

The chairman dabs the corners of his mouth with a napkin, leans over his half-finished steak, and finally looks at me like a man delivering last rites.

"I wanted to tell you," he says, "I really enjoyed your talk. Sharp. Funny. One of the best this week."

I nod, but I'm already bracing for the but.

"You know, I've had plenty of executives come up to me afterward, asking about your role at UTC."

That hits different.

I narrow my eyes. "Then why haven't they come to me?"

He pauses. Rolls the stem of his wineglass between his fingers.

"They're not going to."

"Why not?"

He hesitates, but not out of uncertainty—out of pity.

"Because United Technologies is rewriting their supplier contracts."

The words hit like a punch.

"What?"

"They're squeezing every company that's worked with you. Using your own system—the lean efficiencies, the cost cuts, the throughput—you gave them all the ammunition. Now they're slashing prices across the board. Forcing suppliers to meet impossible targets or lose their contract."

I feel my jaw tighten. My pulse spikes.

"No one told me."

He shakes his head slowly. "No one will. Because if they talk to you—they lose their leverage. Just associating with you puts them on UTC's radar. You've become a red flag."

Teresa looks at me. She doesn't speak, but her eyes say everything.

He leans back. "No one's going to work with you again, Mark. Not if they want to stay in business."

The scotch burns going down my throat.

In that moment, the banners, the applause, the luxury suite—it's all just a stage prop in a farce where I didn't even know I was the punchline.

They didn't shut the door.

They erased me from the building.

After the shortened dinner, Teresa and I go to the pool. Except for us, nobody is on the pool bar deck. The tiki torches have long burned out, and what's left of the evening breeze is brushing the palms like fingers trying to calm a restless mind. Untouched since the last drunk exec wandered off around midnight, the pool glows a silent, still, electric blue.

Teresa sits wrapped in a beach towel, legs pulled up under her, hair damp and clinging to her face like she's just crawled out of the ocean. I'm pacing. Still dressed from dinner. Still boiling.

"That dinner was a waste of everyone's time," I say, too loud for the setting but not caring.

Teresa doesn't flinch.

I turn to face her. "My career ended not because I failed. Not because I delivered crap work. No—I'm done because I made greedy bastards in the boardroom richer than they could handle. Because I helped small companies rise, and now those same companies are being bludgeoned with the very tools I gave them."

I laugh once, bitter and low. "God forbid some little supplier earns an extra two percent. No, no. That's un-American."

Without saying a word, Teresa lifts her arms and whips her wet hair toward me.

Cold droplets hit my shirt. I jerk back.

She grins. "You need to cool off, mister."

I shake my head and sit down hard on the lounge chair beside her, elbows on my knees, face in my hands.

"You know," she says, her voice softer now, "it's a great time to hit the reset button."

I look over. "What reset button?"

She shrugs, casual but razor-sharp. "The one you keep talking about. Getting your MBA. Leaving the snow capital of the universe. Starting something that's yours. Not UTC's. Not borrowed. Yours."

I stare at her. She doesn't blink.

"So let's do it, Mark. Pick your dream spot. Pick your dream university. I'll work. You get the degree. We start over, clean. We take these lemons—"

"And make lemonade?"

"No." She smiles. "We make a lemonade empire."

For the first time all night, I laugh. Not bitter. Not angry.

Just surprised that, even now, she can pull hope out of the wreckage like it was always part of the plan.

A cool wind rustles the palms again.

The stars over the Gulf are clear.

Reset button.

At nine am I call Papa Bertrand and still needing to vent, I explain the events from the day. He picks up on the third ring, voice weathered with coffee and calm.

"Morning, Mark. What's got you spinning this early?"

I don't even ease into it. I spill everything. The dinner, the cold shoulder, UTC's treachery. How they're strip-mining my work and using it to crush the very companies I helped. I let it all out, the venom and exhaustion, and he just listens.

When I finish, there's a long pause. I can hear the soft buzz of morning cicadas and maybe the clink of a spoon in a ceramic mug.

Then Papa Bertrand speaks.

His voice is a slow-burn, deep and thoughtful, like he's seeing every angle at once but only delivering the words that count.

"My daughter has the right idea. You kids have your whole lives ahead. Do it, Mark. Trade in their profit greed for your ladder up."

"They call it corporate profits," I say, "but truth be known, it's stolen wages taken from the working class. The media and education industrial complex has conditioned us to believe that businesses are more valuable than the people who make the business possible. Namely, the employees. In a democracy and a free enterprise system, profits like executive pay should be capped. We had it that way. Roosevelt knew greed had to be regulated. But Reagan and the uber wealthy aligned to remove the cap and initiate twenty-first-century slavery. And the Democrats eagerly agreed. Bill Clinton is doubling down on the momentum."

"As I said before, my daughter's got the right idea. You kids ... you've got time. But what you don't have—what you better learn now—is where to spend that time. What to fight. What to walk away from."

I let that smolder. He continues.

"You're not wrong, what you said about profits. About unpaid wages. Hell, I've seen it for decades. But let me tell you what really eats at the gut of humanity, the part we don't talk about in polite company. People can tolerate success. They can even respect it. But what they cannot—will not—accept is the man who takes without limits."

He pauses to sip his coffee. I can hear it, like a breath between chapters.

"See, there's this old truth buried under all our shiny tech and market theory—people demand balance. We might not say it. We might not even know it. But we feel it in our bones. That's why fairy tales end with justice. That's why the crowd turns on the champion who never falls. Human nature doesn't worship dominance—it waits for it to fall."

I nod slowly, barely breathing.

"There's a force, Mark. I don't know if it's God or just the rhythm of the universe, but there's a law that everything has to even out. The high-flying sons of bitches who stack gold to the ceiling? Eventually, that pile gets so tall it tips. Call it karma. Call it cosmic bookkeeping. Call it the God of Equilibrium. But don't think for a second it doesn't exist."

I close my eyes, gripping the phone tighter.

"And you, Mark—you're caught in the middle of it. You created something valuable. And they used it like a blade. That wasn't your fault. But now that you know what they do with it? What you do next—that's on you."

There's a long silence between us. No tension. Just truth sitting in the open air like sunlight drying dew.

He finishes:

"You've been playing their game, climbing their ladder, building their temples. Now maybe it's time you build your own. Not for gold. Not for empire. Just for balance."

I whisper, "Balance."

"Yeah, kid. Balance. Not the flashy kind. Not the scoreboard. Just the kind that lets you sleep at night."

The line goes quiet, but the words don't fade.

They etch themselves in.

I know exactly where we are going to move.

~~~

The Dzogchen Foundation grounds are still wet with morning dew as I walk the terraced path toward the shrine room, where incense always rides the air just ahead of the first chant. The maple trees have begun their spring transformation—new branches and an abundance of buds, the pinnacle of beauty that humbles you even when your head is full of schemes.

This is my fifth retreat with Lama Sundra Jhinpa, and it no longer feels like an invitation. It feels like a calibration—to strip away the layers, smooth the sharp edges, remember what still pulses beneath all the armor. After a chance meeting with that world famous monk in Costa Rica, I called him two weeks later. He pointed me to this foundation in north central Massachusetts and made the introduction to the Lama.

We're sitting on a weathered wooden bench behind the main hall, sipping tea. Sundra's in a loose cotton robe, legs folded effortlessly in lotus pose. His presence is always a paradox—deeply peaceful, and yet sharp as a blade.
~~~

"You know, Mark," he says, stirring honey into his cup without looking up, "people think the key to a retreat is silence. Trees. Serenity. But really—it's money. Not just to build it. The amount of cash needed to keep it alive is staggering."

He glances up at me with that half-smile, the one that says I know exactly what's ticking behind your eyes.

"You want to bring people here and let them remember who they are? Then you better have a nice bathroom. A clean bed. A stocked kitchen. And you better know how to talk to people with seven- and eight-figure portfolios who think giving ten grand a year makes them humble."

I laugh, but it's just my way of expressing discomfort. My tick. I often laugh when my senses are hurt. Too knowing.

Sundra leans forward.

"You ever think of starting something in Southern California? San Diego, maybe. Ocean air. Sunshine. Earthquake-proof, of course."

"You mean a retreat?" I ask.

"I mean an abbey with rooms for visiting monks from around the world and student residents. Daily sits. Weeklong intensives. A proper Western Dzogchen outpost."

He watches me closely now.

"I need someone to manage these finances. The infrastructure. Long-term investments for growth and stability. Someone who understands the teachings and the money market."

I sip my tea, eyes on the moss-covered stones that grace the garden.

"You mean someone with an MBA?"

"I mean you, Mark."

There it is. Laid out like a koan. One part invitation, one part test.

I nod slowly, letting it sink in.

But my mind drifts. Not to enlightenment. Not compassion. To money.

To the growing number of offshore accounts, I've already built like underground vaults. Corporate veils hide paper trails folded through Panama, Hong Kong, BVI, Grand Cayman and more. To the thousands of wealthy contributors, I could sway with just the right tax incentive, the right phrasing on the 501(c)(3) paperwork.

The internet is young. Nobody knows what it really is yet. Some call it a joke. Others see a gold rush. But I know the truth about it.

Data is power.

User behavior is currency. Whoever controls the pipeline—controls the future. And what better cover than a nonprofit spiritual foundation? What better shield than the robes of Buddhism and the guise of wellness?

I shake the thought loose from my mind, but it lingers.

Sundra raises an eyebrow.

"Dark thoughts, Mark?"

"Just long ones, with fetters," I say.

I pause, feeling something shift inside me—not guilt exactly, but a tightening. Like discovering your reflection distorted in a hall of mirrors, each image slightly more twisted than the last. I glance at the shrine room, its simplicity a direct rebuke to my complexity.

"It's strange," I say finally, unable to look directly at Sundra. "Here, clarity feels effortless. But out there—it's like clarity itself becomes an illusion. Out there, I need a mask."

Sundra smiles, gentle and inscrutable. "Masks aren't the problem, Mark. Believing they're your face—that's when you lose your way."

A chill runs down my spine. He's hit on something deeper than strategy or finance, something buried beneath spreadsheets and offshore schemes. For just an instant, my hunger and ambition seem like symptoms of something older and darker—a hidden wound that demands feeding, no matter how much money piles up.

"The ego always wants to be useful. But remember, Dzogchen isn't about controlling the current. It's about seeing through it."

I nod again, slower this time. But part of me already knows—Wall Street stocks. I recall the email from the San Antonio profit sharing company, using my lean techniques to reward employees. Sweet but there is no money in it for me.

The last light of the afternoon filters through the pines, catching on the curve of prayer flags and the flicker of a brass butter lamp behind the window. We've spent the day pacing the garden paths, tea in hand, ideas too large to fit between breaths.

Sundra speaks softly, the way a man does when he's talking about fire in a monastery.

"A nonprofit isn't just a tax shelter, Mark. It's a powerful vehicle. One that runs on perception and purpose. But it needs to be strategically poor. Too wealthy, and the donors lose interest. Too frugal, and the mission fails. You need to understand distribution as dharma. Stewardship, not ownership."

I nod, but inside—my mind is breaking open like glass under pressure.

Sundra stops walking and faces me.

"You're the right person. I've known it since your second retreat. You've got clarity—and you've got hunger. So let me be clear."

"I'm going to pay for your MBA."

The air shifts. Not metaphorically—actually.

The wind through the trees pauses as if it hears something sacred.

"We'll buy property in San Diego. Build it from the ground up—the model abbey. Not just for retreats, but for training. For transformation. It's not just about enlightenment anymore. It's about infrastructure."

We keep walking, slower now. The leaves crunch underfoot.

"You'll need to understand the legal framework. Charitable corporations, public versus private funding streams, restricted gifts. We'll need to structure endowments and plan distributions. Not just meditate under Bodhi trees—we're planting forests of sustainability."

My mouth is dry. My brain's gone feral.

Stocks and bonds are now traded online.

The market is becoming accessible, pliable, digital.

Speculative currency or liquid derivatives hasn't happened yet, but the whisper of it is out there. The Telnet BBS corner, 4chan.org, IRC Undernet (originator of the hash tag), and Hacker Quarterly regularly discuss these and pass-through banking.

And every whisper from them and now Lama Sundra's words, all of it sounds like opportunity to me. My offshore pipeline is solid and ready for much larger quantities of cash.

"To attract the wealthy," he continues, "you must understand why they give. It's not guilt. Not goodness. It's legacy. Influence. Immortality. They want their names carved into something that outlives their bodies. You give them that, and they'll fund your entire mountain."

I stop. "I don't know where to begin."

He smiles. "That's the right answer."

But he doesn't stop. Doesn't let me off the hook.

"You begin where all paths begin: questions. Not answers. The more questions you have, the more open your mind becomes. Confusion isn't failure—it's awakening. It means you're beginning to see just how deep the structure goes."

My heart's pounding. Not from fear. From possibility. The internet is chaotic. Business is war. Religion is theatre.

But here ... now ...

I'm going to merge them all. Not to exploit. Not to deceive. But to build a new structure—where spirit and strategy aren't enemies.

My mind runs through this conversation like it is on a reel-to-reel tape player set to auto rewind. I'm on the road again. Left Massachusetts and Lama Sundra Jhinpa in my rearview two days ago—retreat dust on my boots, sandalwood still ghosting the collar of my jacket.

Teresa stayed behind at the house in Ferndale to sell it and tie off the last of Michigan's bitter winters. Said she'd join me in San Diego after the closing—once the for-sale sign was gone and her conscience could clock out. She's angry that Sundra's footing the bill for my MBA. She'd planned to gift it herself, as if debt and degrees were acts of devotion. But that's not all she's carrying. There's a longer list, etched behind her eyes. I read it without asking. The writing's on the wall. And me? I'm the Alan Parsons Project—eye in the sky, watching her from altitude, seeing everything, saying nothing.

Right now I'm pushing west through Ohio, where Lake Erie's breath still lingers, and still too early in April for spring to have the nerve to show its face.

I pull into a side road—gas station long abandoned; the sign cracked and colorless sports my biological father's name [Newbury], pumps ripped out like pulled teeth. But the phone booth still stands, leaning like an old priest who hears confessions but doesn't bother with penance.

I fed it coins. Dial the number. Give the code phrase.

The beeper on my hip chirps confirmation.

I read off the tally:

Fifty-two-nine, net.

I write it in my pocket notepad. Grease-smudged. My shorthand scribbles indecipherable to anyone but me—and even then, only if I'm lucky.

This is month seven for the Telecom scam.

New system. New banks. Same programs and improved scripting routines.

The trick isn't making the money. The trick is never needing to explain it.

Curaçao to a San Diego consulting firm.

Consulting firm to a Nevada holding company.

Nevada leases "equipment" to a Panamanian import/export LLC.

All me, front to back. Various names and residences, all me. No more partners in my business enterprises.

Legal? Technically.

Until someone decides it's not. But so far, no one's looking. I hang up. Slide the notepad into my coat. The wind cuts across the lot like a blade. Across the highway, a rust-bitten pickup truck idles alone, its driver nursing a bottomless cup of coffee inside a diner lit by flickering fluorescents. Places like this survive on habit, not hope.

Behind me, the service station squats like a corpse no one's buried. The name makes me wonder about my father and then about my son. Emptiness. A bottomless void.

But I'm still moving.

Kansas City by noon. San Diego by Friday.

MBA classes start in two weeks.

Sundra's contacts are waiting to meet me on arrival. So is the shell nonprofit, the abbey blueprint, and the infrastructure to launder belief and spirituality into capital.

But for now, it's wind, old roads, and the steady hum of a game I've learned well.

It's a longer drive taking the southern route—cutting south through Dallas before angling west toward the Pacific—but it's the first of April. Early spring snow storms in the center of the country are treacherous, unpredictable. I'd rather dodge blizzards than wrestle them.

Besides, I've always liked Dallas. It'll be good to see it again.

By the time I cross into west Texas, a storm out of the north has gathered. Clouds swell up like mountains made of ash, rising into a charcoal sky that swallows the stars. Fifty miles from the New Mexico border, the snow begins to fall—flakes big as fists, swirling in stiff gusts that slam the little Ford Bronco II sideways.

Traffic slows. Then crawls.

Ten miles from the border, the road vanishes under a foot of snow, maybe more. A single lane cuts through the white—ice-rutted trenches carved by a convoy of semis. We follow like cars on rails, no room to pass, no margin for error.

We creep like that for an hour and a half before the New Mexico State Police block the road, waving us off the highway and into a town barely large enough to have a name.

The hotels are jammed full. First place—full. Second—double-booked. At the third, a tired-eyed clerk with a rosary over his register tells me to try a place off the Tesuque reservation, five miles down a side road. He leans in like it's a secret. "No one thinks about going out there," he says. "They got rooms."

The storm hasn't let up. If anything, the wind is worse, and the temperature is falling. Snow comes in sideways now, hammering the windshield, icing over the wipers so badly I have to roll the window down, reach out, and snap the blade against the glass just to maintain vision.

A few miles out, the reservation inn appears like an apparition in the white—a low-slung building with a faded sign and maybe fifteen rooms. Not many cars in the lot.

Good.

I pull in and park. The shortcut worked. I beat the rest of the highway refugees.

Inside, the clerk speaks in halting English, polite but expressionless. Behind him, an electric space heater glows like a red hot coal in the congested corner. It looks more like a fire hazard than a source of warm comfort.

"No heat in room," he says. "But electric blankets. They come soon. One hour to be here."

I nod, pay cash, fill out the form, and take the key.

The room is basic. Two beds, a small table with mismatched chairs, a digital clock radio. I flip it on, turn the dial to the local weather station. Static, static, then the droning voice of a Christian preacher. No weather yet, but I'll leave it playing. Christian religious radio and tightly controlled right-wing propaganda It is the only media the conservatives allow in rural towns and small country cities. I want to know the second the highway reopens, so I let the radio play despite the propoganda.

Outside, the snowstorm is in full swing. Plow trucks are nowhere to be seen and drifts are three quarters up the sides of the few scattered buildings.

The glass frosts. As I sit on the edge of the bed, jacket still zipped, eyes on the window, the preacher drones on about fire and judgment and forgiveness. The wind whistles like it's trying to get in.

An hour later, a knock.

It's the same clerk, a stack of promised electric blankets in his arms.

I pull the top one from the pile. It's heavy, soft, but I see there's no electric cord.

I hold it up. "Where's the plug? The cord?"

He nods. "Electric blanket. Very warm."

I point to the connector slot on the side. "Right here—this needs the cord."

Again, he nods. "Yes. Electric blanket. Very warm."

He turns to go.

"Wait—how do I plug it in?"

He keeps walking. "Very warm."

His voice fades into the storm.

I close the door and stare at the blanket.

No plug. No heat. Just a promise. A thousand political metaphors.

Outside, the snow erases the world.

Inside, I sit in the cold, wrapped in something called "electric blanket." My memories flashback to El Jebel and those frozen days long ago in the Colorado mountains with Josie and me sitting under the blankets while we starve and freeze. The electric skillet with its cord in place was the only source of heat.

When the weather report finally announced Highway 40 was open, it was four-oh-seven in the morning. I was already half-awake, boots on, radio dialed to static-Jesus. Within minutes, I was off the reservation, teeth clenched, behind the wheel of the Bronco, windshield wipers squealing across melting snow.

Fourteen hours later, I round the last curve of I-8, where El Cajon spills west and San Diego opens like a secret kept too long. It doesn't hit me all at once—it pours in the light, the air, the strange comfort of knowing that winter has no dominion here. There are two seasons here. Cool and warm.

The sky is surgical blue, scraped clean by an onshore ocean breeze. The magenta-colored ice plants drape across canyon walls like spilled ink—alive, defiant, thriving on the edges of cliffs. That color doesn't exist in the rest of the country. It's California's alone.

I crank the window down and let the Pacific breeze in. It carries a sharp salty tang, but underneath there's eucalyptus, cut grass, and something floral that The Eagles made famous: colitas. The refuge of air that makes me forget other places exist. It doesn't judge you. Doesn't care where you've been. It just is. My heart sings. I have wanted to be back here for so long.

I cruise Mission Beach first. Volleyball courts, sand-packed muscle heads, girls in sunglasses too big for their faces and bikinis too small for their bodies. Laughter that sounds like a soundtrack.

Then up the coast—Pacific Beach, La Jolla, Del Mar. The ocean on my left, the ridgeline estates on my right. Cardiff, where the surfers ride glassy swells and the coffee shops fill with tanned freelancers and yoga instructors with sandalwood beads around their wrists. I drive with one hand on the wheel, the other dangling out the window. My body aches from the drive, but my nerves? They've gone numb. Like something inside me's recalibrating. A grin stuck to my face.

Same country—but it might as well be another planet. I won't need the chord or the electric blanket here.

Back east, people speak with caution. With history in their throats. Their clothes hide everything, even in summer—sleeves, collars, layers against a cold that's more than temperature.

But here? Conversations bounce. People walk like the sidewalk is optional. Their clothes are made of light. Tank tops and flip-flops and skin tanned into confidence. They smile without suspicion. It's not shallow—it's survival. You don't come here to suffer. You come here to forget you ever did.

Nowhere on Earth finer than Southern California. Not Rome, not Rio, not Kyoto. Here, the sun forgives everything.

I loop back down into the heart of the city, cutting toward Hillcrest. My meeting's at a restaurant just off University Avenue. Ken Kuang. That name carries more than it admits. If there's a play in the world of microprocessor trade routes, startup capital, or ghost-shell finance, Ken's probably wired into it. If he wants to meet, you don't reschedule.

Ken Kuang waits at the corner table, a spot perfectly chosen to survey the restaurant yet remain unnoticed. He's tall but carries himself with the unassuming grace of someone accustomed to moving in shadows—lean without being wiry, mid-forties but ageless in the way some men remain young by never fully revealing themselves. His hair is neatly cropped, threaded with early silver strands, his eyes, odd but sharp and alert, beneath thin, wire-frame glasses.

As I approach, he rises fluidly, extending a firm but unobtrusive handshake. His tailored charcoal suit is quietly impeccable—no labels visible, nothing ostentatious—yet everything about it suggests a careful awareness of appearances, status, and nuance.

"Mark," he whispers, his voice modulated and accent-less, impossible to place geographically, hinting at countless passports and borderless loyalties. "I trust the drive was eventful enough to clear your head, but not too eventful to cloud your thinking."

He smiles faintly, assessing my reaction with the precision of someone who measures risk as naturally as breathing.

His Tibetan greeting was familiar. It is the same as those monks in Boston and the Dzogchen Foundation, the refugee monks who fled the country after China invaded and slaughtered any who remained. They taught and spread Tibetan Buddhist wisdom to the West. It isn't a philosophy that holds on to the past. It evolves and forever continues in the present.

"The wealth of the world is the commodity of data," he says. "Everyone wants to expand their business with an online presence. Soon, everyone will do business online. They are a number and knowing how the number thinks and spends, is key. You call it a cookie. Sweet."

"I'm not sure I understand what you mean."

"Are you hungry?" he asks, undisturbed by my lack of understanding.

Chapter 8: The Veil of Good Intentions
Net worth $26,000

The first week feels like a well-earned vacation. Beaches. Shopping. Late nights at the hotel pool, flirting with women I'll never call and never forget. But the ocean breeze can't postpone real life forever. Today, I dig in.

Six months. That's the timeline I've given myself. Long enough to get my footing, short enough to pivot if I need to disappear. I've chosen the golden triangle—UTC, they call it. University Town Center. It's the welcoming of a place where the streets are newly paved, the trees are just tall enough to whisper about permanence, and everyone's pretending they're not leasing the illusion of wealth.

I find a bank with glass doors that hiss open like a spaceship. The interior smells like paper and polished plastic. I tell the receptionist I'd like to open an account. She smiles too wide and asks me to wait in the customer lobby. A promise that someone will be with me shortly.

Through the windows, I spot the restaurant next door. Italian Seafood. I laugh—quietly to myself. Why ship seafood from Italy when the Pacific Ocean is half-a-mile west of here? Must be a metaphor. Something about importing flavor even when it's already under your feet.

"Mark?" A clean-cut man in a blue tie calls my name. I follow him down a corridor lined with framed posters about retirement plans and community partnerships. His office is a minimalist box, efficient and eager to say nothing personal.

"I'm moving to San Diego," I explain, dropping into the chair. "Just arrived. I'll be renting short term while I scout neighborhoods to buy."

"Six months is the shortest lease you'll find in this county," he says. "Up in L.A. or Orange County, it's twelve minimum. But here you've got options."

He taps at his keyboard. I wait for the paperwork. Wait for the nod. Wait for the simple, adult act of opening a bank account to feel like something other than begging for permission to breathe.

Then he leans back, hands folded, like he's just delivered bad news to a patient.

"I'm sorry. I can't open an account for you unless you have a local address. California banking laws require proof of in-county residency."

No address. No account. No account, no checks. No checks. It's the catch-22 effect of the modern man's trap—nothing functions without something else to prop it up.

I leave Union Bank with a smile that didn't make it to my lips.

Ralphs is nearby. I need a grocery store, but I'm not here for groceries. Out front, by the shopping carts and the kids' coin operated ride-on firetruck, there's a metal rack stuffed with real estate brochures. That's why I'm here. I take a fistful, walk inside, and camp out at the juice bar like it's my temporary war room.

A dozen glossy pamphlets later, I find it. A two-bedroom unit overlooking Rose Canyon. View from the balcony. Five tennis courts. Three pools. Adults only. Billiards room. Gym. The sort of home that smells like suntan lotion and cactus blooms.

The property manager walks me through it like she's showing me her childhood home. She smiles, says I look like I'd be a good tenant. I fill out the application. I write the check—for first, last, and deposit—using my Michigan bank account from the First of Dearborn Credit Union.

She glances at it.

"This check's from out of state?"

"Yes. Ferndale, Michigan. It's my last address. I'm just moving here this week. The bank account's next."

She purses her lips, that subtle shift where friendliness becomes protocol.

"We don't accept out-of-state checks."

I blink. "Okay. Traveler's check? I've got those."

"Nope."

"Cash?"

"We don't take that either."

I stare at her, trying to understand what century we're in.

"It has to be from a local bank," she says flatly. "It's policy and it's California law."

Of course it is. The system isn't built to be welcoming. It's built to delay and dissuade. A revolving door of reasons. Can't rent without a bank. Can't bank without a lease. Can't win unless you're already holding the trophy.

I take the check back, fold it once, then again. It vanishes into my wallet like it never happened.

Outside, the sky is too blue for how angry I feel. Standing in the too-clean shopping plaza, watching the flawless Californian facade—palm trees and faux-stucco elegance. A bitterness blooms in my chest, sharp and familiar. How had I believed, even for a moment, that the rules would accommodate someone like me?

I recall Papa Bertrand's cramped Michigan retirement home, a place where permission was always someone else's to give. He'd spent half his life sidestepping bureaucracy, slipping between cracks. But this time, it feels different. This time, it's not just about escaping.

"What if I build the door instead of knocking on theirs?" I murmur, startling myself with the boldness of the thought. The audacity of bypassing a system designed to exclude me sends a chill through my veins—one I've learned feels more like exhilaration than fear.

Suddenly, the brochures in my hand feel heavier—each glossy photo a blueprint, each neatly typed amenity a promise of legitimacy. If I can't gain entry by their rules, I'll rewrite the rulebook altogether.

Back at the hotel, I slip into something familiar. Not a bathrobe. Not the bar. A glowing computer screen.

The guest computer hums quietly in the lobby's corner, tucked near the potted plants like it's trying to blend in. I log on—dial-up slow—and navigate straight to the new habit I haven't quite admitted to myself yet: AdultFriendFinder.com. The adults-only chatroom loads, pixel by pixel, usernames scrolling like confessions in real time.

She's already there. Sacramento, she says. Or claims. It's not like I've seen a driver's license. But we've been talking. Bantering. Flirting in a way that's just vague enough to be safe and just sharp enough to be dangerous. Sometimes, we type for hours. Sometimes ten minutes is enough to leave the static of the real world behind.

Tonight, she asks about my day.

I tell her: the bank, the apartment, the check refused on account of nothing more than zip code origin. She types back instantly—Yeah, San Diego's brutal. L.A. too. People have run every scam in the book down there. Nobody trusts anyone anymore.

She tells me she has an account at a bank in L.A. It might work for San Diego. Worth trying. Then she pivots:

I have Friday off. Easter weekend. Three-day stretch. You ever been to Sacramento?

Not in a long time, I type.

Wanna meet?

The cursor blinks. I stare at it like it's ticking.

We go back and forth a few more lines. Easy. Almost too easy.

We pick a hotel in downtown Sacramento. Neutral ground. Mid-price chain. Classy enough not to feel seedy, generic enough not to feel like a commitment. Meet you there at three on Friday, I post.

Can't wait, she types back.

I sit there for a moment, screen reflecting off my sunglasses. A travel site is open on another tab. I call them and book the flight before I could second guess it.

And then I just ... sit.

This isn't how my life works. I don't do meet-cutes. I don't chase strangers across state lines. And I sure as hell wouldn't spend three nights in a hotel with someone whose name I only know from a keyboard. This is worse than a plot in a romance novel.

But here I am. Making arrangements. Packing my doubts in a carry-on.

Maybe it's loneliness.

Maybe it's desperation.

Or maybe it's just curiosity. And I've always been terrible at letting a question go unanswered.

Friday April 12, at two forty, I check in at the hotel. Outside, a dry desert wind blows steadily, gusting through Sacramento with a restless edge. In the capital city of California the air is warm, carrying the faint scent of heated asphalt, citrus blossoms, and distant fields. Palm fronds rustle softly beneath an unusually clear sky tinged amber from drifting dust, evoking a subtle but persistent sense of impermanence.

Inside the hotel on the fourteenth floor, I crack the door open, small roller bag trailing behind me like a reluctant sidekick. The room smells like citrus air freshener and hotel linen—a clean, artificial kind of welcome.

Fleetwood Mac is blaring from the clock radio, "Silver Springs"—the '94 version, heavy with that raw, unresolved blues-ache. It spills through the air like the ghost of an argument neither side ever won.

She's dancing.

Barefoot. Jeans low on the hips. Tank top twisted slightly at the hem as she spins.

The Jennifer Aniston resemblance is uncanny—the face, the haircut, the posture, even the way her laugh hitches up when she tosses her head back. Except she's got narrower shoulders, a smaller chest, hips that don't ask for permission. The type of body that's lived through some stories and hasn't apologized for any of them. On the top of her suitcase is a hotel receipt. I see her name. Ana Lorena.

She doesn't stop dancing when she sees me.

She just turns that smile on—full wattage, corner of the mouth to the edge of her pupils. It hit me like déjà vu and wishful thinking collided.

And then she's moving toward me. Still dancing, still smiling. The distance between us dissolves in five steps and one shared breath. We kiss like we've done this before—maybe not in this lifetime, but somewhere, definitely somewhere.

Hands find hips. Fingers tug at fabric. The bed loses its covers in the crossfire. Her laugh rises over Stevie Nicks' voice as the song hits that line—where she screams the haunting crescendo, "You'll never get away from the sound of the woman that loves you ..."

For a second, I let myself forget the internet. Forget the usernames and the city names that may or may not be true. The intuition of her being a woman desperate for rescue.

This isn't about trust.

It's about collisions.

And in that moment, I stop being Mark, the strategist, the ghost, the offshore banker.

I'm just a man in a hotel room with a woman who can dance the weight of the world away.

Four days later, I'm leaning on the black iron railing of my apartment terrace, sipping from a glass of watered-down cranberry juice, watching the late afternoon light spill like honey over Rose Canyon. Even the birds look relaxed here. Teresa's email came in an hour ago.

"The house is sold. I'll be there in four weeks with the van. Don't forget to book the elevator at the complex."

I type back quickly: "The apartment's ours. Phone line gets installed in two days. Internet too. Dial-up, but it'll do."

Hit send.

Now I wait. Watch. Think.

San Diego doesn't do urgency. It leans back. It stretches. Even time moves slower out here, like it's waiting for something better to show up.

Ken picks me up around five. A beige Mercedes that doesn't need to say a thing. It glides past the polished fronts of Hillcrest's boutique cafés and into the part of the neighborhood nobody shows in real estate brochures.

The shadows here come earlier.

Garbage bags split at the sides and spilling like bloated corpses.

Tagging across stucco walls, not the expressive kind—this is just gang code, a territorial pissing contest in neon spray.

A man in a long wool coat—July heat be damned—paces in front of the liquor store, muttering at the air and punching invisible ghosts.

"Up here," Ken says, and we climb concrete steps.

The property sits behind a rusted fence with a gate that swings half off its hinges. An acre lot, mostly dead ground, brittle palm stumps, and scorched desert trees that haven't seen a hose in a decade. But in the back, behind a toppled chicken wire fence, two avocado trees thrive like survivors of a forgotten war—full, lush, their branches heavy with fruit.

The house is ... was ... a mansion. Four stories of turn-of-the-century ambition. Victorian bones and Spanish tile. It leans slightly to the left, like it remembers something it's trying to forget.

Inside, the air is stale—old wood rot, cat piss, and ghosted cologne. Plaster peels like dead skin. Floorboards groan with every step, not in protest but in exhaustion. The banister up the main stair-case is intact, carved mahogany, perhaps worth more than the com-plete structure now.

"Views of Balboa Park from the third and fourth floors," Ken says, pushing open a cracked door. "And east, you get the mountains. On a clear day, you can see straight to Anza-Borrego."

The electric panels in the basement are a not too subtle suicide note. In the dark corner of the basement the furnace looks like it lost a fight with time and ambition and long ago crawled off to death.

Next door, a free health clinic fills the air with wailing. Am-bulance sirens. Babies. Toddlers. Stressed-out mothers shouting in Spanish, Creole, and English without nouns. A boy with no shoes runs past, chasing a deflated soccer ball.

"This is where you want to put a spiritual retreat?" I ask.

Ken smiles, thin and sly. "What better place to prove you can turn suffering into sanctuary?"

I look up at the sagging eaves. At the busted window, an old prayer flag still fluttering from the frame. The metaphor isn't lost on me.

"It's a teardown," I say.

Ken shakes his head. "It's a resurrection."

And behind that? All I see are donors with deep pockets and a savior complex. The elite class of people who write checks because they think suffering's more noble when it's viewed from a safe dis-tance.

I can work with that.

"Sounds perfect to me," I say, brushing the dust off my palms. "Listen, Ken. I won't need Lama Sundra's foundation to buy this."

Ken raises a brow but says nothing.

"Listen, I've learned my lessons about partnerships and I'm set-ting up my own nonprofit here in San Diego. Should be legit in two days. Filing's already with the state. Now, before you get defensive,

I'm open to affiliations and working in concert with the Dzogchen Foundation, but that's as far as I will extend the relationship."

He cocks his head. "And the money?"

"From a corporation in Curaçao," I say, snapping the lockbox back onto the busted doorknob like I'm sealing a tomb. "They'll wire the funds. Just get me a quick closing and I'll have a contractor on-site by next week. We'll start the resurrection."

Ken nods, slowly. He knows better than to ask for details. He just wants it done clean. You know; untraceable.

"You're meeting the most expensive—and most influential—psychiatrist in Southern California in two nights," he says, checking something in his day planner. "He and his wife will be expecting you at Mister A's. Seven sharp."

"Mister A's." I whistle low. "You don't bring your second-tier clients there."

"No," he says. "You bring the ones who might own half the building one day. This shrink has a desire to get his name on everything in the city."

I watch him slide into his car, that quiet purr of imported German confidence. Then I turn back to the property. The house stares at me like it remembers being loved. Like it's daring me to try. In my mind I can hear Robert Cray singing "Great Big Ole House."

Two avocado trees. A clinic full of crying babies. Dead palms that could be firewood or sculpture, depending on the story you tell. The things that seem like a sketch in a Hollywood drama haunt me for two days that lead to the dinner.

The tablecloth is white linen. The stemware sings when touched. Mister A's sits high above downtown, the city lit up like an offering to the night. Dr. Peter leans back in his chair, fork resting idle against his plate, listening. His wife, Treena, watches me over the rim of her wineglass, the tilt of her head sharp with interest.

"We won't call it a temple," I say. "We'll call it an abbey. Because this isn't about worship—it's about presence. Practice. Silence. The kind that speaks louder than sermons."

Peter nods. "You mentioned monks."

"From everywhere," I say. "Bhutan. Northern India. Vietnam. Even South Africa. Not the insulated, unreachable kind. These monks are travelers. Storytellers. Builders. They'll come through San Diego on their way to other cities, other countries. This place becomes a waypoint. A sanctuary with an address."

Treena leans in. "And the house?"

"Already in motion," I say. "Four floors, view of Balboa Park. Needs work, but the bones are perfect. We'll restore it, yes—but not to what it was. We'll make it better. A kitchen that feeds, rooms that heal, a zendo that opens to the garden. Retreat weekends. Silent days. Evening talks open to the public. We'll hold space in the neighborhood, not above it."

Peter raises an eyebrow. "And the funding?"

"Donors are looking for stories that matter. People want to put their name on a future that outlives them. The mansion will carry those names in the stones. But more than that, my connections—Lama Sundra Jhinpa, Thầy Nhất—they bring attention. They bring credibility. One mention from them and every mindfulness and yoga magazine, every wellness newsletter, every slow-living talk show will run with it. This isn't just an abbey—it's a cultural event."

Treena's eyes light up. "It'll be everywhere." Her Michigan accent reminds me of Teresa and Papa Bertrand. I hold her eyes in mine a moment too long. Then quickly catch Pete's suspicious gaze.

I nod. "Exactly."

There's a pause. Not for lack of things to say, but because we all feel the shape of something rising. Possibility has a sound—it's the silence after a pitch that lands.

The check arrives. Peter insists. Treena smiles.

As we step out into the velvet air, I turn to them both.

"Thank you," I say. "For the dinner. For the conversation. For listening."

Peter offers his hand. Treena kisses my cheek and whispers in my ear, "I'll see you at the abbey around ten in the morning."

~~~

In 1995, my full-time job is running the not-for-profit corporation. Which means the rules for moving money are different—but no less dangerous. In theory, I'm a steward of goodwill. A servant to the mission. Every dollar is accounted for, and every expense is tied to "program service" or "public benefit." But behind the IRS definitions and legalese lies the truth: the nonprofit world is just another map for those who know how to draw invisible lines.

My lines run offshore.

The donations come in—small at first. Retired couples writing checks from La Jolla. A trust out of Seattle. Buddhist enthusiasts from Santa Fe who've never sat a single zazen but like the idea of enlightenment with tax deductions. But the difference between those nickels and the gold bars comes from entertaining the wealthy.

I route the contributions to a numbered account in the Caymans. From there, the game begins.

Money moves like weather—if you know how to read it, you know how to ride it. From the Caymans, the funds transfer to a Panamanian shell that pays the building contractor—specialized outfit from the Virgin Islands with zero online footprints. They rebuild the mansion room by room, but no invoice ever hits a California file.

In between? I trade. High-volume, short-window. E-Trade's platform is new and full of bugs and latency, but no one is watching closely. Not yet. And I've built an algorithm—just crude enough to fly under the radar, just sharp enough to scalp percentages on the
~~~

hour. Blue chips. Biotech. Early internet plays no one's heard of. It's not about the company. It's about the signal.

I watch the numbers roll in from a back room off the kitchen at the Hillcrest property. The old walls still bleed mildew and cigarette smoke from god knows when, but my workstation is spotless. Three monitors. Two modems. The hum of the surge protector is my meditation bell. When the trades hit, I can feel it in my chest.

Every gain is laundered through the shell companies. Every expense justified with language so clean you could scrub a confession booth with it.

The key is momentum.

Expedite the permit process. Keep the board minutes signed. Keep the press releases glowing with gratitude and peace and pictures of monks planting succulents on the scorched front lawn.

Keep everyone looking that way while I work behind the curtain.

Because this isn't fraud.

This is leverage.

This is precision.

And this is how you turn spiritual capital into actual capital—without ever touching a single coin.

The ad catches my eye in the back of Forbes Magazine—three glossy pages deep in an article about post-regulation market volatility. Full spread, all caps, gold trim.

WHAT'S THE MONEY SHOW?

Only the largest gathering of self-made millionaires, contrarian thinkers, and renegade economists under one roof.

VEGAS. SEVEN DAYS.

NO BULL—JUST MONEY.

I tear the page out and fold it into my notepad.

No sermons. No robes. Donors won't be asking about retreat schedules or gluten-free options. Just capital. Strategies. Algorithms and breakout sessions on offshore trusts. Keynotes from men who own skyscrapers and don't apologize for it.

I book a suite at the MGM Grand—corner room, mountain view, private concierge. The Money Show runs Sunday to Saturday, but I fly in early. I plan to get the lay of the land. Scout the booths. Shake hands, talk shop, and disappear before they know who I really am.

I light a cigarette on the back patio of the Hillcrest house—where the avocado trees hang heavy with green fruit—and dial her from the kitchen phone.

She answers on the third ring, her voice like the last drag of something expensive.

"Hola, cariño."

"I'll meet you at the Vegas airport," I say. "We're in a suite at the MGM. Corner room should be delicious."

"Ocean view?"

"Desert view. But the money's better."

She laughs—low and real.

"I'll wear something gold," she says.

"I'd expect nothing less."

A week later, I'm standing in the high roller room at the MGM in Vegas. Ana Lorena's flight lands Friday afternoon. Teresa stays in San Diego, house hunting. Ana Lorena descends the escalator like she owns the building, and maybe for the next three days, she does. Gold from head to toe—lamé dress, rhinestone heels, glitter smeared across her collarbones like war paint. Even her eyelids shimmer when she blinks.

She spins once, slow and deliberate, like a ballerina drunk on applause—then lurches forward, arms out, pretending to stumble. She lands against me with the soft crash of perfume and static and heat.

That's when I see it.

The left side of her face is bruised, swollen—a bold lump blooming under a thick coat of makeup that's melting in the Vegas heat. Her left eye's gone slightly purple at the edge, not enough to scream, but enough to whisper.

"What the hell is this?" I ask, jaw already tightening.

She pulls back just enough to keep it playful. "My husband threw my computer at me."

That hangs in the air like a joke only she laughed at.

"I guess he finally figured out that I wasn't just typing," she says, deadpan.

I stare at her. The bruising. The glitter. The gold wrapping paper hiding the crack in the package. There's a thousand things I could say, but none of them belong in the one-armed-bandit pit of the MGM.

So I take her bag, sling it over my shoulder, and say the only thing that makes sense:

"Let's get. Ain't it high time we went?"

The MGM Grand corner suite wraps around us like a velvet lie. Floor-to-ceiling windows soak in the Strip's neon pulse from two angles—glittering towers, endless signage, the desert stars drowned out by the man-made glow. Inside, everything's lacquered in indulgence: a sunken living room with pearl suede couches, black marble counters, a minibar stocked with top-shelf regrets. The bed is enormous, unmade from our making up for time apart. We're not touching it now. Our sex is dirty and a struggle for dominance until her surrender. She plays and pretends and then the action makes the devil blush.

Ana paces, barefoot. Gold glitter trails behind her like she's molting.

"You have to move out of that house," I say. "Come stay with me." The words were out before I could stop myself.

She stops, not turning. Just enough hesitation to let me hear it before she says it. "San Diego is a beautiful place," she says, with that

Jennifer Aniston dryness, as if 'beautiful' is a diagnosis she's not sure she believes in. "But what do we do with Teresa?"

"Teresa and I welcome you to a safe and comfortable home," I say, brushing the back of my hand against the hot bloom on her cheek. "Don't worry about Teresa, sweetheart."

She lifts her eyes. "You won't want me in your lives. I'll be a fly in the ointment."

"You're not a poison, Ana Lorena."

She laughs once through her nose, eyes dropping again. "If you only knew."

"Then tell me," I say. "Explain this. What do you want to say to me?"

She walks fast toward the window. Her reflection glows against the glass—Vegas spilling behind her, lights twitching like a dying star. "It's a fucking ugly story," she says, voice cracking as she opens the sliding door and steps onto the terrace.

I follow.

The air hits me like a slap—dry, thin, desert-sharp. It carries the hum of the Strip: distant bass lines, the whoop of someone winning or pretending to, the dull throb of traffic a dozen stories below. The night sky's clear, all emptiness and electricity.

Ana Lorena leans against the railing, arms folded, face shadowed. Then she starts.

"Four kids. Couldn't get a job. No time. So after the youngest started school, I opened a daycare in my home. It was fine. Full certification, state license, CPR, all of it. Then..."

Her voice trails. She doesn't look at me.

"One day, fifteen-month-old boy swallows a quarter. You can't imagine the sound. That gurgling, breathless gasp. He's turning blue. I'm full panic, but also ... like I'm watching it from outside myself. This can't be. I want to run and never stop until even the memory is gone. Instead, I do everything—everything they teach you. Finger sweep. Back thrusts. I shake him—not violently, just trying to jar it loose. Flip him upside down. Pat his back. What seemed a lifetime later, I got the coin out and several minutes before EMTs arrive."

The story staggers me, and my hand clenches the railing. "Jesus fuck, lady."

She keeps going, stepping further into the night. "But the kid's not breathing. They get him going again, but something's off. MRI says brain damage. He'll live. He just won't be... normal."

I see her eyes now, glassy but dry. All cried out.

"The parents sue. Not malpractice. Not negligence. Shaken baby syndrome. Criminal charges. Prosecutors climb inside your life with dirty boots. Every parenting book on the shelf, every bottle of wine in the fridge, becomes evidence. I got six months. Then they hit me with the civil suit. That's still dragging on, two years later. No insurance payout. No settlement. I'm radioactive."

She pulls her hair back, fingers trembling now.

"My kids ... they get called monsters at school. 'Baby killers.' Strangers whisper when I walk into Walgreens. I try to wear sunglasses. Still doesn't matter. Husband wants me to disappear. Die"

She finally looks at me.

"So yeah," she says. "That's why I glitter up like a fucking Times Square whore. Because no one expects the villain to be wearing gold."

The Strip lights flicker below, pulsing like blood beneath the skin of the city.

I don't say anything yet.

Because some truths sit too long in the chest before you know what to do with them.

The week moves like a hangover without the party—low energy, heavy limbs, a strange sense of floating. But the speakers, the conversations, the raw buzz of ambition at the Money Show in Vegas stirs something back to life. I'm making contacts again. The authentic kind. The kind with second homes in the Hamptons and trust lawyers on speed dial.

Ana Lorena and I draw up a plan. It's not all spreadsheets and logistics—it's emotion. She's done with Sacramento. I'm done pretending I'm not in this with her. Meanwhile, life's events often go past faster than a bullet train from Barcelona to Vealencia. Teresa and I buy a house in North San Diego, tucked high up in Escondido. Good bones, plenty of light. Ana Lorena moves in.

We survive. Mostly. We even thrive. Until Teresa's tortured-shadow shows up again.

I've lived through this with her before. Twice. That slow bleed of joy from her face, the flat answers, the fire gone from her pranks. Then the fights. The passive-aggressive wars over nothing. The tears over breakfast, or no breakfast at all.

But I love her.

So I hold.

The upswing always comes—eventually. Meanwhile, I put them both to work. They get along like old friends.

The abbey's first three-day retreat is on the calendar. Sundra's sending a team down. I've got half a dozen money-show whales attending, dressed in robes instead of blazers. That much wealth in one sacred room will either rupture the space or redeem it. Maybe both.

The prep helps. Something about the shared chaos gets Teresa and Ana Lorena on the same page. I hear them laughing in the kitchen late one night. I stay out of sight, listening, arms crossed, leaning against the cool wall like some eavesdropping monk.

"When he says he loves you," Teresa says, her voice cool, like jazz under city rain, "he's not bullshitting. He means it. All the way down to his core."

"Yeah," Ana says, soft. "I know."

"No. You don't." Teresa's voice tightens—not cruel, just exact. Like clicking the safety off.

"You know that visit I got from hell's sewer?"

Ana Lorena doesn't answer. The fridge hums. A pan sizzles faintly behind them.

"Three feet of pure human horror in my basement. Rancid piss, decades of shit, and a million tampons gone rogue. Every box of memories? Gone. Every keepsake, every dusty maybe-I'll-need-it? Gone. I locked that door like sealing a tomb. Seven months."

A pause.

"Then I take a trip to Greece. Golden beaches and sand for a few weeks. Come back ... and that man? That man had shoveled it out. Every ounce. Bagged it, scraped it, bleached it, painted the walls. Installed lighting. Made it shine."

Another beat.

"And when I asked him why? You know what he said?"

Ana doesn't respond. I imagine her eyes wide, her hands maybe still now.

"He said, 'You shouldn't come home to rot.'"

Teresa laughs. Not big. Just ... real.

"And then he moved in. That was the real gift in my mind and heart. Not the basement. Him."

They fall quiet. A spoon clinks against ceramic. One of them exhales like they'd been holding something for years.

I step back into the hall and up the stairs before they see me. I don't need to hear more. That story's enough. More than enough.

The sun moves slow over the canyon, casting long shadows over the scrub trees and dry grass beyond the cracked retaining wall. But inside the back courtyard, the world has been reshaped. Teresa's eye for design, Ana Lorena's hand with layout. My money—clean and unclean—have turned the crumbling garden into something sharp, striking, and sophisticated.

Gravel paths of polished stones curve between patches of drought-tolerant plants. Meditation cushions form circles on the deck, arranged with precision but never rigidity. A reclaimed wood altar rises from the ground like it belongs there, built from broken fence panels and sanded smooth. Wind chimes sing in languages older than speech.

Thirty people have paid to be here. A few are yoga millionaires, some are professors, one is a former hedge fund manager who now runs a spiritual VC firm out of Sausalito. They look around like they've just arrived at a new version of reality. Because they have.

Inside, the kitchen is half finished—tile ripped up, wires hanging like snakes from the exposed beams. But we've made it work. Nine chairs pressed around a scarred table, a slow cooker gurgling lentils, Ana Lorena plating fruit and passing out thick bread from a local bakery. It's uncomfortable. But it's honest. You can feel it coming together—like bones mending after a break.

But the main event isn't food. It isn't even meditation. It's science.

Dr. Sandhya Ramaswamy from UC Berkeley stands in the shaded corner of the courtyard, framed by salvaged eucalyptus and the drifting perfume of burning sage. She's not in robes. She's not chanting. She's in a vibrant green blazer, white blouse, hair pinned into an elegant knot, and the look of someone who has nothing to prove.

Her voice is smooth. Unhurried.

"Mind. Body. Universe. We've separated them for centuries. But biology doesn't know that division. Your DNA doesn't distinguish between thoughts and chemicals. Between grief and pollution."

She taps a remote and an overhead projector lights the screen as it hums to life behind her. Molecular diagrams. Chromatin loops. Histones unraveling like spools of memory.

"Berkeley and UCSF have been working with chromatin remodeling, histone modification, methylation patterns that shift based on trauma, joy, even silence. And these changes don't just end with you.

They pass down—generations. Epigenetic inheritance. Experience encoded."

Silence falls. Some people close their eyes—not out of boredom, but awe.

"What we call karma," she says, "may just be methylation. What we call liberation—may be the unlocking of a gene suppressed since your grandmother's heartbreak."

She let it sit.

"In our labs, we see spiritual practice—real, sustained introspection—change the epigenetic landscape. It's not belief. It's biology."

I glance at Sundra across the circle. He remains without a nod. His smile is absent. He just breathes, slow and deep, like someone watching an old truth finally find new language.

I scan the crowd. One of the investors—Don Larrabee, from the Money Show, sits upright, lips parted like someone's handed him a new map. Not because it's spiritual. But because he sees the infrastructure beneath it.

That's the hook.

Not the incense. Not the chants. But the data.

The hard, university-backed science that says this isn't all in your head.

It's in your blood.

The last light of day smolders over Balboa Park, turning the canyons and rooftops the color of burnt sugar. From the backyard of the abbey, I watch the sun disappear like it's trying to avoid the burden of expectation.

The bell rings—our borrowed brass bell, tied to a salvaged wooden post. One of the retreat guests, barefoot and smiling, gives it a gentle tug to signal the end of day one.

Teresa gathers the last mugs from the folding tables, moving like someone who wants to be useful but not seen. Ana Lorena's inside, wiping down the counter with a focus that borders on meditative. It smells like bergamot and simmering rice.

The retreat went better than I dared hope. The talk from the UCSF professor on epigenetics left everyone reeling—inspired, intrigued, unsettled. He made it sound like genetic legacy was something you could rewrite with breath, with thought, with conscious living.

It was science, yes. But also myth, reframed.

I slip toward the edge of the yard, where the avocado trees lean into the lot next door. That's when I hear the voice behind me.

"You're on to something."

Don Larrabee. Former Wall Street golden boy, now a seeker in Birkenstocks. He's been quiet all weekend—watching, assessing.

He lights a cigarette. Filterless. He offers me one, but I wave it off.

"You've got lightning in a jar, Mark," he says. "This mix—Buddhism, hard science, transformation—it's new. Or at least it feels new. People are hungry for something different. And this ... is different."

He takes a long drag, eyes on the darkening sky.

"But if you want people to show up—donors, attention—you've got to put it on the map. You need media."

I nod slowly. "That's the plan."

"Start local," he says. "KPBS, maybe The Union-Tribune. Human interest. Science meets spirit. If you get a column or a Sunday feature, someone at The LA Times might pick it up. And from there..."

"National coverage," I say, finishing his thought.

"Exactly." He flicks ash into the wind. "Consider Time Magazine. Think 60 Minutes. Think Charlie Rose—if you can sell the angle right. Not fringe. Not new age. Serious. Academic. Forward-thinking."

He turns to me, more intense now.

"You pull it off, and this little run-down, converted mansion becomes the face of modern Western Buddhism. You don't just host retreats—you build a movement."

I say nothing. Because I know he's right.

Inside, the lights are dim. The retreatants have gone to bed. The kitchen's gone quiet. Teresa gives me a half-wave. Ana Lorena's already up the stairs. The house breathes.

But I don't.

Because the idea is massive. Terrifying. Brilliant.

And all I can think is—

How do I get The Union-Tribune to notice us?

How do I sell this as science, not scandal?

How do I make a candlelit backyard in a sketchy neighborhood worth national airtime?

The bell rings again. Final lights-out.

Chapter 9: Foundations on Sand
Net worth $470,000

The scent of iodine and motor oil battles the salt air inside the narrow, neon-lit shop, somewhere between a body mod temple and a surgical theater. The walls drip with posters—inked gods, suspended rebels, and flaming skulls. A camera crew from Channel 9 Los Angeles is setting up their last shot. Boom mic overhead, the lights searing white.

"I just want to get this straight," the reporter says, her voice sharp, eyebrow arched as if she's talking to a cult leader and not a businessman. "You're saying that tomorrow morning, this man will be hanging by fishhooks the size of encyclopedias over Sunset Boulevard, flown by helicopter in a cross-promotional stunt between your Zen retreat and a tattoo parlor?"

"Implant studio," I say, correcting her with a nod toward the owner, who's stripped to the waist, gauze taped in precise squares across his shoulders, lower back, and thighs.

She turns to him, letting the silence bait him. He doesn't flinch. His name is Vico. He's built like a rock climber—wiry, all tendons and rope-veins—and calm as a monk on morphine.

"Are you nervous?" she asks, the camera rolling.

He smiles. "Not when I drop in."

"Drop in?" she repeats, confused.

"Drop into the breath. Drop into silence. The hooks don't hold pain. You do. I let the pain go."

I step beside him, folding my arms, eyes catching the boom mic hovering just inches overhead. "We're not selling pain," I say, stepping in beside Vico. "We're showing how mindfulness transforms suffering. This is ritual, not spectacle. Vico's a practitioner. A student of breath. The abbey teaches presence, detachment, and awakening.

This,"—I gesture to the gleaming steel hooks lined on the table—"is how we translate that into something people remember. Suspended between earth and sky. It's a symbol."

She narrows her eyes. "So this is a Buddhist abbey publicity stunt?"

"This is a demonstration," I reply, "of what it means to release control. And maybe, just maybe, shake the world awake. We're selling transcendence. This is a ritual. This is focus. People pay six thousand dollars for a silent retreat. This,—" I point to the rigging on the table, glinting steel the size of murder weapons—"this is just the physical form of letting go."

"But a helicopter?" she presses. "You don't think that's a little ... extreme?"

I smirk. "So was walking on fire. So was climbing Everest. Extreme is just a synonym for unforgettable."

Her cameraman pans to the table where two riggers are threading stainless steel lines through sterilized pulleys. One of the tattoo shop apprentices snaps a photo on a clunky 35mm. This footage, this moment, is about to go everywhere.

"Can we film the hookup?" she asks, voice low, conspiratorial now. She's chasing the story under her professional skin. "And the airlift? I want to get an inflight crew and ground crew at the sign."

I nod. "We'll make room for your van and get your guy a harness."

The camera blinks red again as she turns back to face it. "Tomorrow, live from Los Angeles, a man will fly over Hollywood suspended from fishhooks. The question is—what does it mean to elevate pain into purpose? We'll be there. Channel 9. Don't miss it."

The cameraman calls, "cut."

Vico looks at me, unreadable. "You think they'll get it?"

"They don't have to get it," I say, clapping him on the back. "They just have to film it."

Pacific Beach hums with a kind of faded electricity—sun-scorched sidewalks, storefronts painted in peeling neons, graffiti that's less protest than patina. Murals of sea gods and mermaids blend into tag art and anarchist slogans. It's a tableau of contradiction: beauty and burnout, rebellion repackaged as retail.

Out here, nothing's sharp. Even the ocean seems to shimmer in soft focus. Boards lean against stucco walls, waxed and ready, but nobody's rushing. Not in PB. The surfers float out past the break, more meditation than motion. Sand sticks to bare feet, to joints tucked behind ears, to the thin layer of sweat that clings to everybody in sight.

The camera crew winds its way past the line of shops like tourists in a dream. With its blacked-out windows and cheeky red signage, the BDSM store stands out. The New Age boutique, all salt lamps and chakra charts, windows strung with faded prayer flags and crystal prisms that throw rainbows on the pavement. Then the head shops—at least three of them in a single block—bubblers and bongs gleaming like art behind dusty glass, the scent of incense bleeding into the air like a lazy anthem.

It's all color and cool and practiced nonchalance. The beach culture here doesn't shout; it shrugs. Everyone's high on something—weed, sun, their own indifference. Tank tops with ironic slogans. Tattoos half-finished or decades old. Blonde dreadlocks, silver septum rings, sandals with spiritual ambition.

And yet—there's tension under it all today. A spark. A scent of gasoline behind the coconut sunscreen. The camera crew knows it. The vendors know it. Something about hoisting a man into the sky by shark hooks has shifted the vibe from blasé to buzzed.

"I'll see you on the Sunset Strip in Hollywood tomorrow," I say to Vico as he zips the bags closed.

"That's a fact. I only wish we had time to lecture everyone about this jerry-mandering shit the Republicans are pulling in Georgia.

Democrats, as usual, if you can't beat them, join them, do the same in Michigan."

"Political slant won't get us on the prime-time news, brother."

He takes two steps towards me as he points a finger in my face. "Roosevelt didn't flinch. He knew democracy couldn't survive if private wealth ever grew more powerful than public will. So he built the firewall—regulations, labor protections, antitrust. Guardrails, not shackles. Guardrails meant to keep the wolves out of the people's house.

"Reagan was the first to take a sledgehammer to it. He did it with a grin, called it morning in America. Said government was the problem, not corporate greed. He handed Wall Street the keys and told working people to be grateful for the trickle. That was the beginning—when deregulation stopped being a debate and became a religion.

"But Clinton? Clinton is putting it in overdrive. He's dressing it up in bipartisan silk, but make no mistake—he's going to gut Glass-Steagall and sign off on telecom consolidation, let banks fuse into leviathans. He isn't just bending over for the rich—he is going to give them new tools. Legal ones. Sleek ones. Ones that come with lobbyists and champagne."

My head bobbed in agreement. When he drops his hands to his side and takes a breath, I jump on the soapbox. "That's last decades old news. Let's face it we are all sick of hearing it repeated. It's all over except for the Russian flags flying over the city hall in every town across America. But you want to know what could've stopped all of it—all of it—before the first brick came loose?

"Cable television.

"Yeah. That's the part no one wants to admit. Not the lobbyists. Not the professors. Not the talking heads. If the government had stepped in and made cable television free, if they'd broken the broadcasters' spine early—none of this would've happened.

"Think about it. We should have forced the media companies to pay the public to watch. Not just beam propaganda into every living room, but actually compensate Americans for their time, their data, their attention. The government could've mandated that. Instead, we let corporations charge us to be programmed. Networks are paid twice for the same ads; once by the advertisers and once by us.

"Hollywood? The networks? The ad barons? They should've handed out the best televisions, the biggest screens, to anyone who wanted one. No means testing. No subscription fees. And every time they sold an ad slot—every time a politician's face grinned across the screen—the people should've gotten a cut.

"That would've kept the millionaires nervous. That would've made the public dangerous again.

"Instead, we fed the machine. We paid for the privilege of being hypnotized. And while we laughed at sitcoms and sobbed at dramas, the real show—the one with blood and contracts—played out behind the glass.

"They didn't just steal democracy. They syndicated it."

The drive home was calming. Despite the intensity of tomorrow's events and the conversation with Vico, I'm relaxed. It's rare to be going home so early. I usually stay at the abbey until long after sunset. Seeing the San Diego suburbs in the day light reminds me of the beauty of this place.

The smell of salmon on the grill and fresh vegetables greet me as I come through the door. Teresa is busy cooking. Ana Lorena is setting the table outside under the pergola. Each of them seems to be in a good mood and greets me with kisses and hugs.

"Are you ready for tomorrow?" Teresa asks.

I slide my arms around her waist and kiss her cheek. She smells like garlic, olive oil, and something faintly floral beneath the heat. Her smile is easy, but her eyes—always the truth tellers—flicker with concern. She knows the edge I'm walking.

"As ready as anyone can be when a man's about to be dangled over Hollywood by shark hooks," I say.

Ana Lorena laughs from the patio. "You say it like it's a sacrament."

"It is a sacrament," I say. "Theater, truth, guts, and spectacle—that's what it is. It's how we cut through the fog—force the cameras to stop pretending and look dead into the lens."

She finishes setting the wine glasses gracefully; it's a grace she earned, not one she was taught. "Well, the chopper's rented. The rig is stable. The press is hungry. All that's left is the sky."

I nod and lean against the doorframe, watching the two of them move around each other like gears. It's a strange thing, this harmony we've managed. Teresa, the scientist in spiritual garb. Ana Lorena, the wounded alchemist of pain and survival. And me—the architect of systems, ghosts, and gods.

Teresa passes me a glass of chilled white wine. "I saw the CNN piece. They're calling it 'performance activism.' You've officially coined a genre."

"They called Jesus a magician," I say. "If they can't categorize you, they condescend to you."

Ana lights the citronella candles. "They're still sending a second camera team to Hollywood, right?"

"Yeah. One in the air, one on the hill. We're feeding it all back through the abbey's media server. If we're lucky, we'll break into prime time rotation before Letterman."

Teresa snorts. "Nothing says spiritual awakening like a helicopter stunt and corporate disruption."

"That's the world now, love," I say. "You don't dismantle the machine from the outside. You hot-wire it and run it off a cliff."

The telephone rings and Ana Lorena runs to answer. Her head pops outside the patio doors. "It's your grandmother."

I motion to Teresa, indicating we'll continue the jacuzzi after my call. She nods and the gleam in her eyes lets me know she's on a better path.

"I'm supposed to call my kids tonight," Ana Lorena tells me as she hands me the phone.

"I'll make it quick."

Hi Grandma. Are you okay?

"There's something I need you to do for me, Mark. I need you to call your brother."

"Why, what's wrong?"

"Three months ago, he took his kids camping in the woods. He left them at the camp. They were playing around the fire while he went to the river, about a half mile away, to set up for fishing. When he heard them screaming and by the time he got there, a pack of wild dogs had attacked them. It was horrible. He had to beat the dogs with firewood, but by the time he drove them away, the kids were horribly disfigured. Their faces and arms are scarred and disfigured. Dan has always suffered from depression, but this ... this has him lost inside a dark hole. Two days ago, his wife checked him into the clinic. They have him on a 24 hour suicide watch."

The phone tightens against my ear. I stare out at the horizon like I might see the edge of this unraveling.

"Jesus, Grandma ..." My voice is quieter than I expect. "I had no idea."

"He didn't want anyone to know. But now it's different. He needs someone who remembers him before the cracks."

I lean against the patio door, the evening warmth suddenly useless. Teresa is slipping out of her clothes, wineglass in hand, motioning toward the jacuzzi. Ana Lorena watches me from the sofa in the television room with that look—part curiosity, part worry, part knowing that the call has shifted something in the air.

"How bad is it?"

"They stitched the girl's eyelid back on. The boy lost an ear and nose. Their arms ... Mark, they don't look like children anymore. Not in the way people expect children to look."

I sit down. I don't even realize I'd moved. Just that I'm now in the chair, staring at a citronella candle like it's going to give me direction.

"And Dan?"

"He won't speak. Not to anyone. The nurses say he just sits there. Eyes open. No light in 'em. His wife's afraid he's already gone, and it's just his body waiting for permission."

I nod, though she can't see it. I know that silence. That kind of rupture doesn't whisper. It thunders.

"I'll call him."

"Today. Please. I already gave him your number. He may not pick up right away. But he needs to know you're there."

"I will."

She pauses. The static over the line is soft, but it fills the cracks between us like ash.

"Mark. I know you're doing big things out there. But this ... this is family. Do whatever it takes."

She hangs up without goodbye.

Family, she said. Meaningless to me. I have felt, for decades, as though I was born into a void of affection disguised as family.

I stare at the flickering flame, the wax slowly melting like forgotten intentions. Money. Attention. Spectacle. They'd felt like truths, but now? Now they float like brittle lies on dark waters. Dan and I had never been close, but childhood wounds bond deeper than laughter. Grandma's voice clawed open doors I'd sealed with silence and success.

What if tomorrow's hooks weren't steel, but obligation—each piercing through the carefully crafted skin of my life? Had I traded family for fame, intimacy for influence, my brother's pain for public awe?

The candle shudders in a breeze, the flame bowing as if ashamed. I see now—I've built my empire on air, dazzling but empty of a soul. Tomorrow's spectacle might brand me unforgettable, but Dan, my nephew, my niece—they're branded with scars that won't fade. Every time he looks at them he'll remember how beautiful they once were.

My fingers ache to call him, to say something, anything—but words shrink in my throat, useless against the magnitude of his darkness.

Suddenly Teresa's laughter rings softly from outside, innocent and unaware, and my heartbeat stumbles. I stand up, dizzy. How do I balance spectacle with sacrifice? How do I fly, knowing he's drowning?

I return the receiver to the cradle on the wall unit and shrug toward Ana Lorena. "It's all yours."

The sky outside is pure black velvet. I can hear the low churn of the Jacuzzi, its bubbles rising like lazy ghosts into the air. I follow the sound until my eyes adjust—Teresa, half-lit in steam, water rolling across her bare shoulders.

"Get those clothes off and get in here, mister," she says.

The water's hot but welcome, easing into my tight muscles and stiff joints like it knows where the pain lives. I settle beside her. She pulls me close. We kiss—slow at first, then deeper. Our bodies connect, firm and slick, beneath the surface. Sex between us is a ritual act, a spiritual awakening of ceremony. The emotions rise to the top shelf. Every touch and act a holy act of devotion.

After a while, her breath brushes against my cheek. "Why do you still talk to those people?"

I pause, unsure what she means.

Pulled back from the euphoric to the mortal realm.

She holds my face, her thumbs just under my eyes. "Your family. They ignored you your whole life. Now they call when they need something."

I try to answer, but she doesn't wait.

"They're not your family, Mark. Not really. Your parents never taught you love. They taught you survival. There's a difference."

Her eyes search mine, quiet but unsparing. "I've wanted to ask you this for a long time ... Why do you keep your stepfather's last name? That man is poison. He's a scar walking. You don't owe him anything. What is your birth father's name? Do you even know? You could start to heal if you take steps to separate yourself from them."

The words land hard. Not accusations—just truth. Echoes of thoughts I've shoved away for years now stare back at me in someone else's voice.

Newbury. I know his name. The name they stole from me.

Before I can speak, she rises from the spa, water gliding down her body. She stretches out on the warm concrete, arms wide, waiting for me to complete our pleasure.

I move toward her, driven by heat and emotion, but just as I reach her, the Jacuzzi cuts off. The silence arrived like judgment. No hum, no hiss, just the sudden absence of noise—as if the universe had held its breath. That's how truth comes, I realized. Not with a bang or a scream, but with the precise, surgical quiet that leaves you nowhere to hide.

"The damn breaker," I mutter. "Lights and spa together always trip it."

"I'll wait right here," she says, eyes twinkling.

Inside, I pass Ana Lorena fast asleep on the couch, one arm curled over her head. Upstairs, I step lightly into the master closet—where the fuse box's buried behind a wall of her unopened boxes and long dresses.

I shift a stack aside—glass bottles rattle, clink like a bar fight under a pillow. I reach deeper. More bottles. What the hell?

My foot slips against something round. Another bottle.

"Jesus..."

I find the frame, flip open the box, and feel for the blown switch. Snap. Lights back on.

Back outside, Teresa's still reclining on the concrete like a siren waiting for a tide.

"Have you ever heard of Yukon Jack?" I ask.

She opens one eye. "Is that a man or a weapon?"

"It's whiskey. And apparently Ana Lorena collects the damn things. Eighteen empty bottles in the closet. I nearly broke my neck on her little amber graveyard."

~~~

Some mornings roll in soft. Pacific haze draped over the canyon like a memory I didn't ask for. A low, suffocating ceiling is what May Gray feels like. The onshore breeze is faint, but it's there—cool, indifferent. The abbey's stucco walls still hold the chill of night, and the espresso I sip from a chipped ceramic mug is the only thing that feels certain.

I'm on the third floor. The renovation crew has made it halfway to holy—fresh drywall, clean plumbing, no insulation. Their radios buzz static over mariachi and classic rock, and I can hear one of them cussing at a copper fitting that won't tighten.

April 19, 1995. The news headlines are on my chair. I pick up the newspaper and scan. The Nasdaq cracks a record high at 850 and before I finish my coffee, every news station headline screams about a new industrial age, though no one can explain what the age actually produces. I turn the television off and settle in front of the computer monitor. My inbox flooded with hysteria: "Markets Soar on Tech Optimism. Next Stop: 1,000? Silicon Valley Will Eat Wall Street." I
~~~

don't bother opening them. Optimism isn't necessary for me. I have leverage.

Then I see it—forwarded from some overpaid broker with a Capitol Hill kink: Newt Gingrich's morning memo. "The Contract with America is not a promise, it's a revolution."

Right. Less government. Fewer taxes. More places to disappear.

I don't read it like policy—I read it like scripture. Not because I believe, but because I understand. It's not a revolution. It's an invitation.

Then Dennis, the caretaker, knocks. He's always gentle, even when the world's on fire.

"Phone call. Line two. Ruben Meyer."

That's never good.

I walk into the office and pick up the line with a calm I don't feel.

"Mark. I won't waste your time," Ruben says. "We've got a letter from the California Attorney General. They're reviewing religious nonprofit status, and you're on the list. The audit's already started. You need to show $1.3 million in liquid assets. In cash. In a California bank. Within fifteen days."

My spine stiffens. "I know what liquid assets mean. But why do they want cash and not assets?"

"Cash. Not stocks. Not foreign holdings. Not 'pending wire transfers.' It has to be real, unencumbered, traceable U.S. dollars."

I click the mouse. Log into E*TRADE. My positions are solid, but locked—options plays, long holds, foreign funds riding on Hong Kong telecom. I've spread everything out to keep it safe. But right now, safe is useless. Safe doesn't count.

"Jesus," I whisper.

Ruben lowers his voice. "If you can't show solvency, they'll revoke your 501(c)(3). The abbey will become taxable. Retroactively. Every dime you've ever taken in—subject to penalties. They'll bury you."

I hang up.

One by one, I dial in. Cayman. Curaçao. Panama. The shell corporations. The blind trusts. All of them built to hide the money. Protect it. Make it immune.

But now I need it visible. Traceable. And not one of them can give me what I need.

I pace the hall, past unfinished plaster and exposed wires. The abbey's bones are solid, but bones don't pay taxes. I hear Teresa downstairs, laughing—first time in days. Ana Lorena too. They're making breakfast. The place smells like hope and sourdough.

But I'm underwater.

Here's the twist. Not the collapse of wealth—but the exposure of the structure that made it possible. The thing I built to last forever—can't be seen. And if it can't be seen, it doesn't count.

This isn't just a problem.

It's the crack in the glass. And everything behind it is moving.

Teresa knocks once, then pushes the door open with her hip, balancing a frosty glass in one hand.

"Juice," she says, proud of it. "Kiwi, orange, maybe a little ginger. Liquid resurrection."

I'm halfway through calculating a currency shift from Swiss francs to Belizean notes. Numbers clatter in my head like bones in a jar.

"Thanks," I mutter.

She doesn't leave. Instead, she sinks into the chair opposite me and folds one leg over the other. Smiling.

"You're gonna love this," she says.

"I really won't."

"No, no—you will. It's from Noe. You know the one with the e in his name?"

I look up. She's not going to let this go.

I lean back, arms crossed. "Fine. Go."

She takes a deep breath, settles into her act.

"So this Mexican guy from Mexico City, right? He decides he wants to become a Buddhist monk. Hardcore. Goes all the way to the Himalayas in India, to the last real Tibetan monastery. Joins up. Serious business."

I nod, already regretting this.

"The head monk tells him: first three years in silence. No talking. You meditate, sweep, tend the gardens, all of it. But—once a year—you get to say two words."

I already know the punchline. I know the shape of this joke. But she's into it now, face glowing with mischief.

"End of year one, he lines up with the other silent newbies. When it's his turn, he works his jaw around like he's chewing invisible tortillas, clears his throat, looks the monks dead in the eye and says: 'Bed hard.'"

She waits.

I don't react.

She continues, unphased but a bit perturbed. "Back to sweeping, studying, scrubbing. End of year two, same thing—he works the jaw, this time rubs his cheeks, looks at the elders and says: 'Food bad.'"

She laughs once to herself. Even so, still no response from me.

"Third year comes. Same routine. He lines up, jaw stretching, cheeks rubbing—real dramatic. Looks at the monks and says, 'I quit.'"

She raises her eyebrows for the punchline.

"One elder turns to the other and says, 'What did he say?' Other guy goes, 'He said, I quit.' And the first elder goes, 'Good. All he ever did was complain.'"

She snorts. Loud. Covers her face and giggles.

I take a slow sip of the juice. Watch her come apart.

Then I look back at the computer screen. Bank balances. Red flags. The weight of every invisible dollar I can't show.

"I'm glad Noe's still got material," I say flatly. "Do you suppose the guy went back to Mexico City?"

She grins, completely unfazed by my deadpan.

"You're a tough audience," she says.

"Tell me another one when I'm under investigation for wire fraud," I say.

She laughs again. "Oh, I will."

I stare back at the monitor. 1.3 million. And not one goddamn joke to solve it. One point three. Like a curse. It's like a clock ticking behind my eyes.

Behind me, the hallway creaks—her bare feet on old wood, soft like punctuation. "My dad told me you're changing your name to Bertrand," she says. No judgment in her voice. Just observation. "It's got a nice ring to it. Mark Bertrand."

I don't turn around. My eyes are still on the screen, as if the numbers might start moving if I stare long enough. "Papa Bertrand has done more to help me figure out life than anyone else," I say. "He listens. Doesn't interrupt. Doesn't try to fix me. Just hands me a cup of tea and waits until I remember who I am." I finally glance over at her. Her hair's tied up, one stray curl falling against her cheek. She's holding her juice glass like it's communion.

"So yeah," I nod. "I asked him if he'd allow me the honor."

She nods back, quiet for a beat. "He told me it made him cry. Listen," she says, her voice turning to a tone I've never heard from her. "Noe is going to take me to Cancun for two weeks and then I think I'll move to his place."

My head goes numb.

The look in her eyes is half fear and half excitement.

I speak as evenly as I could pose.

"That seems quick?"

"It is, a little, but we've dated for a while."

My head freezes again as I wonder when all this, how did I not see her drifting away? Again, I pose as neutral as I can.

"Are you happy?"

She doesn't answer right away. Just stands there, the juice forgotten in her hand, condensation tracing her knuckles.

"I think I could be," she says.

That's when I know. It's already done.

For one stupid second, a second I'll never admit to breathing, I think about begging her to stay. Not with words. No—Mark Bertrand doesn't beg. But some ancient, ragged part of me—older than the abbey, older than ambition—wants to fall to my knees, grab her hand, and pretend like it isn't too late.

Instead, I tighten my grip on the desk so hard my fingers throb. I nod. Once. Like a man accepting a death sentence written in someone else's hand. Still breathing, though I don't know how. This isn't a test. Not a cry for rescue. It's the briefing before the launch. She's packed it up in her mind, even if the suitcase is still unzipped under the bed.

I swivel my chair just enough to face her. Not fully. I'm not giving her that. Just enough to mark the shift.

"How long have you and Noe been dating?"

Her eyes dart. A reflex. Not guilt—strategy. Gauging how much I already know.

"A few months. It wasn't ... it didn't start as a thing."

She laughs, once. A dry, nervous bark. "I guess it just became one."

My jaw is tight, but I nod, slow. Controlled. Like I'm watching the final act of a play I didn't audition for.

"Cancun," I say. "Nice this time of year."

She shrugs. "He's got a place reserved on the beach and the resort looks cozy. It's easy."

"Easy."

The word lands like a closing door.

Not "better." Not "right." Just easy.

I glance back at the screen.

1.3 million.

And now this.

"I don't blame you," I say.

Not because I mean it. Because she needs to hear it. Because even now, even in this fracture, I won't give her the satisfaction of rage.

She sets the glass down on my desk. It makes a sound like punctuation.

"If you need help with anything before I go..."

"No," I say. "I'm good."

She nods.

Half-turns.

Stops.

Then, quietly, over her shoulder, "Mark Bertrand fits you better anyway."

I wait for the door to click shut before I let the air out of my lungs.

Then I type the login to my Curaçao account.

Because if everything's ending anyway—I might as well start building the next empire.

Several minutes later, Ana Lorena peeks her head through the office door, her hair pinned up in a way that looks like she tried and gave up halfway through. The skirt is one she's worn to too many serious things. The heels are borrowed. Her lipstick is perfect.

"I'm off to trial," she says, one foot still in the hallway. "You alright there, mister? You look like Spider-Man ran out of web."

I give her a half-smile that doesn't reach the surface.

"It's not too late to let me get you a lawyer," I say.

She steps inside just far enough for her shadow to cross the floor. Her eyes scan the desk, catching the banking dashboard still glowing on the screen. She knows what numbers like those mean. Maybe not the details, but she knows enough to stay out of it.

"There's no point," she says. "Might even make it worse."

She shrugs, slow. Like someone carrying a bag with a bomb in it, hoping not to jostle the trigger.

"I have nothing for them to take, right? No car. No savings. The daycare license is gone. If I show up with some briefcase wearing a silk tie, the judge might think I'm hiding assets. He might start looking harder."

Her smile is bitter, but not without dignity.

"Let them dig. All they'll find is empty drawers and four kids who still call me Mom."

I nod. Not because I agree—but because I respect her battlefield.

She walks toward the door, pausing again.

"I'll be back late. Don't wait up."

I watch her go, the click of her heels softer than the silence she leaves behind.

My eyes drift back to the monitor.

Still 1.3 million shy of salvation.

But the thing about numbers is—they're patient.

They don't flinch.

And they don't care who walks out the door.

Only whether you've got the stones to flip them.

My thoughts shift like storm clouds over warm water. The silence in the room breaks apart as something colder settles in.

A voice I heard once—older than me, older than the country, maybe—keeps repeating itself in my skull:

"The value of the internet is not the tech. It's the people. Their habits, their hunger. Their data."

Data is the new currency. And I've been mining it for a decade.

College registration servers cracked open like ripe pomegranates. Texas. Massachusetts. I can name every university by its blind spots.

E*TRADE, before it got its firewall legs under it. Millions of keystrokes. Name, DOB, banking habits, emails, login credentials, browser fingerprints.

Twenty-seven million people.

They don't even know I own them.

I call Ruben again.

"Forty-five days," I say. "Don't ask. Just tell me you can do it."

His voice crackles like tired nerves on a landline. "I'll make it happen. You just need that balance showing for one day. After that, you're golden."

"One day."

That's all it takes to fake legitimacy. Or claim it. No difference anymore.

I hang up and dial the website developer. It's not even noon, but he sounds like he hasn't slept in three days.

"We live?" I ask.

"All but twelve merchants," he says. "Still waiting on merchant account approvals from the banks."

"Screw the banks," I say. "Use my merchant account for all of them. Process through my shell. Just get it live."

"You sure?" he asks.

"I've never been more sure of anything."

If I do this right, if the data flows and the transactions don't raise flags—this could be the moment.

The lever.

The pivot.

The jump from survivalist to overlord.

My cursor hovers over the database window—twenty-seven million lines of pure leverage.

All I need is for no one to look too close ... and for the game to stay rigged just one more day.

The sun melts the last of the marine layer like candle wax off the blue. That San Diego light—the sort that makes you forget what gray ever looked like—crawls across my desk. Warm. Patient. It touches the rim of my coffee mug, my forearm, the old envelope where I've scribbled figures too volatile for software.

It's quiet, except for the ceiling fan clicking in slow orbit.

I've been staring at the screen too long.

And yet ... there's something to say.

Email to Thầy Nhất

Subject: You Are Always Welcome at Hillcrest

Dear Thầy,

The morning sun reaches my desk now with a kind of reverence—quiet, warm, aware. It reminds me of your teaching: the sun shines with no need to prove anything. I find myself breathing a little slower when I think of that.

The Hillcrest Abbey is nearly complete. The walls are still humming with fresh energy, the earth still settling around the foundation. But the spirit here—teacher, it's real. People come with open minds. The silence holds.

It would mean more than I can say if you would join us for our first gathering. A soft opening, a humble offering, but one we believe can ripple. The media may call it a "spiritual venture," but we know better. This is transmission. Presence. The Dharma in the West, anchored in the here and now.

Your presence would be a lantern for all who attend.

With deep respect and gratitude,

Mark Bertrand

Hillcrest Dzogchen Abbey

San Diego, California

I hit send. Then I pivot to my scheme.

— Investment Forecast Email —

Subject: Timing the Turn: Strategic Insight into Market Pulse

Dear Investor,

Financial markets aren't subtle anymore. Not with this administration. The Clinton White House has mastered the art of deregulation through distraction—cloaking massive shifts in consumer data laws, telecom structures, and international trade access in the language of economic expansion.

This week, the real players are moving.

If you're paying attention, MOT (Motorolla) is the play. The undercurrent of post-NAFTA infrastructure spending and microchip manufacturing subsidies is building pressure. Our proprietary models suggest a substantial movement—timed right, it's harvest season.

Forecast: Sharp Rise Before Friday Close.

The rules haven't changed. Only the players.

—Equinox Strategies©

I hit send. But not to everyone.

I split the master list—13.5 million each. Half got the bullish prediction. The other half got a mirrored version, forecasting a downturn in Motorolla based on overextension and speculative drag.

Why?

Because by Friday, one of them will believe I'm a prophet.

And the other half?

It was necessary to let them go.

The truth doesn't matter.

Perception does.

Chapter 10: Trading on Trust
Net worth $1,478,000

The sun cuts sideways through the eucalyptus haze as I park under the brittle shadow of a jacaranda tree. The air tastes like metal and sage—San Diego's signature cocktail of coastal light and drought-season nerves. I kill the engine but don't move. The dashboard clock ticks loud in the hush. A clipboard with laminated schedules rests in the passenger seat. My name is printed across it in bold. The name they expect. The one that still opens doors.

Three hundred people have paid to listen. To learn. To find stillness.

And I'm here.

Mostly.

The driver's side mirror reflects a campus lawn being mowed into obedience by a student worker who doesn't know he's shaping the backdrop of a dream I no longer fully believe in. I adjust my collar. My hands feel disconnected, like they've been trained to move without instruction—habit over intention. There's a massive rental space reserved near the Trade Center downtown, rooms filled with folding chairs and meditation mats. A freight truck delivered signage and speakers yesterday. Flyers were posted in coffee shops and yoga studios from La Jolla to Tijuana.

And I'm the headliner.

But my mind? It's off-grid. Somewhere dark. Still circling the scorch mark where something beautiful used to be.

I feel like I'm back on that reservation. Inside that icy room at the hotel and wrapped in that electric blanket without the cord. Despite the appearance, I'm cold to the bone.

The meeting room smells like electric ozone and copy toner. Third floor of the university annex, east-facing windows painted with a marine layer sky. They've set the chairs in a loose circle, all ergonomic and mismatched—some academic nod to egalitarianism. I recognize a few of them: the monk from Plum Village with a voice like wind moving through pine, the epigeneticist from UCSF who published the methylation study, and the woman from UCSD's mindfulness lab—calm face, cut-glass stare.

They don't greet me with applause. They nod, the way researchers nod when they've already read your bio and filed it under 'possible utility.'

Sundra is seated already, robes folded, presence grounded like a stone in still water. He meets my eyes and smiles, but it's the type of smile that sees through things.

No small talk. The woman from UCSD taps a laptop cabled over to a screen illuminates behind her, a bright flicker that fades into a real-time brainwave display—slow waves, sharp peaks, bursts of blue and green like sonar from the deep.

She motions toward a mat on the floor. "We thought you might like to see."

"See what?"

"How thoughts feel," she says. "And how feelings think."

I don't respond. I kneel, sitting back on my heels. My mind chasing her words round and round inside my head as I struggle to comprehend meaning from what she said.

The Plum Village monk begins the breathing count, low and even. Inhale, two, three, four … exhale, two, three, four...

My eyes close.

Somewhere behind my skull, the gamma waves rise—fast, fleeting signals across a sea of gray. I feel nothing. Then everything. Heat in my chest, the sharp push of grief between my ribs. A sudden cold in my hands, like memories flooding backward. The machine picks it up—green lights spike into gold.

The mat feels like a raft drifting loose from a sinking ship. I close my eyes, but it's not peace that fills me—it's the sensation of falling inward. Of sliding between ribs and cartilage into some vault sealed since childhood.

And there it is.

Not grief. Not shame. Hunger.

A howling, starving core that no million dollars ever touched. The biofeedback machine stutters, then spikes, the screen flashing gold like a storm tearing open the seabed.

My mouth goes dry. My fingers curl into fists without asking.

This isn't alignment. It's ignition.

The fuse is inside me.

"You're not meditating," the epigeneticist says softly. "You're aligning."

"What does that mean?"

"Your thoughts are the language of your mind," the UCSD woman answers. "Your feelings are the language of your body. When they say the same thing—your genes listen."

I open my eyes. The room looks different. Or maybe just truer.

Sundra is watching me, silent.

The UCSD woman sits forward. "Change your thinking and your feeling—at the same time, with coherence—and you signal your body to express new genes. New chemistry. New reality."

"Like turning on a light," I whisper.

"No," she says. "Like igniting the sun."

The monk rings the bell. The sound hangs in the air, soft but final.

And in the silence that follows, I feel it:

Hope, not like a fire—but like a fuse. Joy!

My mind slides into a memory

Just two weeks ago to the day, everything I ever wanted in this life happened. The memory floods.

The audit report stared back at me like a confession typed in Helvetica. Under "Assets—Liquid," in bold, black ink: $1,441,819.55.

My first million. Came in on Friday, May 12, 1995.

I stared at it for hours. Kept refreshing the screen like it might vanish. Or grow. Or speak to me.

I wanted to touch it. Hold it. Feel its presence in the world. Not the idea of wealth—but its mass. The way a brick feels different from a pillow even before you lift it. My name next to seven digits, and no one can take that away from me.

I have split the list three times. Calibrated every line. Half the crowd got a sunrise, the other half got a funeral. One of them was always right. That was the secret. That was the trick. If you tell both sides of the future, you never lose.

Then I pulled the trigger: "Want to keep receiving my money-making predictions? $350 and sign up here."

The page went live at midnight. By morning: $1.2 million.

No product. No meetings. No inventory. Just a promise in pixel form.

Eureka.

And then—twelve days later—the Federal Trade Commission ruled all unsolicited financial marketing via email illegal. Boom. Done. Shut down overnight. Politicians, once again fixing laws to regulate new technology so the population doesn't share the wealth and only a select handful of already wealthy individuals benefit.

Game over.

But I was lucky. I had my million before they slammed the door. So...

It's not the collapse that gets you. It's the echo. The questions that follow you around like a cold draft in your own house.

Now what?

Now who?

Now why?

But I tell myself the truth I need to hear—because some truths grow in the dark like mushrooms, only useful if you don't inspect them too closely.

I have my million. So...

(And the silence that follows isn't peace. It's the sound of the fuse still burning.) The memory turns away from the joy.

The sky outside had curdled—low clouds smearing the coast like a dirty bandage, the seasonal marine layer once again familiar taste like copper and unfinished arguments. Salt and exhaust soured the air, pressing against the windows, as if the world had been over-cooked and left to simmer. I breathed it in. Because it matched the burn in my throat—the taste of scorched resolve and last chances blistering on the tongue. Even in celebration, I feel the oppressive persistence of life and the lies it wants people to believe.

But it kept getting worse.

After the FTC erased my million-dollar Eureka, the ripple turned tidal. The Pacific Beach merchants started circling like vultures that hadn't eaten in weeks. Disappointment turned quickly into blame. Their websites were up, their carts were functional, the pixel storefronts were spotless—and no one was buying a damn thing.

They'd spent thousands. Some second-mortgage homes, others pulled from savings. All of them lured in by the dream that the internet was the new mall, the new gold rush, the new gods.

But clicks don't mean customers.

Orders trickled in like condensation—enough to make you hope, never enough to drink. Some saw a handful of purchases. Most saw none.

They weren't alone. By now, the entire country was squinting at the screen like maybe it had tricked them. The news started muttering about "the online business fad." Tech stocks trembled. Investors quietly ghosted. Corporations reversed course and went analog again. It wasn't yet the burst, but the bubble had started to swell.

And me? I became the face of their failure.

Their scapegoat.

The man who'd promised them the stars and delivered dial-up.

Doesn't matter that I built the sites. Doesn't matter that I gave them tools, strategies, full-service. To them, I was the magician who vanished their money. The architect of empty carts and unfulfilled expectations.

The dream was turning, souring in their mouths—and I was the one who sold it to them.

One by one, they started calling.

Some were polite. Most weren't.

The I-15 freeway is a slow suicide in asphalt. Taillights flicker like dying embers all the way from the 805 split to Escondido. The FM dial keeps looping the same top forty songs, and the cassette deck's chewing up my Miles Davis bootleg. I'm cooked by the time I pull into the driveway—three hours of brake lights and fumes, and a stack of pink message slips waiting for me at the front desk of the abbey, all scribbled in the same panicked handwriting.

Ana Lorena meets me at the door. Her face is slick—tears, sweat, mascara, maybe gin. The glass in her hand is more ice than liquid, and the look in her eyes is pure collapse.

"I'm ruined," she says. Not a greeting. A verdict.

Inside, the house smells like perfume and despair. The blinds are drawn, but the television blares—something plastic and laugh-tracked on a loop.

I sat her down. Get the drink out of her hand. Her voice is warped, rubbery from crying for too long without breathing. But I got it out of her, eventually.

One point five million dollars.

That's the civil judgment. Her name on it like a tombstone. The daycare lawsuit came to collect.

"You don't have anything," I say, trying to stay calm. "They can't get blood from a stone."

She laughs—raw, deranged, the type of sound that makes walls lean away.

"I told the judge I'd pay. I'll make it work. I have a plan."

I wait.

"I want to start a website," she says. "An amateur porn site."

Silence.

She thinks I'm shocked. I'm not. I'm numb. Something deeper.

We meet couples. Content creators. Industry veterans. People who live off humiliation and pixels. We go to shoots behind blacked-out windows in warehouses that smell like latex and liability. I learned things I never wanted to know about lighting, about angles, about how desire is marketed like dish soap. The line between performance and pathology blurs until I'm dizzy.

Weeks pass. The money never comes. Her plan is a fantasy scribbled in lipstick.

There's no exit. No parachute. Just the ledger and the weight of her crying in the next room.

So two months later I do the one thing I swore I wouldn't.

I pay.

I liquidate every account. Sweep up the last remaining threads of my offshore system. Watch the zeroes flicker as the money vanished. Twenty years of clawing, scamming, scripting. Twenty years of dodging regulators, manipulating code, outmaneuvering every system built to keep men like me small.

The account clears. Just like that—a million and a half gone. And for the first time, I don't feel lighter. I feel clean. This money isn't fuel anymore. It's poison I've bled out. Maybe that's the trick: to keep the engine running just long enough to pull over and walk away. I'm not saving Ana Lorena. I'm saving what's left of me.

My net worth is now three hundred and sixteen dollars.

I sit in the dark for a long time. No music. No television. Just the hum of the fridge, the echo of choices, and the sound of one man breathing like he's trying not to disappear.

While I lean against the doorframe, the drywall cool on my back. Ana Lorena is curled up on the sofa, barefoot and mute now, spent. Her glass hangs from her fingers, catching the last thread of kitchen light. I don't need to ask if she's okay. Nothing about this is okay. Not the $1.5 million settlement. Not the site idea. Not the slow, quiet way she's starting to disappear from her own life.

I walk into the office. The lamp buzzes when I turn it on. My ledger's open, where I left it—page titled "Options." The rest of the house is still. Too still. I turn to the window. The city glows beneath the coastal haze like it's been lit from below, and I remember the screen at UCSD—the real-time readout of my mind. Gold lines across black.

"Change your thinking and your feeling—at the same time, with coherence—and you signal your body to express new genes. New chemistry. New reality."

That was only months ago. A different man in the same skin.

And now?

Now, I'm broke.

But I'm not erased.

The fuse is still lit. Even if everything else is burning.

Journal Entry

Napoleon Hill said in his book, Think and Grow Rich, "Every adversity, every failure, every heartache carries with it the seed of an equal or greater benefit."

In three weeks, I'll have an MBA. Add it to the museum of degrees gathering dust on my wall—souvenirs from the endless chase for legitimacy in a game that was never meant to be fair. At some point, learning stops being growth and becomes a weapon. Another forged credential, another blade for cutting through red tape—or slicing clean through the façade of civility.

The brutal truth is cooling beside my coffee: either burn it all down, or keep running fast enough to stay ahead of the fire. But that's the lie, isn't it? That you can outpace a system engineered to devour you. That you can succeed without becoming part of what you loathe.

You'd think I was a Republican, the way I justify crimes when the math works in my favor. The way I move assets in the dark and turn legality into a parlor trick. But I hate Republicans. I hate their war on empathy, their worship of hierarchy. I grew up under that brand of control—my stepfather with his rigid spine, hollow morals, and closed fists. He didn't teach me discipline. He taught me how to hide the bruises and the fear.

But don't mistake me for a Democrat either. They wear softer faces but sharpen the same knives. They brand their betrayal with compassion, then hand your future to Wall Street and call it progress. They kneel, they cry, they write speeches while the machine grinds on, unchallenged and well-fed. It's not about sides. It's about survival. And they've all sold out their tribe for a seat at the table.

So, where does that leave me?

Looking for exits in a building with no doors. Calling it strategy when all it is—is adaptation.

You want the truth?

Anarchy is the only honest option.

Not chaos. Not Molotovs in the street. I'm talking about freedom. The kind that doesn't come with tax brackets or donor tiers. The kind where you don't need a license to live or permission to think. They fear it because it makes them irrelevant. No leash. No master. Just the echo of your own choices in a world that's forgotten what that even means.

No votes. No saviors. Just you.

They want you addicted to structure. Numbed by safety. But what they fear most is the man who sees the whole system for what it is—and still walks away.

Not broken.

Not bitter.

Just done.

Getting a million dollars is damn near impossible.

Keeping it? That's the crucifixion.

Well, I have killed before and if that's what it is going to come to...

I'm not afraid to do it again.

Chapter 11: Three Names for One Man Networth $1,799,508

She's seated when I arrive, the hostess barely keeping pace as I slide past the patio and into the intimate dining room where the wine list comes with a pronunciation guide.

La Perla is low-lit and lush with scent—burnt rosemary, garlic in olive oil, saffron rice crisping on the edge of a steel pan somewhere behind the kitchen wall. The waiters move like shadows, trained in invisibility. A jazz trio in the corner paints the air with brushed snares and upright bass, nothing obtrusive, just enough to remind you you're somewhere money goes to exhale.

Teresa watches me approach, her glass of tempranillo half-full, her fingers tracing the condensation like she's sketching invisible truths.

Then the familiar voice filters in through the clink of silverware and the filtering hush of high-end conversations. "Hey, Bertrand," she says.

"You remember that night we took Archbishop Timothy to The Fairlane Club?"

Her brow lifts, amused.

"Ferndale?" she asks.

"Right on the border," I say, nodding. "Could've been North Detroit, but you know how borders blur in winter. My favorite local group—Orange Lake Drive—was doing those Thievery Corporation and Oasis covers. Remember her voice? Like smoke on glass. And that horn trio—God, they were tight."

I can feel the rhythm in my chest again. The heat of scotch in my throat. The red velvet walls. The way time got lazy when the trumpet swelled.

"I was watching Timothy," I say, "the way he rocked his head and shoulders. That jazz sway. A man who spent seventy years inside Greek Orthodoxy, fifty of them in South America, surrounded by marble and incense and the ancient rigors of How Great Thou Art. And here he was, letting that black Detroit groove work through him like it had always been waiting."

She smiles gently, tipping her wine glass in salute to the memory.

"He loved that night," she says. "He never would've found that on his own."

"No," I murmur. "We gave him a piece of life most people only dream about."

The waiter arrives. Black suit, silver tray, the kind of courtesy that expects no recognition. He presents the bottle with reverence, recites its pedigree like scripture, then pours. We nod our approval with the choreography of people who used to pretend more than we do now.

The tempranillo rolls across my tongue—dark fruit, cedar, a breath of ash. It tastes like something survived.

"Do you think he's passed on?" I ask. "He went back to Greece over a year ago. Doctors said six months."

She sets her glass down, looks at my hand. Her eyes flicker. "You're wearing the ring he gave you."

I glance down. The white gold band and the star sapphire glint in the ambient light, bold and exacting—like his faith.

"Every day," I say. "It reminds me that belief is more than liturgy. It's what you do for others when no one's watching."

She doesn't respond. She doesn't have to.

Outside the window, the bay stretches out like a breathing animal, lights from the harbor winking through the marine haze. A soft mist has gathered, blurring the cars into half-forgotten memories.

I watch her across the table, eyes tracing the line of candlelight reflected in her wine glass. She's still got that Ferndale frost—cool, poised, a little wry—but something warmer's breaking through. Not just nostalgia. Something like commitment.

"I know you want me to help with the first offsite retreat," she says, her voice lower now, sincere. "I'd be honored. Can I meet, Thầy Nhất?"

I smile—barely—but it's there. Real. She doesn't ask for much, not anymore. And the fact that she wants in? That means more than she'll ever admit.

"You'll meet him," I say. "You'll meet all of them."

And just like that, we're already driving into it. It's been a long transition from being a young engineer at Bell Helicopter to here.

As we step out into the night, the air tastes like salt and eucalyptus. Teresa lingers before climbing into the car, her eyes scanning the skyline.

"You ever think we got here too fast?" she asks.

"No," I say. "Just late enough to be dangerous."

The next morning, the sky breaks open clean and blue. The marine layer burns off early, like it's clearing space for something bigger. I'm standing in the echo of our rented retreat space downtown—bare concrete walls, high glass, sunlit silence—while freight crews wheel in stacks of folding chairs and audio cables. Banners unfurl with my logo on them. Flyers pile up by the door. Three hundred attendees confirmed, and walk-ins expected.

No longer the meditation leader whispering rebellion under incense smoke.

Now, I'm the architect of something that looks like salvation.

And if I do it right, they'll believe it is.

Three days after the last teaching, the abbey doesn't sleep—it hums.

Retreat guests have become donors. Donors become disciples. Disciples want influence, investment opportunities, and naming rights to the next breakthrough in conscious evolution. I find myself playing interpreter in a new dialect—half mindfulness, half ROI. It's a strange fluency, but I speak it better than most.

The abbey is booked out months ahead. Downtown's off-site venue is under contract for quarterly events. Three new researchers from UC Irvine are asking for grant money. And every night, I'm at dinner with someone who once used their hedge fund to dismantle public housing and now wants to fund "the science of wholeness."

I no longer sip smoky scotch for myself—I do it because that's how these people talk. They read epigenetics the way priests once read scripture—mystical, misinterpreted, and endlessly quoted out of context.

Dinner One: La Valencia Hotel, La Jolla

The dining room is all ivory linen and echoes. The Pacific outside is all posture and blue. Across from me, Lawrence D'Marin, who owns the largest commercial property trust on the West Coast, swirls his pinot like it owes him an apology.

"I'll be direct," he says, tucking a cloth napkin across his knee. "Your man Thầy changed the game. And your scientist friends—they turned it into something measurable. Quantifiable. That's rare. I've seen trends come and go, Mark. Yoga. Crystals. Fasting. But this?"

He leans forward. "This is replicable. It's data-driven transcendence. And people are buying it."

I offer nothing but a nod. Let him keep talking.

"I want to fund three of your research tracks. One in emotional coherence. One in gamma field mapping. And one in trauma imprint reversal. But I want first-look rights at the results. For my wellness division."

I keep my tone mild. "You're not worried about conflict of interest?"

His grin is feral. "Mark. I've made millions from conflict. I'm offering you alignment."

He cuts into his duck confit, the silverware making a sound like old money clinking in a cathedral.

"What do you get out of it?" I ask.

He dabs his lip. "Legacy. And immortality. Or the appearance of it. Which, in this town, is the same thing."

We seal it with a nod. I don't shake his hand. He respects that.

Dinner Two: A private club above Sunset, Los Angeles

It's called Zodiac. No signage. No menu. The wine list reads like a ransom note. At the table are five women and one man—all VC royalty. Founders of biotech firms, ex-CEOs of pharmaceutical giants, one whose company patented the gene-editing process for pet longevity.

They're not here for me. They're here for the idea.

"Epigenetic recalibration," says the bleach blonde in white linen. "If I can fund a study that proves it, I can restructure my company's entire product line around experience-based healing."

"Define prove," I say.

"Quantify outcomes," she replies. "Control variables. Replicate the shift. Offer predictable results."

The man in the group—thin, spectacled, skin like parchment—leans in. "What if we could show a link between meditation and the down-regulation of the cancer gene clusters? Just the hint of it."

One of the women taps her pen on the table. "You'd be overnight heroes. Pharma wouldn't know whether to buy you or burn you."

I sip my scotch. Let the silence fill.

"The research exists," I say finally. "But we'd need to separate 'spiritual wellness' from 'conscious intervention.' One they'll tolerate. The other, they'll kill."

"You mean like the CIA killed psychedelics," someone says.

"No," I say. "Worse. Like the FDA buries nutrition."

That shuts them up.

Later, the linen woman whispers as we walk to the elevator. "What you're doing? It's more than wellness. It's the next arms race. But inward."

Dinner Three: A back patio in Point Loma

This one's quieter. Just me and a man called Felix, who once ran security for three governments and now spends his days reading Sanskrit and lifting weights.

"You want to know why this works?" he says, gesturing to the research packet I brought.

He doesn't wait for me to answer.

"Because for the first time in history, people believe it might be possible to control their suffering without permission. That's what epigenetics is. It's the science of un-permission."

I frown. "What do you mean?"

He cracks his knuckles. "You ever look at a man in war who knows he's going to die? He stops thinking. He just is. That's alignment. The body doesn't wait for permission to survive. It just does."

He flips a page. "You're not selling science. You're selling the end of dependency. And that, my friend, is treason in a system built on addiction."

He pours us each a finger of Lagavulin 24, neat.

"So what now?" I ask.

"You already know," he says. "You're not running a retreat anymore. You're starting a movement."

I sip. The peat smoke fills my mouth like old books burning in a church.

Dinner Four: An Uncomfortable Seat at the Table

Location: Mister A's, Bankers Hill—old-school elegance, skyline views, a place where white linen meets whispered power.

We're seated in the back, away from the windows. Less light. More privacy.

Across from me sits Thomas Whitaker III, a second-generation wealth manager with a voice like old vinyl and a jaw carved from Wall Street. He's fifty-eight, Protestant, tailored to within an inch of his neurosis. He believes in capital the way monks believe in relics. He's also a major donor to two of our meditation labs.

He cuts into his filet without looking up.

"This retreat of yours," he says, "it's got legs. But some of your messaging—the language—concerns me."

"How so?"

He chews. Swallows. Drinks.

"You talk about dismantling systems. About privilege. That word gets thrown around like napkins at these things. White privilege. Like it's some sin baked into skin tone. I find it... reductive."

There it is.

I let it sit a second.

"You think it's a distraction," I say finally.

He nods. "We're building something extraordinary here. Bioenergetic alignment. Neural plasticity. Conscious evolution. And you want to drag it into the mud of social grievance?"

"Thomas," I say calmly, "the mud is the ground we're standing on."

He leans forward, brow tightened.

"I've worked for everything I have," he says. "My father might've opened the first door, but I walked through all the rest. You want to tell me I'm privileged—fine. But tell that to the twenty-hour days I pulled building my first fund."

"You're not wrong," I say. "You walked through the fire. But Thomas—did anyone ever ask to see your ID when you were just trying to walk into the fire?"

His eyes flicker.

"You ever worry your zip code would get your loan denied? That your surname might sink a job interview? That the cop pulling you over might shoot first and ask if you're an angel later?"

"That's not privilege," he says sharply. "That's injustice. And I agree—it exists. But we don't solve it by punishing success."

"Who's punishing you?"

He doesn't answer.

I push my plate away. The wine glass is full but untouched.

"White privilege doesn't mean you didn't work hard. It means your hard work didn't have to break through a firewall of inherited disadvantage. It means the system was set to 'neutral' for you, while others were stuck in reverse."

He exhales through his nose, slow.

"And what about Black privilege in South Dallas? Or Asian privilege in Cupertino? You want to tell me there's no advantage there?"

I nod, slowly. "There are advantages in context. But white privilege is systemic. It's global. It's the default in advertising, in hiring, in media, in law, and health care. The system itself was built by and for whiteness—through colonialism, conquest, cultural dominance. That's not a theory. It's a footprint."

"Slavery ended," he says.

"Did it?" I ask. "Or did it just change costume?"

He shakes his head, jaw tight.

"You're romanticizing suffering," he mutters. "Making a market out of grievance. People don't want guilt—they want results."

"No," I say quietly. "They want truth. Even if it breaks the glass they built their lives behind."

I watch him. He's thinking.

And I know that thinking hurts men like him. They built their identities on certainties. But the new world has none.

"You said privilege was being born with the door open," I continue. "I don't blame you for walking through it. I just want you to stop pretending it was locked."

He looks at his wine. Swirls it. Doesn't drink.

"This movement," he says, "what exactly are you building, Mark?"

"A path," I say. "Where biology meets belief. But it won't work unless we're honest. And the body knows when we lie."

He studies me.

"Do I still have a seat at the table?" he asks, voice quieter now.

"Only if you're willing to see who built the table," I answer. "And who was never invited."

He nods, once.

And we sit here, in this uneasy peace—the kind that comes when old gods are questioned, and new ones have yet to speak.

The bathroom is silent. Too silent.

A single wall sconce flickers above the mirror, old filament trying to remember how to shine. I lean into the basin, fingers braced on cold marble. Everything smells faintly of lavender and brass polish—money's attempt to cleanse what it can't name.

I look up.

The man in the mirror stares back like he just heard something he's not ready to believe. Collar sharp. Jawline tight. Star sapphire catching the light like it's still in ceremony. But something beneath the eyes is off. Not fear. Not yet. Something quieter. Thinner.

For a second, I can't tell if I'm proud or ashamed. I'm remembering Whitaker's voice—gravel and glass—saying the word privilege like it was a slur. Remembering how he reached for his wine, not for comfort, but control.

And I'm remembering my own voice—reasonable, deliberate, wearing its empathy like armor that fits too well.

I splash cold water on my face. Not to wake up. To see if I still feel it.

The truth is, I can't tell if I won that conversation or just negotiated the terms of my surrender. Every time I translate suffering into funding, it gets harder to remember if I'm helping or harvesting.

The mirror doesn't blink. Doesn't forgive.

I adjust my jacket, smooth the lapels. The reflection complies. Polished. Prepared. But I know that somewhere beneath the silk and symmetry, I am shifting.

Not into someone else.

Into someone more usable.

I kill the light as I leave, letting the mirror keep its secrets.

As I walk back to my car, the city presses in—glittering, carnivorous. I sit there a moment, engine off, window cracked to the salt air. For the first time since this all started, my hand shakes slightly as I pull the seatbelt across my chest. A simple tremor. A warning shot from whatever part of me still remembers.

You're drifting.

I sit there longer than I should, tasting the bitterness behind the pride. If I ever needed proof that belief could be bought, tonight gave it to me. The trick isn't selling out. It's selling just enough to still recognize your own face in the mirror.

I start the car. I don't drive home. I drive until the gas light blinks, past places I once couldn't afford to dream in. Past places I barely see now.

When his check came in the mail a week later, it made me laugh—one of those deep, throat-hollow laughs that leaves something sour at the edges. It was signed in fountain ink, thick and dark, with the same precision he used to cut his filet.

And then it made me proud.

Maybe the conversation mattered. Maybe something shifted. Or maybe this was just how men like Thomas Whitaker III atoned: by writing their way into the next chapter, hoping someone else would footnote the guilt.

I folded the check into the day's deposit and turned my attention south. Courting the rich was time-consuming. I needed to find a way to automate. But until then, I had to actively manage multiple projects.

Managing Sundra's finances had given me a kind of clarity. Central America wouldn't be any different—just warmer, looser, more plausible deniability. The numbers weren't huge yet. A few hundred thousand a year. Investments were simple, non-threatening. Most of it wrapped in municipal bonds that sounded like philanthropy: bridge replacements, water system upgrades, new parking lots for local markets that had no customers.

Low-risk, long-hold, tax-sheltered—perfect camouflage. They were the kind of instruments old men trusted and young men ignored. Nobody ever went to jail for buying a bond.

But I wasn't interested in jail.

I was interested in invisibility.

And municipal bonds? They're just the smoke.

And where there is smoke...

~~~

The problem isn't the plane ticket. It's the name printed on it.

Mark Bertrand.

Just Mark Bertrand.

Not Emanuel Torres. Not the other one—Carlos Adrián Viedma, the Panama alias I thought I'd retired but always kept in my back pocket like a counterfeit saint's medal. Bertrand, plain and legal, with a US passport that tracks back to a Social Security number.

The invitation from the Nicaraguan foundation arrived via fax. Two pages, heavy with ceremony. My name—my name—appears
~~~

nine times in eleven paragraphs. Their expectations are clear: they're not expecting a whisper. They're expecting a man.

The trouble is, I'm not sure which one.

I lean back from the desk; the fax crumpled in my lap. The office smells like oolong and dust. Outside, rain hisses against the gutters in that low San Diego murmur that never gets truly wet—just damp, like the city's trying to remember how to cry.

If I fly under Mark Bertrand, everything's visible. The flight. The destination. The customs declarations. A foundation wire out of the country under a name that matches the nonprofit's filings. Everything legitimate.

That's the trap.

Because the IRS has started sniffing around the edges. Not a full audit. Just questions. Letters. Small inquiries pretending to be curious when they're really laying the perimeter for a kill shot.

If I use Emanuel Torres, I vanish. I slip through Houston under a false passport and surface in Managua like a ghost with a good tan. But the Nicaraguans won't recognize the name. The contracts aren't in that alias. The land deeds, the wire transfers, the environmental exemptions—they're all tied to Bertrand. If I show up as Torres, they'll shut the door before I even get through the gate.

And Carlos Viedma? He's too polished. Too foreign. Too attached to a shell company that got gutted by Panamanian regulators in '95. He's radioactive.

I turn the desk lamp down a notch. The low bulb catches the rim of my teacup, half-drunk and growing cold. Somewhere down the hall, Ana Lorena is awake again—murmuring, moaning into a microphone. Another live stream. Another night of keeping the lights on with a body half the world thinks they own.

Her voice floats like a spell through the air vents. It's always just low enough to keep me from forgetting where the money comes from.

I turn back to the problem.

What matters more? Anonymity—or legitimacy?

If I go as Bertrand, the mission gains credibility. The foundation gets photographed, documented, praised. My name climbs into the quarterly reports and settles like a trophy on someone's donor wall. I can fundraise off that.

But if the IRS is already circling—and I know they are—then walking through customs in D.C. six weeks later with a tan and stories about sustainable aquaponics in a country I "accidentally" funneled seven million dollars into?

That's not a story I can spin.

But if I go as Torres, I look like a criminal. No paper trail. No welcome. Just a stranger with a smile and the wrong name.

I stare at the fax. My name, again and again, like a drumbeat.

Maybe the truth is, I'm tired of hiding.

Maybe that's what this chapter of my life is.

I rise. Cross to the closet. Open the lockbox with the passports. The real one. The two fakes. And the expired Panamanian ID.

Three lives.

Three lives, and not one of them is enough.

I hold the real passport a moment longer than the rest. The photo is from three years ago. Thinner. Cleaner. The eyes were less worn down by belief.

I set it on the desk. Not a decision. Just a placeholder.

Tomorrow, I'll call Teresa. Ask her to draft the Board a statement about the Nicaragua trip. Something clean. Something sanitized. We're expanding operations. Exploring educational partnerships. Looking into clean water solutions and temple-based trauma recovery programs. They don't need to know everything yet.

All of it's true. And none of it is.

Because the actual story is: I'm about to walk into the next version of my life. Without armor. Without aliases.

And with the IRS watching.

A terrible idea.

A necessary one.

But first—I jot a note in my journal, the red leather one Ana Lorena gave me when I still thought this was just a phase.

Journal Entry

February 3, 1997—4:06 a.m.

The walls here are thin. Ana's working again—moaning into some stranger's screen, half-acting, half-bleeding—and it wakes me like it always does. Not the sound, but the reminder: every dollar I ask from the wealthy is another coin I'm not taking from her. Or from the banks I used to rob with paperwork and a grin. But there's a sickness to it. The way these dinners blur into performances. I talk about wholeness while mapping their portfolios behind my eyes. I taste the scotch, but only to mimic their gods. I tell myself this is a better crime. A legal crime. And maybe it is. But I still wake up in a sweat. I still hear Ana Lorena perform. And I wonder which of us is selling the bigger lie.

In-Flight Journal—February 6, 1997

Somewhere over the Gulf of Tehuantepec—first leg

Altitude: 34,000 feet and dropping like a broken promise

Bilking the Rich Requires Four Strategies

That's what I write across the top of the page. The ink skips, catches, then drags. Turbulence—sharp, sudden. My pen bleeds a crooked stroke that mars the line.

The air smells like overhead plastic and recirculated cologne—cheap, citrusy, someone in seat 14B probably. Sweat, too. Not mine. The nervous kind, sharp and thin, freshly made.

I shift in the seat, elbow braced against the armrest, trying to steady the journal against my thigh. The vibration hums through the fuselage like a warning—subtle but cumulative.

This isn't theft. Not really. It's alignment. Perception alchemy. It's learning their longing and selling them the lie they need to sleep at night.

The wealthy give for four reasons. Always four. Every donor I've ever met—VCs, hedge fund cowboys, third-wife-on-her-second-reincarnation—they all fit.

—

1. Immortality Seekers

They give to outrun the grave.

They want their name etched into time. A university wing, a genomic patent, a foundation with an elevator logo. Anything that outlives their liver.

Strategy: Build them a monument that never looks like a tombstone. Immortality isn't about being remembered. It's about pretending death is negotiable.

Pitch to practice:

"You're not just funding research, you're rewriting the human expiration date."

—

The plane lurches. Not gently. It felt as if something large and angry hit the belly of the fuselage.

Someone two rows back yelps. Up ahead, a can of soda spills into a seatback pocket. The hiss of carbonation hits the air like static.

I feel the slap of pressure in my sinuses, then the buckle and thud of a sudden altitude loss. My stomach stays where it was; the rest of me is down here now.

I grip the pen tighter. The line under the word Strategy is jagged.

Annoying. Not terrifying. But I keep the tray locked. I've seen enough overhead bins unhinge to know what a Samsonite swinging loose at 500 mph can do to a skull.

Still. We fly on.

—

2. Guilt-Washers

They want to be forgiven.

Not with words. With wiring. With hospitals. With wells dug in the third world by men they'll never meet. Usually ex-tobacco. Oil. Pharma. Developers and Insurance who built their mansions on poor people's leveled homes.

Strategy: Offer atonement without shame. Reframe sin as opportunity. Let the damage fund its own repair.

Pitch to practice:

"This isn't about repair—it's about redemption that works."

—

Another bounce. Overhead compartments groan. One opens. A duffel falls, hits the aisle like a corpse.

I don't flinch. But I do stop writing. The ink runs where my hand smudged the bottom of the page.

I curse softly. Not at the weather. At the smear.

Ink on sweat-slick skin, mixed with the scent of overheated plastic, sharp lime soap, and the mechanical ozone of circulated air.

—

3. Vanity Vultures

They want to be seen.

Red carpet donors. They want their name on the banner, their face next to the Dalai Lama's in a photo they'll frame over their toilet. They don't care about results. They care about resonance.

Strategy: Applause. Mirror their image back at them in marble and LED. You don't need their belief—just their brand.

Pitch to practice:

"With your leadership, this initiative becomes a movement."

—

The turbulence hits again. Harder this time.

A shriek. Overhead bin claps open. A backpack bounces down and catches a man on the shoulder.

He gasps. Everyone tenses.

The lights flicker, then dim.

I tap the tip of the pen against my knee. Count the rhythm. Anchor myself.

One. Two. Three.

The smell now is sweat, fear and burnt coffee.

We're nowhere near descent, but this plane is fighting something stronger.

—

4. True Believers

They mean it.

They see purpose in your eyes, not marketing. They cry when you talk about neuroplasticity like it's scripture. These are the ones who'll follow you into ruin if you let them.

Strategy: Echo. Don't lead—reflect. Let them feel the cause belongs to them. Give them depth without control.

Pitch to practice:

"This isn't a donation—it's alignment with your deepest purpose."

—

I cap the pen. Close the journal. Fold it into the leather satchel I keep at my feet.

We're still shaking. Still climbing. Or descending. It's hard to tell anymore. The captain's voice has gone conspicuously quiet.

The woman next to me crosses herself. Catholic, probably. Latin fingers, wedding ring. She's watching the wing like it might fall off.

She smells like rosewater and panic.

I wonder, for a flash, too brief to name, if this is it. Not just the plane. Me. If I built a life so thin, so patched, that the sky itself can tear it open without warning. Maybe this is what it feels like when the body finally catches up to the fraud the soul's been living.

No aliases to hide behind. No clever contracts or shell companies or saint's medals. Just one name, one breath, one seatbelt pressed against me while a dying engine decides if I get to pretend again tomorrow.

Maybe that's the real reason I came up here, above the clouds—not to escape the IRS or spin another hustle—but to find out if a man with three lives can survive losing all of them.

I exhale slowly through my nose. The breath tastes stale.

This is nothing. I've been through worse. A back alley in Argentina. A boardroom in Cleveland. A backhanded threat inside a Geneva bank.

Air is just another element you learn to negotiate.

The rich don't give because they believe in good.

They give because they believe in themselves.

And my job?

My job is to become the thing they wish they believed in more.

Even if it means bleeding ink on a shaking plane full of people praying to gods, I've already outgrown

In-flight Journal—February 7, 1997

Over Panama, descending into Managua. Second leg.

Scalping Salvation: Four Market Trading Strategies for Harvesting Donations

They think it's funding healing. Conscious evolution. The great epigenetic awakening.

But I'm not here to save them. I'm here to scalp the windfall. To strip the donations of their ceremonial robes and march them, quietly, into my offshore trading ecosystem.

This isn't theft. This is orchestration. This is a strategy.

Four market states. Four ways to win.

1. Bull Market: Higher Highs, Higher Lows

The rich love this phase. The news is good, optimism grows contagious, and stupid money flows like sangria at a Sonoma retreat.

Strategy: Momentum scalping. Small margins, quick exits. Let the illusion of growth fund the operation. Skim 2–3% off each cycle like a monk shaving a coin in the dark.

Operational move: Route donations through the Curaçao shell, mask trades under the nonprofit's "sustainability fund." Use DAO-simulated reports—nobody checks what they don't understand.

Mantra: Ride their hope. Exit before it peaks.

Before moving on to the second trading strategy, something odd haunts me. It is something I've noticed about this La Costeña flight crew.

They don't flinch. Not when the nose dipped like a diving hawk. Not when the engine stuttered so hard I counted the seconds between thrusts. Not when the panel above row nine cracked open with a groan like a crypt yawning for air.

They smiled. They poured juice into cracked plastic cups.

Like this is how the sky behaves in Nicaragua.

Like turbulence is an old friend who just barges in without knocking.

I shake it off and return to my strategies.

2. Bear Market: Lower Highs, Lower Lows

Everyone's afraid. Even the wolves turn sheepish. But fear is fertile.

Strategy: Inverse ETF siphoning. Liquidity crunch means higher spreads. Take short-term positions that bet against the market, but paper them as "temporary defensive allocations." No one questions hedging.

Operational move: Move funds to the Panama account. Pair a dummy loss report with a hard-pivot "counter-cyclical" statement for the board. Say it's protecting donor funds. They'll nod. Fear makes sheep obedient.

Mantra: Bet against the faith. Blame the storm.

I cap the pen for a moment and look the airplane over from tail to nose.

It's not one sound. It's a full orchestra of protest.

The propeller stutters as if it's rethinking its life.

A high-pitched electrical whine stabs the cabin inhabitants like tinnitus.

Floorboards rattle with the rhythm of my pulse—no, faster. Out of sync. Resembling Morse code from a dying god.

Then—silence.

Not peaceful silence.

The type of silence predators make before they strike.

I feel it in my chest. I can't breathe. No one speaks. Even the baby two rows back stops crying.

The engine starts again with a growl like gravel under bone. Everyone exhales.

Except me.

I'm calm. But not still. Not stupid.

I know how systems fail—this one's stitched together with rot and routine. I pull the cap off the pen with my teeth.

3. Consolidation Market: Trapped Between a Ceiling and a Floor

The market stalls. Sideways chop. Smart money sits it out.

Strategy: Delta neutral scalping. Long and short simultaneously on uncorrelated sectors. Let the volatility bleed out through options. Your win isn't growth—it's the illusion of stewardship.

Operational move: Roll trades in hourly cycles. Use a rebalancer shell in Nevada to justify high-frequency commissions. Cloak gains in "consulting fees" to a Belizean LLC.

Mantra: When nothing moves, move everything faster.

4. Shorting: The Quiet Art of Decline

Not just betting against stocks—betting against myths. Against companies, currencies, countries, even people.

Strategy: Target hype. Gut it. Use donations to borrow shares through a Cayman mirror, dump into the market, then buy back at a loss. Cloak it as "strategic exit." Meanwhile, extract the spread into the trading ledger of a St. Kitts holding corp.

Operational move: Use delays in nonprofit financial reporting to mask 90-day positions. Nobody notices until Q3. By then, the money's recycled as "forward-committed programmatic disbursement."

Mantra: Profit from decay. Preach resilience.

I look around the cabin again. The cabin decor that still screams 1974. Floral vinyl on the seats, cracked and sweat-stained. Seatbelt buckle from a defunct insurance firm.

The safety card instructions laminated in a decade I barely survived.

The overhead bins creak, warped from tropical heat. When they pop open mid-flight, a purse drops hard onto the aisle and doesn't move.

No one stands to fix it. Not even the crew.

They've seen worse. I return to my journal.

Four plays. Four masks. One gospel: Appear sacred. Trade ruthless.

I close the notebook—but not before my pen jerks violently, dragging an ink scar across the margin. The plane shudders again, deep this time, a hard drop like a body flinching in sleep. The ink smears. My handwriting, ruined. My wrist throbs from gripping too tight.

Mountains close on the left wing—too close. I wonder if the pilot's aiming between clouds or cliffs.

The descent isn't coordinated—it's instinctual. Spiritual. It's like he's feeling the landing through the soles of his shoes.

The runway shows up late, jagged, narrow, flanked by mango trees and children with soccer balls. The wheels hit like a courtroom gavel.

No bounce. No grace.

Just done.

We taxi over broken concrete. We stop. The door hisses. I step out into humid air that smells like diesel and wet bark.

I'm sweating, but not from fear.

Not entirely.

The air hits different here. Thicker. Sincere. The pace is like people used to waiting for someone who never shows up.

The driver holds a sign that just says "Dr. Benton." I figured he spelled my name close enough. He's thirty, maybe younger, with the leathery skin of a man who's spent more time in sun than shadow. He says my name like it's both a question and a warning.

"Bienvenido, doctor. Yo soy Marvin. El coche está aquí."

The way he says it, clipped and fast, I catch maybe two or three out of five words. But I nod like a man who belongs.

The vehicle is a dusty Toyota Hilux with a cracked windshield and a small sticker of the Virgin Mary weeping into a cigarette. I throw my duffel in the back and climb in.

He talks the whole way—pointing out things I don't ask about. Rivers. Churches. Political scars that still have blood under them. I let him talk. Let the rhythm of the country slide into my bones.

The hotel is a low-lying concrete retreat wrapped in bougainvillea and shadows. American in design. Latin in soul. The kind of place NGO executives use when they want to pretend they're roughing it.

I sign in under my real name. First time in years. The woman at the front desk reads my passport like it's a confession. I can feel the curtain being pulled back already. No more Emanuel Torres. No more Gabriel Montoya.

Room 304. End of the hall. The AC buzzes like it's got a grudge against God.

I drop my bag. Strip to the waist. I should shower. I should unpack. I need to call the Foundation rep and confirm tomorrow's meetings.

Instead, I sit on the edge of the bed. Outside, a rooster is crowing like it's his last song on Earth.

The city below moves in lazy swells—motorbikes, tin-roof echoes, the ghosts of revolutions still bleeding into graffiti.

I light a cigarette. Thinking of Ana Lorena. She's probably still filming.

Probably still whispering into a webcam, telling anonymous men to send tributes and pretend it means something.

I stare out over Managua and tell myself the truth:

I don't need love.

I need plausible deniability.

And a plan.

Because tomorrow, I stop being a ghost.

Tomorrow, I become someone real.

And if I screw this up?

I don't get a fourth identity.

I get a prison cell with my real name on it.

Chapter 12: Nirvana by Design
Net worth $1,017,800

July 1997—San Diego, California

Tuesday. It starts with silence.

The kind that isn't empty—but taut. Like a violin string pulled tight across a godless altar.

Three monitors burn in the dark, their low glow reflecting off the brass trim of the desk like stained glass in a criminal church. The numbers on-screen dance in perfect tempo—red to green, green to gold. The offshore accounts tick forward. Not in leaps. Not in explosions. But in measured, monastic breath.

I lean back into the leather chair. Not a throne. A cockpit.

The fabric of my dress shirt sticks to my back. The room is warm—too warm—but I haven't opened a window in two days. Outside, the Pacific hammers the shore with a steady, exhausted rhythm. The market of the sea, relentless as ever.

On the desk: a crystal tumbler. The Lagavulin inside is two fingers deep and untouched. Smoke spirals up, faint. Peat and iodine. It smells like a bonfire soaked in memory.

I click to open the Cayman interface. The shell company bleeds out another passive gain. Forty-eight thousand this morning. Mostly clean. Masked through NGO consulting "transfers." The Belize fund shows even better—sixty-three, thanks to the short squeeze. And none of it links.

Lama Sundra's foundation. My foundation. Thầy Nhất's Nicaraguan temple initiative.

Three separate empires of purpose. And flawless detachment characterizes every cent moving between them.

That's the brilliance of it. Not that the money flows.

But that it flows without ever touching the same fingerprints twice.

The IRS has nothing. The AG in Sacramento has nothing. Even the internal accountants, the ones who believe in what we're building, wouldn't know the difference between divine intention and derivative trading if it lit their yoga mat on fire.

I sip the Scotch. It cuts my tongue like a lit prayer.

My fingers hover above the keyboard. I enter the last transfer of the day. Thirty-eight thousand reallocated from the Nicaraguan "Spiritual Literacy Endowment" to a dummy research hub in Austin, Texas, run by a Korean neurologist who hasn't taught a class since 1991.

It routes through Curaçao. Hits St. Kitts. Backdoors into the Nevada rebalancer. And shows up on the balance sheet as a deferred consulting expense related to cross-cultural trauma mapping.

That's what it says.

What it means is: I've made another eighty-six thousand dollars today without opening my mouth.

The air smells like hot metal and dying sandalwood. The candle burned out hours ago, leaving a string of black wax that curls like a question no one will ever answer.

I reach for the mouse. My hand trembles—just a little. Not fear. Not even adrenaline.

Satiated.

It's working.

The architecture holds. The trades land. The reports bluff.

And I am—finally, unmistakably—in control of something that was never meant to be tamed.

Outside, the street is quiet. No sirens. No knocks.

And here, the only sound is the quiet click of money becoming memory.

Later in August, 1997. It starts, as these things often do, with a compliment that doesn't blink.

Sunday afternoon. The abbey's mainline rings twice before Teresa picks up—she's been screening all media since the wellness profiles started appearing in Vanity Fair and the LA Times. But this one has pedigree. The Atlantic. A piece on "the transcendent economy of wellness." Her phrase, not ours.

Teresa forwards the call with a clipped warning: "She's charming. Very charming. Say less than nothing."

I invite her to lunch.

We meet at a bistro perched like an eyrie over the Del Mar cliffs—white stucco, sun-bleached tablecloths, waiters who serve with the disinterest of the highly paid. The Pacific unspools behind her in wide, endless blue, a visual lullaby for men who don't want to admit they're being watched.

She arrives on time, which I already don't trust.

Linen pants. Frayed-blazer sleeves—intentional, branded humility. Her scent is a trace of neroli and vetiver, faint but curated. She's the kind of woman who's been to Bali twice and called it pilgrimage. Her smile is efficient. Her handshake dry.

Her recorder stays in her pocket. A performance of discretion.

"You've built something extraordinary," she says, stirring her lemon water like she's coaxing a confession out of citrus. "A faith-adjacent revenue structure that doesn't feel extractive."

I nod, as if that makes sense. "It's about alignment," I offer.

She lifts an eyebrow. "It always is. But let's be honest—people don't give millions because they feel aligned. They give because you make them feel inevitable."

She's good. Better than I'd expected.

I like her more for it.

And less.

"You're not writing a profile," I say, cutting my salmon with practiced calm. "Profiles start with names. You've barely said mine."

She blinks, once. Slow.

"Oh?" she asks, fork suspended like a question mark.

"You're triangulating," I say. "Your questions are soft, but your shape is sharp. You're not looking at me—you're tracing the negative space around me."

Her eyes don't widen. They narrow. The right move.

She sets down her fork.

"You mean the separation between your foundation, Lama Sundra's retreat fund, and the Nicaraguan sanctuary initiative?"

I breathe in through my nose, slow. The salt air stings. She's done her homework.

"Three distinct legal entities," I reply, keeping my tone as clean as the plate I've just emptied. "There are no board members in common. No consolidated audits. No cross-border liabilities. There are three EINs. Three missions. Three geographies."

She leans in, dropping her voice just enough to imply intimacy.

"And yet," she says, "every major donor in the last six months has touched all three. Indirectly. Sequentially. Electric current through a closed loop."

I smile, eyes steady. "Coincidence."

She laughs—not loud, but honest enough to cut. "Coincidence," she repeats, rolling the word like a rosary bead made of arsenic.

No recorder. No notebook. Just a smile lined with teeth and the memory of someone who won't forget a syllable.

"Off the record," she murmurs, wiping her fingers on the linen napkin. "Do you ever worry it might unravel?"

I sip the espresso—burnt, bitter, good. My eyes drift to the horizon where the surf slaps the cliff side like it's making a point.

"No," I say. "I don't build things that unravel. I build things that evolve. Three not-for-profit corporations hire me as CFO or CEO because I help people find peace within a world where people want them to suffer. That's why they give. Not because they trust me—but because I don't need them to."

She stands without saying another word. No handshake. Just the sharp scent of intention and Tommy Girl perfume trailing behind her.

As she walks away, her linen pants sway like a curtain parting before a revelation.

She's already writing the story.

But she won't find the seam.

Because I haven't hidden the bridge, burned it.

And left behind smoke shaped like structure.

That's the trick. That's the architecture.

The journalist was never a threat.

She was the canary. The soft-singing harbinger.

The threat is inside.

And it's already breathing my air.

It arrives folded in clean white stock, uncreased, unsigned—just a board request printed in sharp helvetica, the type used by men who don't raise their voice because their authority already hums in every serif.

Subject line: Request for Transparency—Strategic Audit Review (Non-Financial).

They never call it what it is.

The envelope smells faintly of recycled paper and toner heat. Institutional. Sterile. No fingerprints, but I can feel the nervous sweat of whoever sent it. This wasn't approved unanimously.

I crack the seal with a letter opener shaped like a miniature katana—a gift from a Japanese hedge fund manager who thought he was being poetic. I kept it because sometimes violence needs form.

Inside: a formal suggestion—no, a demand—that we perform an internal audit. Not from the IRS. Not from the feds. From within. A rogue board member. One of the minor ones. Too smart to ignore, too small to threaten me directly. The audit is focused on "alignment of donor intent, procedural transparency, and operational integrity across international partnerships."

They're coming for the seam.

But there isn't one.

I lean back in the leather chair—top-grain, stitched by men who've never flown coach—and stare out the window of the office. The sun's coming down over the Pacific like it owes someone money. Low, wide, indifferent.

The ocean doesn't care if you're clean. It cares if you can float.

I spin the letter between my fingers. The texture is soft, but the tone is steel.

They want records. Ledger trails. Meeting notes. Understanding how funds flow is their objective. They want to catch a glimpse behind the velvet curtain, but they don't know the stage is deeper than they can see.

There was a time when I used to believe the map was the territory. That if I could name it, ledger it, margin it—I owned it. But something shifts now. Not in the market. In me. It hits like a wave I can't hedge against: maybe all I've built is just another craving. A prettier kind. A smarter kind. But craving all the same. And craving never ends. It just hides in sharper suits.

So I give them the show.

We host them in the San Diego suite. Windows tall, espresso black, air like chilled confidence. They sit in those stiff-backed ergonomic chairs we keep for visitors—chairs that keep your spine upright and your lies rehearsed.

I open with a joke. A small one. Something about accounting being tantric—slow, deliberate, full of trust. One of them laughs. Others don't. Perfect.

Screens lower from the ceiling. I click the remote. Slide by slide: donations logged, trades cloaked as "impact investments," the shell layers broken down into trustable visuals. The Belize consulting contract. The Curaçao sustainability fund. The Panamanian "Educational Futures Asset Pool."

Each entity perfectly legal. Each transaction airtight. No overlap. No leaks. The language is neutral; the tone composed. I don't explain—I let the paperwork explain itself. I speak only to correct their assumptions.

And they have many.

The lead on the audit—Ron something, ex-finance, still wears cufflinks—asks why we don't cross-report between the three major projects.

I sip water.

"Because we don't cross-fund," I say. "Transparency starts with clean separation."

He nods. It's the kind of nod that feels like he's filing something away for later.

Then he says it.

"We just want to be sure this doesn't blow up. You've built something big, Mark. And big things get attention."

I lean forward.

"I don't build things to survive attention," I say. "I build them to outlast scrutiny."

That line sits heavy. The room stays quiet long enough for the HVAC to sound like a threat. Then someone clears their throat and it breaks.

The audit wraps.

They leave with packets that weigh exactly as much as they're supposed to. No more, no less. Nothing to fear, nothing to find.

I close the door and walk back to the window. The sky's gone darker now. Blood orange. Fading.

I feel the tension in my shoulder blades loosen. Just a little.

It wasn't the IRS.

It wasn't the Attorney General.

It wasn't a reporter with a flash drive and a vengeance.

It was the family, knocking on the walls of the mansion they helped build, wondering if the foundation had shifted.

And what did they find?

Just walls.

Just smooth—polished stone.

Because the seams don't exist.

I didn't hide the money.

I orchestrated it.

Each piece plays its part. Lama Sundra's trust. The Nicaragua project. My foundation.

Never once touching.

Always singing in harmony.

This is the new gospel.

And they just heard the first hymn.

The actual proof that you've won isn't the money.

It's how you spend it without leaving footprints.

The Abbey has scheduled its gala for Friday, but tonight is Thursday, and I am field-testing success.

Without red carpets. No donors. No monks with scripted gratitude.

Just the penthouse level of a private property in Torrey Pines, doors locked, lights low, kitchen staff imported from Baja Norte, and a bottle of Bruichladdich Black Art that retails for more than most people's monthly rent. I didn't buy it. It was a gift. That's the key.

Nothing I own appears to be mine.

The room is full of men who know the game. Portfolio chameleons. Former covert ops turned financial strategists. One used to run black bag logistics for a defense contractor; now he's got a wellness company that helps hedge fund managers microdose psilocybin between earnings calls.

No one here asks where the money came from.

They ask what you did with it.

One of them—gray-bearded, black-suited, glass of Barolo sloshing like blood in a velvet glove—leans over and says, "You've made it work, Bertrand. Clean flow. Fast. No regulatory whiplash. That's rare."

I give him nothing but a nod. Let him keep talking.

He does.

"You know the joke, right?" he grins. "If you wanna hide a body, become a nonprofit."

They laugh. All of them. The laughter men use to confess to crimes they haven't committed yet.

Outside, the Pacific shrugs against the cliffs, moonlight skimming the surface like a rumor it doesn't want to confirm.

I pass around Cohibas that aren't for sale anywhere in the continental U.S. My name isn't on the import manifest. Nothing ever is. The man who gifted them is long gone, his signature still looping inside a numbered Swiss lockbox.

This is the layer the IRS never sees. Because it isn't real estate. It isn't cars or art or stocks. It's access. Flavor is what it is. It's smoke and silence.

I spend from my ghost accounts. Use donation rebates routed through consulting shells in Anguilla. Pay the cooks in cash. Tip the valet in cash carried by someone else.

The money moves without my fingerprints.

I move through the world like I've always belonged.

This is the moment I know: I'm not just holding wealth.

I'm breathing it.

No need for the purchase of a jet. I charter one under a different name. No yacht—just a corporate membership that lets me walk aboard like I was born to salt and teak.

The key isn't ownership.

It's permission.

And I give it to myself now.

A man pulls me aside. Leans close. His breath smells like scorched oak and ambition.

"You could scale this," he says. "Ten countries. Double blind. Wrap it in academic partnerships and call it conscious capitalism. We'd get the Saudi wellness funds involved. You want that?"

I let the silence stretch.

Not because I'm unsure.

Because I want him to sweat just enough to respect the next word out of my mouth.

"No," I say.

He waits.

I smile. "Not yet."

The party moves. I drift. But I feel it. In my spine. In my blood.

This isn't the high.

This is the plateau.

The long, wide ledge where gods walk before they fall.

But I'm not falling.

Not tonight.

Tonight, I exhale. Light another Rocky Patel Toro.

And think of tomorrow.

We take the cruise out of Puerto Vallarta.

Not a carnival deck full of drunks and discount buffets. This is different. Charter-only. Unlisted in civilian registries. A 180-foot stealth-class yacht retrofitted by a Japanese billionaire with a love for naval silence and impossible acoustics.

It slides through the water like a question no one dares to ask.

Ana Lorena joins me. I fly her in first class—not because I have to, but because I can. She arrives in a silk wrap and no jewelry, her hair tied up like a rebellion waiting for nightfall. The minute she stepped aboard, I knew I'd made the right call.

The crew is minimal, discreet. The champagne is dry, cold, and unlabeled. I paid for everything through a consulting fund routed out of Cyprus. The yacht? Owned by a media start-up that technically doesn't exist outside of an annual retreat for "mindful creatives." I am, legally, a guest.

I spend nothing.

And I spare no expense.

Dinner is fresh catch, shaved truffle, dark chocolate grown in volcanic soil. The cutlery is matte black. The table is rosewood. The sea beyond the deck rails is velvet and endless.

We toast Noé and Teresa's engagement—though I don't let the night orbit them. This isn't their celebration. It's mine. I just let them borrow the shine.

They're grateful.

Everyone is grateful.

That's how I've structured it.

As the meal ends and the glasses get lazier, one guest—Reid, a partner in a firm that arranges biotech joint ventures between Norway and São Paulo—leans back in his chair, eyes soft from mezcal.

He asks it casually. Like it's nothing.

"Hey—why does your assistant always book your travel through a legal group in Bermuda?"

The question hovers just above the table, catching the breeze but not the tone.

I smile. The kind that buys time and warns the table to enjoy the moment while it lasts.

"Because," I say, "I believe in local expertise."

It gets a small laugh. One of those polite, corporate sounds that men make when they don't want to be the last one to laugh. But I see it behind Reid's eyes now. He's not drunk. He's testing.

That's fine. I respect the move.

I pass him a refill. Mezcal with the faint taste of smoked lime and cartel forgiveness.

"You think I'm laundering?" I say lightly, privately.

He shrugs. "I think you're smart."

I let the silence thicken just enough.

Then: "What I do is simple. I keep three projects insulated. Each with its own mission, its own reporting, its own audit trail. Lama Sundra's fund handles rural mindfulness infrastructure. My foundation supports U.S. university research. Nicaragua's project is purely environmental and trauma-focused. None of them touch."

He raises a brow. "But you touch all of them."

"That's the game," I say. "No one gets indicted for being consistent."

He studies me. Then he smiles.

And sips.

No more questions.

Later, I stand alone at the bow. The air tastes like salt and steel. Ana Lorena is below deck, already in a drunken sleep. The ocean hums like a satisfied machine.

And me?

I feel it. Not the wealth.

The structure.

I wonder, for a flicker of a second, if this is what kings felt the night before their murder in their sleep—not fear, not guilt, but the aching certainty that nothing they built could follow them into the dark.

Structure isn't salvation.

It's scaffolding for a pyre.

The quiet miracle of a system so precise, so airless, so beautiful that even my enemies would hesitate to tear it down.

Because it works.

The IRS won't touch me.

The journalists can't reach me.

The donors adore me.

And the money?

It keeps arriving.

Wired through belief.

Disbursed through precision.

Multiplied through leverage.

And masked by a faith I no longer have to fake.

I lean against the rail; the cold biting my palms, and I wonder—not if I'll be caught.

But if I'll ever want to stop.

~~~

It's two minutes before 8 a.m., early March 1998 and the abbey is already alive—quietly, like a body stretching before it remembers it's human and the leg cramps set in again. The sun breaks through the coastal haze in ribbons, catching dew on the succulents and bougainvillea that border the back garden. This is the only place in San Diego that still remembers how to hold silence.

We've experienced many hectic days in preparation. Seventeen guests. One bathroom broken, fixed. Thirty meditation cushions cleaned, fluffed, spaced with the geometry of reverence. Ken Kuang arrives before dawn, hands me a thermos of pu-erh, eyes already scanning the guest list like it owes him an apology. He doesn't speak much—he never has—but when he does, it's a signal. Today, it's just a nod. All systems go.

Most of our attendees are locals. Carlsbad, Solana Beach, a few from as far north as Ventura. But this week's buzz pulled in a couple
~~~

from Juneau. Juneau. As if whatever's cracking loose inside people has no latitude. They're here for epigenetics, they say. For the mind-body frontier. But I know the truth. They're here to remember something the modern world tricked them into forgetting.

I take the long way to the garden. Past the small koi pond. Past the circle of white stones that used to be a chapel until it burned, or was torn down—I can't remember which. The garden unfolds before me like a held breath.

They're already waiting.

Seventeen men and women in loose clothes, borrowed silence, and the soft twitch of unprocessed grief behind their eyes. Some sit with perfect posture. Some fidget, blinking against the sun. One guy in a Patagonia vest keeps checking his watch like peace runs on a schedule.

They all look up when I step onto the polished gravel path.

I don't speak.

I let the sound of the wind through eucalyptus take the first word.

And then I take my place in the center.

The silence deepens.

This is the moment.

My palms rest on my thighs. My breath slows.

The first bell rings.

A second, slower.

The third follows like an echo from a deeper room.

I begin.

"Let your body settle—not into perfection, but into presence. Sit like a flame on the wick—upright, yes, but not rigid. Still, but not fixed.

"You are not holding the body. You are letting the body rest in itself."

The wind moves through the eucalyptus with the dry hush of parchment turning.

"Let the inhale find you.

"Let the exhale leave you untouched."

Pause. I see the light flashing on the corner of the office window. Letting me know my emergency phone is ringing. Offshore lawyer calling. Something is wrong. I have to stay focused. He'll have to wait.

The hush thickens. A car door slams faintly three blocks away. Then quiet again.

"As you sit, the mind will move. That's its nature. It will want to know what's next. It may chase the taste of this morning's coffee. Or draft tomorrow's apology email before you even remember who it's for."

A low, distant rumble begins—an airliner overhead. Not loud. Just present, like a god that's stopped speaking but still hovers.

"You may hear the plane above us. Good.

"You are not the sound. You are the awareness of the sound."

The jet passes, slow and steady, like time's own pulse.

"This isn't distraction. It's invitation. Each interruption is not a mistake. It's a bell—not a barrier.

"It shows you where your mind hides."

A long pause here. Just breathe and breeze. The chirp of something in the garden. The scrape of someone adjusting their spine on gravel.

"When you realize you've been distracted, you're already awake.

"That moment—that click of awareness—is not failure. It's brilliance.

"Thoughts are not enemies. They're fireflies on the edge of a forest path.

"You need not chase them.

"Just witness the flicker. And remember: you are alive."

Another long pause. The garden holds its breath. Then—

A siren, far off, howling through some inland street. Closer. Louder. Rising. It rushes past with authority, then fades into static.

"If you hear the siren, good. You didn't choose it. It entered. It passed. That's all.

"You're not in the siren. You're in the noticing."

Soft silence returns. Someone clears their throat. The gravel crunches under a shifted foot.

"You don't have to silence the world to know peace.

"You just have to stop believing that silence is peace."

A single bell sounds. Low and round, like a lake forming inside a mountain.

"Now we sit."

Ten minutes of silence, newly defined, follows. Eyes lowered. Hands resting. The garden breathes. The light blinking again.

"If a memory comes, watch it gently.

"If boredom arises, bow to it.

"If restlessness stirs, smile—as if it were an old friend arriving early."

Time moves like breath. Not forward. Not back.

Eventually, the last bell rings.

"Nothing went wrong if you were distracted.

"You only proved you were capable of waking up again. And again. And again.

"That's the practice.

"The mind's brilliance is not in its silence, but in its return."

A long bell. Then two more.

The last hangs in the air like a note no one dares end.

"I have to go," I say to Ken as he steps into the center to lead the retreat. His face becomes tense. His jaw drops. "Sorry, Ken, I have to go."

Before I call the lawyer, I contact Schubach Aviation to have them ready a crew in thirty minutes. Destination either Panama or British Virgin Islands. I let them know when I arrive. Then I call the lawyer. Twenty minutes later I'm in the air.

The hum inside the cabin is almost meditative—deep, balanced, tuned to disappear. Leather and lacquer. Polished teak folding tray. Cut crystal tumblers set in chrome recesses. The only sound besides the engines is the hiss of altitude and the gentle pop of cabin pressure modulating through the air ducts.

I lean back into the cream leather seat, eyes half-lidded, shoes off, a folded cashmere blanket resting over one knee. The Gulfstream's altitude monitor reads 43,000 feet. Somewhere below us, the isthmus narrows. In forty minutes, we'll descend into Panama, like myth rewritten as arrival.

The satellite phone rings once—then again, slower.

I already know who it is.

I press the receiver to my ear.

"Go," I say.

A sigh on the other end. Legal, brittle, cautious.

"I hope you're sitting down," the voice says. He doesn't know I'm reclining in a jet worth more than some countries' GDP.

"Is this about Curaçao?" I ask, half to test him, half because I already feel it in the atmosphere—the laws are changing. Again.

"No. Well—yes. And not just them. Luxembourg's tightening. Lichtenstein is drafting legislation. The Caymans are quiet—but that's what worries me."

I say nothing. Let him pour the poison first.

"Panama's been flagged for soft cooperation with U.S. inquiries. Not a list, not yet. But the banks are being watched. Wire movement between certain nodes—Curacao, Geneva, BVI—is now considered a red flag if the timing looks irregular."

Irregular.

The word tastes like iron.

"And let me guess," I say. "My timing looks like a jazz solo."

He exhales. "You're trading at frequency levels that don't match donor behavior. It's not just the amount, it's the latency. Too fast, too sharp. It's not 1995 anymore. Regulators are hiring coders now."

I shift in my seat, a strange vertigo slipping into my bones. It's not fear—not yet. It's the deeper thing that follows it: recognition. Like when you dream you're being chased, and suddenly realize you're the one who taught the monster how to run.

The system isn't hunting me.

It's learning me.

I sit up, slowly. My knees crack. I pour a half-inch of Glenfarclas from the decanter beside me.

The taste is wood smoke, chocolate covered cherries, and black licorice. I swirl it, but don't sip.

"Are we exposed?" I ask.

A silence follows. The kind that doesn't trust itself to speak too soon.

"Not yet. But they're building tools that won't need subpoenas. New FinCEN protocols include mapping metadata—server lag, routing architecture. And your offshore shells ... they're starting to look like lace."

"Tell me the firewall still holds," I say, voice low.

"It does. But don't lean on it. Some of your architecture is built on latency."

"I know," I say, tapping the rim of the glass. "The illusion of slowness buys time. But time's catching up."

He shifts tone—softer now. Less the technician, more the advisor with a war story.

"Mark ... there's a reason the old players are winding down. The new compliance acts are back dooring through payment processors.

It's no longer about Swiss secrecy. If you can't explain the velocity, they'll fabricate motive."

I stare out the jet's porthole. The sky is black at the edges now—like we're flying into space instead of toward Panama.

"And?" I ask.

"You need to unwind. Not everything. Just the layers. The opaque stuff. Keep the Panama fund visible. Make the BVI account your 'anchor donor holding.' Fold Curaçao into a DAF platform in the States—something Chase will underwrite. We'll build a new cover story around it. Spiritual legacy, eco-mission, trauma science."

"And Sundra's?"

"Keep it clean. Keep it local. Make it look like the origin, not the laundromat."

A long pause.

I sip the whisky now. Let it coat the inside of my mouth.

"You know what the problem is?" I say.

"What."

"I finally made it real. The money. The structure. The pitch. The belief. All of it. And now it's the infrastructure that's the risk, not the crime."

"That's how it ends," he says. "Not with a bust. With a new law that makes yesterday's genius tomorrow's indictment."

I hang up.

Let the phone rest in the receiver cradle like it's holding its breath.

Outside, the clouds shift. Thunderheads on the horizon. I watch them. They don't look angry. They look inevitable.

I glance down at the notebook on the tray table.

A new page.

March 4, 1998—Gulfstream en route to Panama City

Journal Entry

They're closing the loopholes. Not all at once. Not with force. With latency. With architecture. With connection speeds and metadata fingerprints. They're not chasing me with badges—they're auditing me with silence.

The rich still believe in the myth. The donors still call. The meditation retreats are full. But the infrastructure—the shell that holds it all—is starting to hum wrong.

I may have to burn some of the web. Let the illusion flicker out in select places.

But not yet.

Not while the sky still makes space for this jet.

Not while the descent into Panama still feels like purpose.

And not while I'm still the only one who understands how to turn their longing into liquidity.

—

Next morning. Outdoor cafe. I'm eating a half peeled banana. The lawyer walks past me like he doesn't know who I am. Three men in matching blue suits in tight formation follow behind.

Must be feds. Emergency protocols.

Three streets north, I check into the hotel and pick up the messages he's left me.

—Stay out of sight until Tuesday. Come to my office at 16:00.

Long delays mean time on the beach.But Tuesday comes.

The lawyer finishes the meeting with a figure I don't like.

"$180,000, minimum. That's just to get the new Panama stacks up, make them airtight. Nominees, silent directors, compliance backfills going back three years—if we want legitimacy on paper, it has to look like it always existed."

"And next year?" I ask.

He doesn't answer at first. I hear the flick of his Zippo.

"We'll be back at it. The systems are evolving faster than the regulators. But the regulators ... they've started hiring the guys who built those systems. That's the shift."

The room at the Bristol smells like cigar ash and citrus polish. I crack the window an inch and pour myself a double espresso from the chrome La Pavoni I had flown in last year. The hiss of the machine sounds like a serpent giving advice.

Strategy Layer One: Entity Fragmentation

Each foundation gets its own shell—distinct IBCs set up under unrelated nominees. Names you wouldn't recognize unless you used to drink with trade ministers at the Gamboa Yacht Club.

The trick isn't hiding the money.

The trick is making the structure so tedious that no regulator wants to unravel it.

One entity feeds a second as "fiscal sponsor." That second donates to a third's "emergency research initiative," which just happens to lease its servers from the fourth's side project in machine learning meditation.

You want to find the money? You'll need two tax attorneys, a linguist, and a tolerance for recursive headaches.

Strategy Layer Two: The Ameritrade Infiltration

I ditch the boutique trading firms. Too bespoke. Too noticed.

By 1998, Ameritrade's interface is crude but effective—speedy for its time, real-time data, and they'd just introduced 15-second refresh rates for active traders. Rumors of high-speed internet over DSL and cable television are abundant but not available. I'm stuck with 56kbps dial up. That's my window.

Each IBC gets its own Ameritrade account, each with different "donation objectives" for the IRS to read later—clean water, educational robotics, neurofeedback for veterans.

But the real engine is swing trading.

In and out of volatile tech plays before they stabilize. I treat Amazon like a jungle gym, Yahoo like a speedboat, and eBay like it owes me rent.

Ameritrade doesn't flag intra-account movements fast enough. So I transfer stock positions between accounts at valuation cliffs. Wash trades on paper—perfectly legal—while I scalp the float gains into dormant cash positions.

Then I re-inflate the narrative: "Investment gains held for future disbursement cycles."

What I'm really doing?

Scalping the zeitgeist and laundering it through purpose.

Cayman and Panama for liquidity.

Luxembourg and Switzerland for long-term parking.

The returns get routed through a high-fee advisory firm in Zug that specializes in "legacy protection," which is code for we don't ask who built the castle, we just help you furnish it quietly.

Each repatriated chunk gets funneled into clean, boring things: hotel real estate trusts, timber portfolios, pollution credits.

But one of them?

One account in Zurich gets a monthly $9,700 wire—a psychological play.

Every month.

Twelve times a year.

Like a heartbeat that never triggers the stethoscope.

Every new shell company gets a $1 invoice from a defunct telecom startup in the Philippines.

Why?

Because when the IRS or a foreign auditor sees "foreign telecom consulting" on a line item for one dollar, they always think the real money is somewhere else. It's too absurd to question.

But it's actually a tripwire.

If anyone ever flags that invoice, I know they're onto me.

I keep a Rolodex of fax numbers that don't go anywhere. Random numbers in Argentina, Moldova, and Saskatchewan.

They're listed on fake consultant letters attached to the foundations.

The feds can send all the verification requests they want. And they do. The numbers ring to nothing. The real paperwork lives in three separate safety deposit boxes—Mexico City, Lisbon, and a strip mall branch of HSBC in Guam.

The coffee I drink when I'm being watched?

Espresso, neat. Double.

When the heat is off?

Cafe con leche with a cinnamon stick and too much sugar.

Ana Lorena knows the difference.

If I ever ask for sugar twice in a row, she knows to pack.

The espresso steam fogs the corner of my glasses. My shirt clings slightly to the small of my back—Panama's humidity doesn't wait for you to get ready.

Downstairs, the hotel lobby piano plays something jazzy and off-tempo—an American pianist with more nerve than nuance.

I light a cigar, Cohiba Siglo VI, and open the Ameritrade console.

Three trades already clear. My Zurich account pings back with a timestamp confirmation.

Everything's running smooth.

For now.

Ten days later, I return to San Diego.

The house is cool, still, spooky quiet. No Ana. No scent of incense or the faint whir of her streaming rig humming from the back room. Just filtered air and hardwood silence.

On the desk in my upstairs study sits a single envelope.

Not government-issue. Not a threat.

Worse.

The accountant.

My name written in sharp, efficient pen. Postmarked three days ago.

I open it. The paper inside smells like toner and panic.

"Client Note: Urgent."

Then in bold:

"The Massachusetts escrow from last fall has decayed. Held at your instruction for five months. $190,000 is now $27,441.62.

"Awaiting direction for tax disbursement. Please advise."

No explanation. No apologies. Just math and a countdown.

It's not embezzlement. It's entropy.

The market cooled. The trade stalled. The liquidity pool dried up and took most of the illusion with it.

I sit in the leather chair by the window, the city breathing beneath me. Somewhere below, a siren stretches its cry across the boulevard like a torn vowel.

I stare at the number again.

Twenty-seven grand.

I owe six times that before the end of the week.

And the only accounts flush enough to cover it belong to a different name, in a different country, under a mission that can't know this one even exists.

I close the envelope.

The gears in my head ground—slow at first, then surgical.

I'll have to move funds sideways. Quietly. Without leaving the popcorn trail that connects two otherwise clean foundations.

No transfers. No wire noise.

I need sleight-of-hand.

I need smoke and magic.

And I'll need it by Thursday.

Journal entry, March 3, 1998.

In the name of fairness, freedom dies. Not for the rich, but for those who never crafted the loophole in the first place.

Chapter 13: The Third Noble Truth
Net worth $5,963,722

At twelve years of age, I learned that flight doesn't come from wings—it comes from the wind-up. With enough horsepower, you can make a brick fly.

Balsa wood kits from the corner hobby shop. Cheap, warping fuselages. If you had money, you flew with a Cox .049 engine and real nitro fuel—ripped the sky open with noise. But I was poor. My aircraft flew on rubber bands, thick ones, coiled until they hissed with tension. My hands would shake from the torque—fifty, sixty, sometimes seventy turns before the airframe begged me to stop.

You'd wind it past reason, then let go.

And for a few seconds, if everything was perfect—if the prop didn't stall, if the wings didn't twist, if the rubber didn't snap—it would fly. Half a loop under power. Two, maybe three tight circles on dying momentum. The most beautiful things I ever saw were gliding into failure.

Now, decades later, I feel the same hiss in my chest. But it's not a model plane in my hand—it's twenty million dollars of donor-managed illusion. The IRS is winding the clock in reverse. The Department of Justice wants to trace every thread of silk I pulled through Panama, Belize, Curaçao, Zurich. They're twisting the rubber band backwards—trying to see where it all began.

My operations have to withstand any scrutiny. Today, my two biggest benefactors arrive—both uneasy, both obsessed with visibility. And both expecting to be the only shadow in the room when we go over the books, the plans, the "how do we keep this thing from eating us alive" part. It's the second time their visits overlap.

Crossing paths in a financial transaction—especially off-shore—is like crossing streams in a gunfight. Technically survivable, but not advised.

It's a red flag. Not a siren. Not a takedown. But the kind of detail an underpaid analyst in a windowless treasury cubicle might tag in an algorithm someday. A blip on a future audit that grows teeth when they find just one more thing. And that's all it takes for the rubber band to start unwinding.

One more thing.

It was the first time I'd felt it. That flicker. That risk. Not to the foundations, or the movements, or even the traders running my synthetic options strategies out of Curaçao. No, this time the risk touched me. My revenue source. The pulse that keeps my body in tailored linen and my name off subpoenas.

So I moved it.

Everything.

Clean.

Dismantled the shared vaults and restructured each project into its own offshore shell. Cayman for Lama Sundra's retreat continuity fund. Nevis for the trauma-informed education grant. Belize for the Nicaraguan project's health corridor.

The funds roll one way only—always out, never across.

Then the magic: I funnel everything into Ameritrade through a corporate account based in the British Virgin Islands. No one questions it. Everyone's busy looking at mergers and IPOs. The dot-com bubble hasn't burst yet—it's still inflating like lungs in a confession booth. Some people think it is all going to end tragically at any moment.

Trading goes well. More than well. My long/short straddles scalp half a million over eight weeks. The gains? Those go quiet. Into Switzerland. Into Luxembourg. Then, sometimes, back to the States—but always as repatriated income from personal investment gains. Or through the Internet advertising company. Our Marketing Guys LLC.

Legal. Painfully legal. It's the sort of legality that doesn't comfort like safety. It feels like air before a lightning strike.

The rest—the donor funds—stay quarantined. Projects. Stipends. Delayed disbursements masked as "programmatic scheduling conflicts." Invoices late on purpose. Contractors float their time like it's an act of devotion.

I use the money until I can't use it anymore.

Then I move it.

Every dollar has a role. Every entity has a tone. Each spreadsheet a different signature font. There are no shared accounts. No round-trips. Just corridors that curve gently enough to look like walls.

Because that's the rule.

Clean paths. Logical lines. Separate money.

Always.

Still ... I know the truth.

I know the sick little ache that comes when you brush up against exposure. The pulse that thumps not in your wrist—but in your ledger. That feeling that if even one decimal wandered too far? You wouldn't need a warrant. Just a rumor.

That's why I don't sleep much. That hasn't changed.

Not because I'm scared, though. Not any more.

Because I can't afford to blink. I often think it's time to walk away while I still can. Would I miss any of this? What would life be otherwise?

Then the first of the benefactors arrives. He doesn't bring a bag. Just a folded robe over his arm and the soft silence of someone who no longer traffics in hurry.

Thầy arrives before noon. The air outside is coastal and warm, too early for fog, too late for dew. He enters without announcement—no assistant, no translator, no fanfare—and I'm already on my feet when I feel his presence before I see him.

We bow, palms together. No words, not yet.

In the small meeting room adjacent to my office, I've arranged the figures: printed ledgers, donor tallies, build-out expenses, updated architectural drafts from the Nicaragua project. Nothing extravagant—just numbers with breath behind them.

He studies the documents like they're calligraphy. Not reading for math. Reading for essence. I watch the way his eyes move—not quick, not slow. Just exact. As though his gaze isn't looking at the page, but into it.

After a while, I speak.

"We've spent just under seven million. That includes labor, supplies, the permits, customs issues at the Corinto port, and security for the Dharma goods coming through San Salvador."

He nods once, thumb gently turning the edge of the top sheet.

"The inner wall is complete. Roof design is finished. The reliquary base has been poured. We still need to fabricate the gold-leaf cap, do the tile work, and finish the dormitory extension."

I slide the next sheet across to him. The projection. I've circled the line: $2,060,000.

"I recommend another two million. Conservative. It would finish everything within the original schedule."

He doesn't speak. Not yet. Just breathes, eyes flicking to the small architectural rendering clipped beside the numbers.

"There have been delays," I say. "But they were purposeful. Necessary. I kept it tight. I didn't want to float debt. And the funds from the third tranche were routed through the Nevis foundation as planned—clean, no crossing paths."

At that, he looks up. Not stern. Just present.

"You have a beautiful office," he says, his voice like rice paper brushed with rain.

His eyes move—not to the floor plans, not to the ledger—but to the wall behind me.

The diplomas.

Framed. Hung with space between them like museum pieces. My B.S. in Aeronautical Engineering, Embry Riddle. M.S. in Mathematics from Boston University. MBA from California State University.

Degrees that cost me nothing. The US Navy paid for the first one. United Technologies the second. Lama Sundra's foundation paid for the MBA.

His gaze lingers.

And when he speaks again, it's not about the stupa. It's not about money.

He says, "So much knowledge. So many shapes for the same mind. Why?"

He's not accusing. He's inviting.

And I know this next part isn't about balance sheets anymore.

It's about the hunger that built them.

When I pause to flip the folder closed, his gaze lifts.

His eyes track the frames on my office wall—degree by degree.

Aeronautical Engineering. Mathematics. Business.

"You studied air. Then numbers. Then people," he says.

"Machines. Patterns. Systems," I correct gently.

He smiles. "Still air. Still numbers. Still people."

I shrug. "I love knowledge."

"Why?" he asks, not with suspicion, but with disarming curiosity.

"Because I don't know enough," I say.

The answer surprises even me in its honesty.

He tilts his head. "That's not hunger. That's truth."

I lean back in my chair. "The more I learn, the more I realize how little I actually understand. Every answer fractures into new questions. Every system I master reveals a second system I didn't even know was running in the background."

He folds his hands in his lap. "So you believe you are chasing knowledge?"

"I do," I say. "Always."

He looks at me for a long moment, then leans forward, voice quiet.

"You are not chasing," he says. "You are remembering."

That stills me.

He continues: "The universe holds everything—including knowledge. Everything. All truth. It is the great container. And you," he taps the folder between us, "you are part of that container. Not separate. Not a student looking in, but a fragment looking back."

I don't respond. I wait.

He nods once, gently.

"To learn," he says, "is not to gain. It is to recall. You already know everything the universe knows. You are made of the same knowing. But the self forgets. The ego forgets. So we sit. We listen. We remember."

He closes his eyes.

"That's what the word means," he adds softly. "Learning. Not inventing. Remembering. Putting the pieces of what is already there ... back together. You cannot learn what is not already known. You simply remember what you have forgotten."

The wind brushes against the glass outside. The leaves move like prayer flags.

I think about balsa wood planes, rubber bands wound too tight. I think about Ameritrade servers and offshore corridors. I think about the absurdity of knowledge, and how much I've confused it with control.

Then I say what I've never said aloud.

"I don't know if I'm learning the truth. Or just better illusions."

Thầy opens his eyes, slow. "That is the most honest thing a wise man can say."

He studies me—not as a man studies another man, but as silence studies a bell before it's rung.

Then, without flourish, he says, "If you want to pursue more—if you feel this remembering needs form—I would like to sponsor your doctorate."

My hands still. No reaction on my face, but inside, something lifts. Like a lever clicked into place. A breath I hadn't known I was holding moves through me in full.

He continues, "A PhD in epigenetics. I've spoken with the dean of admissions at UCLA. He agrees. You're already doing the work. You're already shaping the discourse. It's time the credentials matched the current."

I blink once. "You're serious?"

"Of course," he says, as if offering someone a glass of water in a desert. "Knowledge should not be guarded by gates. It should be used like breath—given freely and returned clean."

"I'd be honored," I say. And I mean it. Not the kind of honor that belongs in press releases or grant proposals. The genuine kind. The kind that feels like being seen.

He gestures toward the window. "You are already a builder. This would simply formalize your materials."

I nod. The thoughts layer in real time.

"I'd want to focus on the behavioral side," I say. "Gene expression affected by ritual, discipline, intention. Not just chemical inputs. But volitional ones. The edge where spirituality becomes biology."

He smiles wide. "Yes. That edge is not an edge. It's the stitching. And you know how to thread it."

I feel it again—that pull, that gravity of purpose, the clean hunger.

Not for money.

Not even for recognition.

But to know.

To remember.

And to build something from that memory that makes the world less forgetful.

"When can I begin?" I ask.

He laughs softly. "You already have."

A knock at the open door, then a voice like wet gravel smoothed by decades of chanting.

"I thought I heard a familiar voice."

Lama Sundra steps in from the hallway, barefoot as always, loose cotton draped over his frame like a flag that's seen too many winds. His beard's grown in since I saw him last—whiter, longer. His presence carries the scent of old cedar and something earthy. Vetiver, maybe.

Thầy rises. They bow to one another with full spine, no affectation. Monastics of different geographies but the same soil. Their clasped hands linger a beat longer than necessary. No words exchanged for the first few seconds—just a shared look that asks: Still here? Still breathing? Still remembering?

"I didn't expect to see you until tomorrow," Sundra says, smiling toward me after they part. "You two cooking something dangerous in here?"

Thầy replies, "Only forgotten memory. And maybe a little fire."

They both laugh, soft and confident. Then Sundra clasps his hands behind his back and glances toward the window. "The stupa's foundation looks good from the road. I saw the new prayer flags on the south fence. Your colors?"

"Thầy's," I say. "I just poured the concrete."

He nods. "That's always been your gift. Making the invisible walk upright."

A few more pleasantries, a brief return to shared dharma companions they both knew in India in the '70s and '80s. Something about the rains in Sarnath. Something about the way memory gets lodged in the ankles. Then Thầy touches Sundra's arm.

"Stay well, brother," he says.

"I'm trying," Sundra replies, and there's something unsaid in his tone.

Thầy bows again and exits, quiet as paper folding into a drawer.

Sundra waits until he's gone, then lowers himself onto the cushion across from me.

"All right," he sighs, tapping the folder between us. "Let's see what fire you've walked these donations through now."

We go through it line by line.

Three hours. Two pots of tea. Every transaction, from the Massachusetts foundation project down to the air conditioner repair at the Oceanside retreat center. He's sharper than usual today. Asks about vendor overlap. Asks why the conference rental in San Francisco was double the prior year.

He's not accusing. He's being precise.

But I feel it. A shift in the air. I am no longer the man who built this. I am the law it obeys.

Finally, when the books are closed and the sunlight has turned gold, he leans back against the wall. One hand covers his ribs as if something aches deep inside him.

"I'm going in for surgery," he says.

I look up.

"It's serious?" I ask.

He shrugs. "Define serious."

"That's not an answer."

He exhales, long and dry. "Liver, mostly. And some soft tissue near the spine. They think it's manageable. But I'll be grounded for a while. Off the grid."

I wait.

Then he says it.

"The foundation will need to pay the bills. Insurance won't cover it all. I've asked the board to release one hundred twenty thousand."

It's said gently. But it doesn't land that way.

Not because I don't want to help. But because I already know where that hundred and twenty lives. Or where it should live.

I nod. Slowly. Quietly. Inside, my mind watches the rubber band twitch.

It's that old sound again—the hiss of torque building up in a fragile frame. I feel twelve again. Bare feet on dry grass. Wrist sore from winding. Watching the plane rise, then dip, then hold—just barely—before it falls into an arc that looks almost like grace.

Back then, failure as expected. The beauty was in the, almost.

But this isn't balsa and glue. This is flesh, money, karma—and the glide has to hold.

The part they never printed on the side of the model kit box: how to land without wings. How to walk away when the air runs out.

And now I'm not holding a rubber band. I'm holding his life. One twenty, trapped in Zurich. Waiting on a conversion rate that won't respect prayer or prognosis.

For a split second, I see it: a treasury agent flipping through these ledgers, stalling on a mismatch. A soft inquiry that hardens into a subpoena. Offshore shells collapsing in a daisy chain I can't stop. Lama Sundra waking from surgery, asking for a balance sheet that's been frozen. Headlines my son would read before he understood what I'd built: Charity Frontman Linked to International Fraud Network.

Not a storm. Not a fire. Just ... an unraveling. A rubber band unwinding in reverse, faster than I can coil it. And me, standing there, stupid, empty-handed, explaining to men with cold badges how the failure wasn't in the math. It was in me.

Average me.

~~~

The house smells like steam and cannabis. My feet slap wet tile as I cut across the master suite, towel clenched. Outside, somewhere under that coastal haze, an entire operation waits for me to catch up.

Ana Lorena is already perfect. She leans toward the vanity mirror with a small compact in one hand, lashes curled into upward symmetry, lips pressed in concentration. Her robe is still half-open, catching light with every movement. "We're thirty minutes late," she says, not looking at me. "The PO is gonna be so PO'ed."

"Jesus," I mutter. The PO—the probation officer moonlighting as crowd control for the retreat—has no humor. Not at this hour. Not when I'm the one who still owes him two hundred in hazard pay for last fall's VIP tantrum. I make a mental note: fold the cash into the check-in folder. Bribe as grace.

The shower is still running, hot water fogging up the mirrors like the house is trying to sweat out my sins. I step in. No time for rituals. No time for silence. Just pressure. Clean skin. Neural reset.

But my mind? It's already in motion.

This is why I never lose.

I remain focused!

Twelve noon: the community radio crew shows up with their gear. I need to give them access to the back gate and the east hedgerow—cordon off the monk's entrance, so no one captures Lama Sundra dropping f-bombs under his breath about the garden acoustics.

One P.M.: the caterer arrives. Vegan sushi, finger-breaded jackfruit, ceremonial tea sets. I still haven't confirmed if they're using organic soy sauce or if I'm about to be crucified by some sectarian macrobiotic from Encinitas.
~~~

Two P.M.: guests begin arriving. Seventeen from San Diego. Four from Oregon. One from Alaska. A couple with his-and-hers mala beads who flew in from Nova Scotia and left a voicemail about how the Buddha told them to take this retreat. That's always a good sign.

Three P.M.: Lama Sundra's guided meditation. The big one. The ultimate act. The silence that's supposed to justify all the chaos that came before it.

The hot water beats across my shoulders. I want to stay there. Just another minute. Maybe five. Maybe forever.

Ana Lorena's voice cuts in again, sharp but melodic. "You did remember to sign off on the lighting permit, right?"

"I delegated," I shout over the cascade of water.

She snorts. "You forgot."

I don't answer. The truth's already pooling around my ankles.

Behind the fogged glass, the eucalyptus trees bend in the breeze, blurred shadows moving like monks in procession. I close my eyes. Let the heat bake something loose in my spine.

This is what peace looks like now.

Deadlines. Permits. Facial serums. The scent of matcha hiding the panic beneath every email confirmation.

I rinse fast. Kill the water. Towel off.

Today, I'm the host of a hundred sacred expectations.

But right now, I'm just a man trying to find clean socks before the Sangha arrives.

Ana Lorena stands in the doorway holding the receiver like it's radioactive. "It's the caterer. They're short-staffed—need to set up at noon instead of one."

I bite down on a curse and finish buttoning the cuffs on my linen shirt. Third time I've worn this one for a public event—creases in the wrong places, collar a little too high. But no time to change. No time to argue. The only answer is movement.

Thầy's wire transfer came through this morning—two and a half million, even. Another miracle disguised as a line item. I'll have to carry it to Panama next week, disguise it under consultancy clearances, make it look like an endowment. But for now, it's just a note in my ledger and another reason to sweat under this jacket.

"I'll call them back," I say, kissing her forehead as I pass. "Tell them to set up on the west side, near the water feature. Avoid the south path—the ground's still soft."

I snag the folder from the counter, the one with the gate code sheet and the catering schedule, and head for the garage. The Corvette is staged like a caged animal in the morning sun. I pop the door, toss the folder onto the passenger seat, slide in, and—

Wrong keys.

I stare at the ignition. The teeth don't match.

Back inside. Fast. Through the kitchen, past the tea kettle, still hooting like it knows more than it should. I grab the right ring off the hook by the fridge, the one with the classic gold fob. Ana Lorena's following behind now, her eyes bright, sharp, ready.

"You okay?" she asks, half in jest, half in code.

"No," I say. "But I'll pass."

I tap the counter twice, an old ritual, then we're back out the door. This time, the engine snarls into life like it missed me.

Next stop: downtown San Diego. Ana Lorena's appointment with her probation officer.

"I still don't see why he insists on meeting in person," I mutter as we merge southbound onto the I-15. "You're clean. You've been clean."

She slides on her sunglasses. "Because I'm beautiful, and he's not. Power's a drug too."

I glance over. Her jawline's hard, but her voice is calm. She knows the game. We both do.

The sky is brutally clear. Blue like judgment. I weave through traffic like the road owes me a favor.

We have seventy-five minutes to solve five problems, and I'm the only one holding the keys.

Ten minutes, she says, then with a spin on her six-inch heels, swings the door closed and trots toward the state building. My patience is running thin. A discomfort I have learned to avoid. Those ten minutes turned into fifteen and then twenty. I'm considering going in after her or leaving her here.

The radio station and caterer are thirty minutes from showing up. Ten minutes to get to the abbey from here. I go over the possible routes as my grip on the steering wheel tightens.

She jumps in the car. "Kiss me, baby, I'm free," she says as she climbs into my lap. Smothering me with a kiss.

"We have to go. What the hell happened in there?"

"Humph." She slips into the passenger seat and I take off down the road. The folder slides off the dash and lands in her lap.

She goes through the folder. "That was my last meet with the probation office. I signed the last check in and he signed off on the completion of the court order. I'm free!"

"Far freakin' out!" I shout the old school words, not knowing how to best the expression. "That is tight!"

She holds up a check. "That's a fucking expensive catering check. Are we serving filet mignon today?"

"It's for Noe and Teresa's wedding. They told me if I didn't pay in advance from now on, they won't cater my events."

When we pull into the parking lot, I see Ken Kuang. The man is my sidekick. Always appears when I need him most. He's already met with the radio station and the caterers. Most of the guests have arrived. My heart goes quiet. I've built something that has, for the first time, made me proud. Into the garden, my eyes wide open, taking it all in.

The sun's still climbing, lazy and golden, casting angled light over the back gardens of the abbey. The lawn, recently cut, gives off that green, earthy sweetness—the kind that doesn't smell like grass but like time returned. A row of folding chairs flanks the stone path, backs straight, arranged without symmetry but with care. They are already filled. A hundred and thirty guests. Some local, some pilgrims from as far as Europe. A few stand barefoot on the edge of the gravel, preferring the soil to seating.

The flowers nod in the wind. Somewhere behind the gate, a bird offers three uncertain notes and goes quiet.

Sundra stands before them. He's thinner than last year, paler in the cheeks. But there's something fierce about him today. Not sharp, but clear. His robe whispers as he turns, smiling at someone in the front row. He doesn't raise his voice.

He doesn't need to.

"We begin," he says, "by remembering there is nowhere else to be."

He waits. The crowd stills. Someone coughs. A child rustles in her seat. Then—

One bell.

A second.

A third.

Long. Low. Measured.

The wind quiets.

He begins.

"Of the Four Noble Truths, the third—the cessation of suffering and stress—is the one we talk about the least. It's the result of the practice. And so we focus on the cause. But we must never forget what we're walking toward."

He pauses. Lets them feel it.

"The third noble truth is not nibbana. That's something different. The third noble truth has a duty to be realized. To be understood. It is the act—not the destination. Nibbana carries no duties. It is simply ... being done."

There's a stillness in the audience now. Even the trees seem to lean in.

"When we abandon craving—when we cease the hunger for sensuality, for becoming, for not becoming—we will begin to see. The abandoning is not absence. It's presence without need."

He looks out over the gathered faces. Some closed-eyed. Some weeping.

"The Buddha spoke of six faces of this abandoning. Not synonyms. Steps. Nuance. Each a different door.

"Viraga. Nirodho. Cago. Patinissaggo. Mutti. Analayo."

He turns to the side, letting the names echo like stones dropped in a deep well.

"First, viraga—dispassion. It's not detachment. It's the loss of interest in feeding on things that never fill.

"Some dispassion arrives like rain. Quiet, slow. Other times, you must rip the root from your ribs.

"To get there, you must first be sick of craving itself—not just the things you crave, but the hunger for hunger.

"Look at what you feed on. Pleasure. Grievance. Fear. Victory. They don't satisfy. They seduce."

He raises his hand as if plucking something unseen.

"Only when you see this clearly does nirodho come—cessation. The factory closes. The machine stops. Craving ends."

He breathes in through his nose. Long. Deliberate.

"After cessation, there is cago—giving back. And patinissaggo—relinquishing.

"You realize none of it was yours. Not the success. Not the trauma. Not the righteousness you wore like armor.

"So you give it back. Like a fire releasing the log. Like a thief returning the loot after realizing it burned in his hands."

He paces once along the edge of the chairs. Barefoot on polished gravel. The stones don't seem to notice.

"Then—mutti: freedom. Not as achievement. But as default. You unhook the chain, and suddenly, the chain was never hooked to you."

"And finally, analayo. The most dangerous seed of all—nostalgia.

"You let go of the craving ... but you still remember it fondly.

"Like a bitter ex. Like the cigarette you swore was your last.

"Nostalgia is craving in disguise."

He lifts his head.

"You say you've let go, but your hand still rests on it. Ready to reclaim.

"But when you spit it out—when you stop even missing the craving—that's when the fire stops feeding.

"That's when you are free."

The garden is utterly still.

Sundra's voice softens. Slows.

"Freedom does not mean silence. It means no longer mistaking noise for meaning.

"No longer bargaining your breath for something you already were."

He steps back to his mat. Kneels. Bows.

"So today, as we close this cycle, this retreat, this chapter—

"Ask yourself not what you are still seeking.

"Ask: What craving have I stopped missing?

"And what lives in that absence?"

He raises the bell once more. A single tone. Then another. Then the third.

This one longer than the rest.

A note that does not end.

It floats—unclaimed—above the lawn.

Above the folding chairs.

Above the money, the plans, the passports, the lies.

Above it all.

And in the stillness, there's a knowing.

Something in me exhales—not the air, but the ache that has carried it.

Suddenly, it sneaks up on me: a memory I haven't touched in years.

I'm eight years old again, knees scraped, the old swing set in my parents' backyard rocking empty in the twilight. I'm crouched behind the toolshed, fists balled, ashamed of a spelling bee I lost to a girl I liked.

No one is coming to find me.

And for the first time, it had occurred to me—I could stop needing to be found.

I could just ... be.

That hollow settles in my chest again now. Not loneliness. Not triumph. Just air where a wall used to be.

Freedom is not the prize.

It is the fire gone cold.

And no longer needed.

Lama Sundra remains still after the bell, as if listening to something older than sound. A breeze rustles the eucalyptus just enough to brush the edges of his robe. Behind him, the abbey's terracotta roof holds the last of the midday sunlight like its memorizing warmth.

Then, softly:

"The third noble truth isn't about ecstasy. It's about ending. And not the ending of life, or desire, or ambition—but the ending of the needing. Of the restless becoming."

He gazes out across the group—130 souls, quiet and breathing together.

"We talk about nibbāna like it's far. But the Buddha never said it was elsewhere. He said it was the moment you stop needing anything to be other than what it is."

The space of the garden holds still. No throat clears. No foot shifts. Even the birds seem paused at the edge of a branch.

"And what's remarkable," he says, "is that it doesn't require adding anything. It requires subtraction. You subtract the grasping. The needing. The craving."

He inhales deeply, then exhales through his nose.

"It's not dramatic. It's not glorious. It's simple. Like when a fever breaks. Or when you put down a bag, you didn't know you were carrying."

Someone sighs. A breath that sounds like relief. Or grief.

Lama Sundra smiles.

"When the Buddha spoke of mutti—freedom—he said it wasn't something you create. It's something you uncover. Because it was always there, beneath the habits, beneath the story, beneath the self."

Then his voice lowers again, softer than dusk.

"You will not find liberation in fire. You will not find it in the teachings. You will not find it in the future. You will only find it in the precise moment your hand opens and stops trying to hold the world."

He lets the words settle.

A single jacaranda petal flutters onto the stone path between mats.

Then, with the same tone he might use to offer tea, he says,

"Let us sit together."

No command. Just invitation.

He closes his eyes. Hands rest on his knees, palms up. His breath moves like a tide that's forgotten how to rush. And one by one, the circle returns to stillness.

This is no longer instruction.

It's a transmission.

Stillness becomes atmosphere. Thought becomes echo. And what remains ... is enough.

Ten minutes pass. Or an hour.

Then a final bell. Low. Resolute. No flourish. Just truth.

He opens his eyes. Folds his hands at the chest.

"May you remember," he says, "not what you've learned—but what you've uncovered."

He rises. His robes gather around him like a curtain falling after a story well told.

And for once, no one claps.

Because something sacred has already answered.

Lama Sundra steps back toward the abbey's rear walkway, where the polished gravel crunches under his sandals and the last light halos the back of his shaved head. No ceremony. No farewell. Just a quiet return to where the tea might still be warm, where silence resumes its rightful place as host.

The guests don't stir. Not yet. Something has shifted. Not in doctrine. Not in belief. But in posture. As if each of them is a flame learning how not to burn.

I remain seated. Legs crossed. Hands open in my lap.

In the distance, a late commuter plane arcs across the pale orange sky, its contrail scribbling something impermanent in the firmament.

And I wonder—for the briefest, unguarded moment—if it's possible to live this way. To move through systems and capital and secrets with a heart that doesn't flinch. To stay hidden and still be seen. To let go without letting down.

Then the wind shifts.

Eucalyptus.

Ash.

And the faint, unmistakable scent of bougainvillea opening its petals.

A bell echoes once more from somewhere inside the abbey.

I don't move.

I let the sound pass through me.

And in that hollow, in that pause—

I disappear.

Journal entry. August 1, 1998.

There are no names left to sign, no gates left to guard.

The systems hum without a conductor now—loops self-sustaining, funds arriving like weather. Somewhere in a file no one will ever open, a transaction moves in silence.

Clean. Precise. Unnoticed.

And somewhere else, a man no longer answers to the name that built it.

Because the real ending isn't exile, or wealth, or arrest.

It's subtraction.

A slow release of wanting.

A breath no longer bargained.

What remains isn't the architect.

It's the architecture.

And it no longer needs a witness.